No. 10 DOYERS STREET

No. 10 DOYERS STREET

A NOVEL

RADHA VATSAL

First published by Level Best Books/Historia 2024

This novel is entirely a work of fiction. The names, characters and incidents portrayed in it are the work of the author's imagination. Any resemblance to actual persons, living or dead, events or localities is entirely coincidental.

Radha Vatsal asserts the moral right to be identified as the author of this work.

Author Photo Credit: Juliette Conroy

Cover Photo Credit: Library of Congress

First edition

ISBN (paperback): 978-1-68512-775-6
ISBN (hardcover): 978-1-68512-774-9

Cover art by Joe Grossman

This book was professionally typeset on Reedsy.
Find out more at reedsy.com

Praise for No. 10 Doyers Street

"[A]n immersive historical novel in which social constructions of race impact politics on a grand scale."—*Foreword Reviews*

"[A] descriptive, engaging thriller set in the dark alleys of New York's Chinatown more than a hundred years ago."—*Asian Review of Books*

"[A]n engrossing read about the erasure of people and their homes and culture in the name of so-called progress."—*Historical Novel Society*

"This book begins with heartbreak and ends up being an extremely deft portrait of the way politics work… Archie and the story of a bursting New York City is indelible."—*Deadly Pleasures*

"[A]n absolutely fascinating story, richly told with vivid descriptions. I finished this in a day and a half, and when I wasn't reading it, I was thinking about Archie and Mock…"—*Kings River Life Magazine*

"[A] richly layered historical fiction novel of power, identity, and belonging… Vatsal's writing is a love letter to a city in transformation."—*Brown Girl Bookshelf*

"[Vatsal] has a unique talent for connecting the past and present in meaningful ways that just might alter the views of some readers unfamiliar with the struggles faced by minority groups in this country. By juxtaposing higher society against those with much less, *No. 10 Doyers Street* feels both timely and relevant."—*BOLO Books*

"[A] crackerjack mystery… Trailblazing journalist Archana Morley has both the strength and sensitivity to cut to the truth in this fast-paced tale that illuminates the history of Asian immigrants in Chinatown."—Sujata Massey, internationally bestselling author of *The Widows of Malabar Hill*

"Radha Vatsal's skill as not only a historian, but a crafter of gripping and character-driven mysteries, are in full effect in the pages of *No. 10 Doyers Street*—as readers are guided through the streets of a lost New York from the perspective of an Indian journalist embroiled in a real-world underworld caper. Pitch perfectly accurate and enthralling, I was rapt until the last page."—Alex Segura, bestselling and acclaimed author of *Secret Identity* and *Alter Ego*

"Gripping and vibrantly original. Radha Vatsal has a gift for unearthing those seemingly small moments that change the course of history. Both a brilliant tale of the plot to destroy New York City's Chinatown and a heartbreaking courtroom drama, *No. 10 Doyers Street* is a fresh, unforgettable look at 1900s New York."—Mariah Fredericks, author of *The Wharton Plot*

"Vatsal has wonderfully captured 1900s Chinatown, breathing life into the complicated character of gangster Mock Duck… Gentrification, mixed-race identity and discrimination against immigrants are all evergreen issues that come to light through Vatsal's protagonist, a South Asian female journalist. *No. 10 Doyers Street* reflects a new stage of reality-based fiction—a pan-Asian exploration of American history."—Naomi Hirahara, Edgar and Mary Higgins Clark award-winning author of the Mas Arai mysteries and the best-selling Japantown mysteries

"Vatsal's riveting story of early 1900s Chinatown will pin you to your seat. Her deft writing has rendered legendary gangster Mock Duck an empathetic character. Vatsal's intrepid journalist narrator uses wit and pen to stride through prejudice and red tape, and pulls along the reader to find what we're all looking for: The truth."—Ed Lin, author of *David Tung Can't Have*

Praise for Radha Vatsal and The Kitty Weeks Mysteries

"This lively and well-researched debut introduces a charming historical series and an appealing fish-out-of-water sleuth who seeks independence and a career in an age when most women are bent on getting married, particularly to titled Englishmen. Devotees of Rhys Bowen's mysteries will enjoy making the acquaintance of Miss Weeks."—*Library Journal* Starred, and Debut of the Month

"[A] spirited debut… Vatsal deftly intertwines the tumult of the era, from emerging women's rights to spreading international conflict, into this rich historical."—*Publishers Weekly*

"The fascinating historical details add flair to this thoroughly engaging mystery starring an intelligent amateur sleuth reminiscent of Rhys Bowen's Molly Murphy. Vatsal's debut will leave readers eager for Kitty's next adventure."—*Booklist*

"This first in a planned series is a nice combination of mystery and thriller seasoned by historical facts and a look at women's lives before woman's liberation."—*Kirkus*

"An impressively well written and consistently compelling read from beginning to end, Radha Vatsal's *A Front Page Affair* is the first book in what is justifiably expected to be an outstanding series featuring rising journalism star Kitty Weeks."—*Midwest Book Review*

"The novel's strength lies in its exploration of complicated wartime politics, and the difference between neutrality and innocence."—Shelf Awareness

"Delightful, intriguing, and relevant historical fiction!"—*Historical Novels Review*

Who's Who

NEWSPAPER ROW

- Archana Morley (Archie): reporter for the *Observer*
- Hervé Dupont: her editor
- Pike: reporter from the *Sun*
- E.K. Hornby: reporter from the *Times*

CHINATOWN

- Mock Duck: leader of the Hip Sing Tong
- Tai Yow Chin: his wife
- Ha Oi: their daughter
- Bedelia: their maid
- Grace Woo: a downstairs neighbor; mother to Lily and May
- Tom Lee: leader of the On Leong Tong
- William: his grandnephew
- Corsair: tour guide and raconteur

CITY HALL AND ADJACENT

- George B. McClellan (Georgie B.): Mayor of New York City
- Georgiana McClellan (Lady Mac): his wife and advisor
- Dr. Phillip Morley: Archana's husband, official at the Health Department
- Vincent Pisarra: agent of The Society for the Prevention of Cruelty to Children (the Gerry Society)

TAMMANY HALL (THE DEMOCRATIC PARTY ORGANIZATION)

- Charles F. Murphy (Silent Charlie): Tammany boss
- George Washington Plunkitt: Tammany philosopher

THAW TRIAL

- Harry Thaw: murdering millionaire
- Evelyn Nesbit: his wife, and former showgirl
- Daniel O'Reilly: Thaw's lawyer
- Stanford White: architect, and Thaw's victim

ARCHANA'S PREDECESSORS

- Pandita Ramabai: Indian woman who traveled to the United States and wrote *Conditions of Life in America* in the nineteenth century
- Dr. Anandibai Joshee: first Indian woman to become a doctor in the United States, also in the nineteenth century

* Apart from Mock Duck, all names appear with the given name first.

Chapter One

The bump in the road came out of nowhere. Or rather, everywhere. Constant use and shoddy repairs had left the streets and sidewalks cratered and veined. But usually, I kept my wits about me. Usually, I didn't trip and have to catch myself. That day, however, a swarm of newsmen buzzing uptown grabbed my attention. I waited a few seconds for them to pass, and then followed, a small, matchstick-like figure in trousers, jacket, and a hat, scarcely worthy of notice.

The skies were still light, and vendors were out. The air had lost winter's sting, and spring was beginning to take hold. I kept the newshounds in my sights as I dodged the crowds. Something out of the ordinary must have taken place. Whatever it was, it would make a welcome change from the Thaw trial, which we'd been covering morning, noon, and night for nearly a year.

The pressmen streamed past City Hall and the Tweed Courthouse, past the sumptuous Hall of Records and the Brooklyn Bridge. They continued beneath the elevated railroad tracks, skipped Mott Street, and hooked a quick left on Doyers.

No more than a few hundred feet long and maybe ten or twelve feet wide, the street hung from Pell like a sock on a line, bent sharply at the heel, and emptied out onto Chatham Square and the Bowery.

The newsmen slowed as they approached the curve. It was known as the "Bloody Angle" because it had been the site of so many shootings.

A lone copper stood on guard in front of wooden double doors below a metal fire escape. Locals milled around outside, ashen-faced and in silence.

A sign read: Chinese Opera House. The newsmen went in.

The copper looked me up and down.

I'd never covered the district—my editor believed it wasn't a job for a woman.

"And you are?" the lawman asked.

"With the *Observer*." A scrappy, by-your-bootstraps rag to be sure, but not unknown among New York's dozens of dailies.

He frowned, muttered something under his breath, but grudgingly stepped aside, allowing me to enter.

Once inside, it took a few moments to adjust to the dim light; then I made out the scene: a stage had been set for a performance. But the ornate backdrop painted with soaring trees and a gold palace had been punctured with bullet holes—so many that it almost looked intentional. Benches placed in neat rows for the audience had toppled helter-skelter, shattered glass glittered. Bodies lay sprawled on the floor. I counted four. They were pooled in their own blood, eyes wide open.

I rested my head against one of the metal columns, trying to breathe, while coppers replied to the newsmen's questions.

"The On Leongs and Hips—at each other's throats again."

"In the middle of a performance?"

"That's right. But this time, they've crossed the line. The theater's supposed to be neutral territory."

"Do we know who fired first?"

"The Hips."

"Who planned the attack?"

Cackles in the gloom.

There was no need to answer.

Chapter Two

My editor wouldn't hear of my going back. "There's no point, Mrs. M.," Hervé Dupont, a New Yorker by way of Louisiana, said. "We have it right here." He tapped the pages I'd handed in. "A shootout at the Chinese Theater. Fuckin' Celestials. What's next? A gunfight at City Hall? Machetes at Madison Square? And that Mock Duck, just thumbing his nose at American law and order, as though it doesn't apply to him. Those fellas should blow each other's heads off, as far as I'm concerned. Then we'd be done with the lot of them."

Most of the reportage that followed framed what was quickly dubbed "The Chinese Opera House Massacre" as the most vicious in a series of escalating battles between the two gangs and connected it in vague terms to Mock Duck's ruthlessness and the general lawlessness and unsanitary nature of the district. Similar claims, with a few alterations for local color, had been made about all kinds of places, even Bombay—where I'm from—and I felt the need to dig deeper.

Scarcely out of his late twenties, Mock Duck was already a local legend. His dead, expressionless eyes gazed from the backs of playing cards and souvenir matchboxes. Street urchins sang ditties in his honor. They said that he could hear a pin drop, see around corners, and that his rhinoceros-thick skin protected him from injury. But I wanted to find out who he really was, what fueled his enmity with the On Leongs, and, most importantly, whether he truly believed he could flout all the rules so brazenly and get away with it.

I waited a week or so for the dust to settle, during which time Dupont kept me busy with mindless tasks, and it became clear that while the Hips had definitely caused the carnage and fired without warning on their rivals, Mock Duck would not be arrested.

Not only had no one seen him at the theater, his alibi was unassailable. When the shooting occurred, he had been bailing out a couple of friends right under the noses of the cops at the police station. It was almost too rich, as though he was daring the authorities to catch him.

As I scoured the newspaper's morgue for old reports, I discovered that this was a pattern with Mock. Although he'd been implicated in and arrested for dozens of crimes, he always managed to produce a watertight alibi or hire expert lawyers and argue his way out of the situation. In one instance, when he was identified by a white witness, Mock maintained that the witness must have been wrong since all Chinese looked the same to Americans.

His various strategies paid off: He had never yet been convicted.

I returned to Chinatown on a slow afternoon. All around me, the city was growing. Buildings shot up like weeds, chains for the Manhattan Bridge dangled expectantly above the East River, and farther north, the two sides of the bridge to Queens strained to connect in the middle. Elevated trains clattered overhead on the Bowery, and I recalled a story I had heard at the *Observer*: One of the reporters had been on the train when Mock Duck entered his carriage, which was empty save for him, and a drunk who was fast asleep lolled across three seats. Mock took one look at the inebriate, picked him up, and coolly tossed him out onto the platform as though he was a sack of potatoes. Then he brushed off his hands, opened a newspaper, and began to read.

"Never seen anything like it," the reporter said. "The fellow couldn't have hurt a fly, and still, Mock Duck couldn't resist dumping him."

As I neared Chatham Square, I wondered whether I was in over my head. Whether the leader of the Hip Sing Tong was best left to other, more hardened types. I reminded myself that I hadn't done anything yet. I hadn't spoken to anyone, I hadn't written a word. I was only getting the lay of the land.

A uniformed roundsman patrolled the square between Doyers Street and the Bowery. Workers in black trousers and tunics hauled bundles while passengers hurried back and forth from the station. The roundsman beckoned a vendor with an imperious gesture of his hand, spoke a few sharp words, examined the unfamiliar vegetables in the man's basket, and started to haggle over the price of leafy greens.

A childish voice chortled, and I looked over to see a little girl in bright pink pantaloons, hair festooned with pink ribbons, riding on her father's shoulders. She was about five or six years old and was pulling on his ears to direct his gaze. He was slim, with chiseled cheekbones, and dressed, like most of the other men, in loose black trousers, black canvas slippers, and a black tunic with a high collar. He wore a black skullcap, and his hair was pulled into a bun.

A train rumbled out, and the father raised his arm, pointed at the carriages, and began counting them one by one in English. The little girl repeated the numbers after him, enunciating carefully. The pair were lost in their own world, and for a moment, memories of home came rushing back. Then I tore my attention away and moved on to Doyers.

The street possessed a curious, rundown charm despite the horror that had recently occurred. Three- and four-story wooden tenements leaned in toward each other, so close that they seemed to be whispering secrets. And the bend was the result, or so it was said, of the path of a stream that had once flowed there. Whatever the cause, it was a welcome respite from the unyielding right-angled grid that had taken hold farther uptown.

A couple of grim-looking fellows appeared from behind the curve. My pulse quickened, and I averted my eyes, minding my own business. We passed each other without incident.

Mock Duck lived a few doors down and across the street from the theater, right on the curve, at No. 10. It was an unremarkable tenement, not unlike its unremarkable neighbors. To my surprise, there was nothing the slightest bit distinctive about it, nothing to indicate that it was home to one of the city's most notorious highbinders. A flea-bitten mutt groomed itself on the strip of sidewalk outside, and a shingle painted with a camera and the words "Woo's Photography" hung by the front door. From its windows, you could get a clear view of the theater, now barricaded.

If Mock happened to be at home, I didn't want him to notice me, so I hurried on to Pell.

Shops were open, and people were out. Signs hung everywhere, both vertically and horizontally: from awnings, balconies, fire escapes, and grilles attached to walls and lampposts. Most displayed only Oriental characters; others also announced their goods and services in English. Clock Repairs. Shoes. Herbal Medicine.

A ragged urchin approached, his hand outstretched. I threw in a penny. A fellow pushed a wheelbarrow loaded high with crates of squawking chickens. Men in quilted vests transported loads on handcarts or from tumplines looped across their foreheads. Nuts and seeds in all colors and sizes overflowed from sacks outside a grocery store. I could have been in Canton…I could have been in Calcutta, but I couldn't afford to become complacent.

Across from me, its name painted in bright gold letters on a green awning, the Hung Far Low Restaurant was a reminder of a recent tragedy. A few years previously, a vat of grease in the kitchen had caught fire. An On Leong, who was asleep in the dormitory above, awoke to find his bed engulfed by flames and hurled himself off the balcony. Neighbors said his skull shattered the instant it hit the sidewalk.

He had been slated to testify against Mock in a murder trial.

Mock, who was in jail at the time, told reporters that he could hardly be responsible for the man's death. He wasn't some magician who could kill his enemies from behind bars. He couldn't make things happen just by wishing them into existence. And with the chief witness against Mock Duck gone, the city's case against him crumbled. He walked out of jail a free man, as he had done on numerous occasions.

I moved away from the restaurant and toward the Pelham Café, a storied tourist establishment. The proprietor, a Russian Jew, hired singing waiters to entertain his motley clientele, who ranged from eccentric bohemians to the Astors and the Vanderbilts. Even the Duke of Brandenburg had stopped by during his visit to New York.

There could be no harm in stepping in for a moment.

That afternoon there were no singing waiters, just a lone pianist, two pocket-squared gents chatting with a bluestocking, and a rouged lady munching on a plate of fried chicken.

I took a seat behind the bar and ordered a pint. My reflection stared at me from the mirror lining the back wall. Small face, alert dark eyes, brows like wary slashes. Perhaps a bit stern and unwelcoming, but not too bad for a woman in this line of work, nudging thirty.

"Where're you from?" the bartender asked.

"Uptown."

He laughed. "No, really."

"I'm not joking."

"Well, what brings you to these parts?"

I hesitated before replying. Although I wasn't speaking loudly, it felt as though everyone could hear. "I'm considering writing a story about the neighborhood."

"Is that so?" He set an overflowing tumbler on the counter. "You know much about Chinatown?"

"Why don't you tell me."

"I've been working here twenty years and still can't figure it out."

I took a sip of the drink, savoring its bitterness. "What have you heard about the shooting?"

"Same as everyone else. That Mock's behind it, but they're never gonna catch him. He'll get away with it, like he always does."

"Have you ever met him?"

"Sure. Seen him out and about, though he never comes in here. And before you ask, he's nothing special to look at. And sounds like any other fella. You best be careful, though. You never know what's coming next with him...."

I took another few sips, paid, and stepped out into the early evening. Leaves dangling from its mouth, a goat sauntered over. A man clattered by on his bicycle, and another carried baskets on his back.

"Pssst." A scrawny figure beckoned from a few feet away. He must have been about eight or ten years old, his neatly combed hair parted to one side.

I looked over my shoulder.

"Hey, you." He pointed at me. "You from the papers?"

I nodded uneasily. "How did you know?"

"You wanna write about Chinatown," the boy continued, "you come with me." He began to walk and, unsure what else to do, I followed. He turned onto Mott Street and stopped in front of a store with the letters L-E-E painted across mullioned windows.

"What'cha waiting for?" He pushed open the front door.

I hesitated for a second, then stepped over the threshold.

Chapter Three

The cloying, sweet scent of tobacco hit me first. It rushed into my nose and throat, seeping into every pore, my lungs, my jacket. Leaves the size of elephant ears hung in great bunches from the ceiling. Boxes of cigars, packets of cigarettes with pictures of camels and exotic harem scenes, pipes, cigarette holders, varieties of snuff and snuff boxes, lighters, and other paraphernalia filled every available nook.

"So, you met William," an ancient voice crackled through the dusty mist. "He's my nephew Lee Toy's boy. He's seen you before—at the Opera House, on the day of the shooting." Wreathed in a cloud of smoke, an elegant gent reclined in a teak planter's chair behind a glass-fronted counter. His face was narrow, wrinkled and crepey, like onion-skin paper. A wispy gray goatee and the tendrils of his mustache trailed beneath his chin. He sported a nattily cut beige suit and waistcoat, gold watch fob, and a tie pin that shimmered with diamonds.

William scampered off and squatted in the corner. A broad-shouldered clerk silently removed items from the shelves, dusted them one by one, and carefully returned them to their places.

"I got a question for you, Observer." The old man puffed away on a cigar, his index finger curled around the top. He seemed to know a lot about me. "You wanna know what's going on in the neighborhood, why not come speak to Tom Lee straightaway?"

I shifted my weight from one foot to the other. Although the papers made a big to-do about Mock Duck's savagery, the On Leong chief was no angel either. His men gave as good as they got, and sometimes worse.

"Sit," the old man commanded. "Make yourself comfortable." He motioned to his assistant, who brought over a stool. "You think you can stroll into the neighborhood and Tom don't hear? All you gotta do is dream about us, and Tom Lee knows." He tapped an arthritic finger to his forehead.

The little boy crouched in the corner, neatly writing in his copybook and murmuring the words out loud.

"What'cha doing?" Lee asked his grandnephew. "Tell the reporter."

"Practicing my penmanship."

"Read it out loud."

"'Tis the star-spangled banner,'" the boy read. "'O long may it wave. O'er the land of the free and the home of the brave.'"

"Y'see what he can do? Y'see what they're teaching 'em? Good stuff." Lee pushed himself upright and opened a hinged box that his assistant had brought over. It was filled with cigars, and he offered me one.

"No, thanks."

"C'mon. Give it a try." It was an order.

I picked it up, though I seldom smoked. He struck a match. I took a cautious breath and coughed. The old man grinned. "Too strong?"

"I hear they call you the mayor of Chinatown, Mr. Lee."

The leader of the On Leongs inclined his head modestly.

Photographs and newspaper cuttings tacked around the store testified to his standing amongst his people: here he was, marching at the head of parades and cutting ribbons. There, he was accompanying a group of locals and powerful politicians to a picnic on Staten Island.

A blurry image showed him celebrating Chinese New Year at a banquet hall in the company of several bigwigs. "That's the police commissioner, the district attorney, and the Chinese consul general," Lee said, pointing. "You gotta have friends if you want to survive. Tom knows that. But fellas like Mock Duck, they pull down their pants, piss wherever they want, and leave everyone else to clean their mess." He warmed to his theme.

"Trouble with Mock is, he don't care about no one except Mock. He don't care about our people. You think all this shootin' and fightin' is good for business? It ain't. Coppers show up and start askin' questions. Tourists get scared. Even the Chinese stop visitin'. Too much attention ain't good for us. But Mock, long as he's satisfied, long as he gets what he wants, he don't give a damn."

Lee's voice rose, and he tugged at his beard. "At the theater, *boom, boom, boom,* no warning. Outta nowhere. He kills four of my best guys. Family men. Grocer, laundry guy. Never hurt nobody."

I found that hard to believe.

"Mock don't need no excuses. He wanna shoot, boy, he just starts shootin'. A couple of the fellas, they saw him go inside. This business about the alibi? It's garbage."

"Are you saying he wasn't at the police station?"

Lee shook his head vehemently. "The copper who saw him there—it was a mistake. And before the theater, he shot my nephew, William's pa. Lee Toy was out deliverin' lucky money to the kids on New Year's Eve, and Mock clips him right here." Lee touched his jaw. "Ain't that right, William?"

The boy looked up from his book and nodded.

"Lucky that my nephew is sturdy like an ox. Else, he'd've been a goner."

The chief held up his hand. "But Tom always says, 'an eye for an eye, and we all go blind.'" He spat a fleck of tobacco from his tongue. "So, what's your name anyhow? They told me *Mrs.* Morley."

"That's correct."

"You a gal"—he peered at me—"in trousers? Why?"

"It helps me move about freely."

"And Mr. Morley, he don't object?"

"We have an understanding." It had taken a while for him to see my side of things, but he slowly came around.

"If my Minnie Rose ran about town like that…" Lee picked up a framed photograph, rubbed the glass with his sleeve, and held it up so I could take a closer look. A buxom white woman posed in the center while two boys in sailor suits gazed up at her adoringly.

"That's Minnie with little Frank and Tom. They're both grown men now. Frank's on his way to China to convert the natives," he said with pride. "And Tom Junior, he aims to be a mechanic." He returned the photograph to the shelf. "You got any kids?"

"I'm afraid not."

"'Course you don't. If you did, you wouldn't be here. You'd be home with them.… Where you from? Lemme guess. Istanbul? Persia?"

The cigar burned in the ashtray. I'd barely touched it. "Bombay."

"Bombay…" He nodded. "That's far…land of the Maharajas." He produced a box of Maharaja Brand tobacco to show me. I murmured a few words of admiration.

"You ever see an elephant?"

"Yes."

"Traveled through the Suez Canal?"

"On my way here."

"You know, your people, they bring opium to China?"

I nodded. Bombay had been built on the profits from the trade. Prominent families, like those of my friend Cyrus Merchant, had done business in China for generations.

"Well, it ain't your fault, I suppose." Lee stroked his beard. "How long you been in New York?"

"Ten years, give or take."

"Ten. Not too bad. Tom's been here forty. That's how it goes in this place. You come, think you'll stay maybe a year or two, earn a few dollars, go home—then you look up, and more'n half your life's gone.… How long you been at the paper?"

"About four years as a reporter." I had started as a secretary, writing travel columns and typing articles.

"And I ain't never heard of ya?" He fixed me with a stare.

"I don't come here very often." And unless the paper had some pressing reason to publicize a particular reporter, they never printed names.

Stooped over with age, his cane supporting his weight, an old man stood at the doorway and bowed. Lee waved him in. They spoke in their language for a few minutes before Lee's clerk pulled out a ledger and wrote something on the page. The On Leong chief pointed to an empty spot, dipped his pen in ink, and handed it to the visitor, whose trembling hand marked the spot with an X. The elderly visitor bowed again before he departed.

All I followed of their conversation were two words:" Mexico," then, a few minutes later, "Vancouver." I couldn't guess why they were discussing Mexico but later learned that many Chinese had settled there. As for Vancouver, it was also a port through which many Chinese—and some Indians—made their way to the United States. Sikh farmers from the Punjab were known to sail across the Pacific, travel down the West Coast, and settle in California.

"Okay." Lee closed the ledger with a thud and secured the closure with a string. "Where were we? Oh, yes. When Tom came to New York many years ago, Chinatown was small. Just Pell, Mott, and Doyers, and not too many Chinese. Now we're everywhere—Brooklyn, Bronx, New Jersey, even Boston…. You listenin', Observer? You gotta write this down.

"You reporters, you talk about the tongs, but you got it all mixed up. We ain't gangs, we ain't here to fight. At least, the On Leong Tong ain't. The Hips, now, that's another matter. But Tom and his On Leongs, we're here to assist. When the new fellas come over, we find them work and a place to stay. When a fella dies, we pay for his funeral. We send his bones back to China. You gettin' all this?"

I nodded, scribbling furiously. The chief's chattiness was an unexpected gift. "So how did the trouble with Mock begin?"

The old man rolled the smoke in his mouth and released it in slow puffs. "Maybe six, seven years ago, he shows up from 'Frisco, dressed all sharp. Like a choirboy, some say. Nice suit, leather shoes, laces and all. Fedora. Real American guy. Pals up with Reverend Parkhurst"—the noted reformer— "and tells the Reverend he's gonna help clean up Chinatown. You know how he does that? He says Tom Lee runs all the gamin' joints in the district.

"Now Tom, he don't run nothin', you understand? He just helps out his friends when they need some little assistance with the police. Ain't nothin' wrong with that. But Mock, you know what he does? He gives the Reverend a list of all of Tom's friends' joints. The next thing Tom knows, the cops have raided twenty, maybe thirty parlors." Lee grew animated.

"Why? Our boys don't cause no trouble. So they game a little in the evenings. A little *fan tan*, a little *pak kop piu*—what the Americans call 'policy.' There ain't no harm in that. The fellas, they're lonely, they work hard, they deserve a little enjoyment… And then, when the owners of the gamin' joints get out on bail, they come straight to me.

"They say, Tom you gotta do somethin' about this Mock Duck fella, now he wants money from us to keep our places safe.… You see what I'm talkin' about? And that's when the shootin' starts. If my boys get outta hand, what can Tom to do about it?" He pointed to a clipping. "Look at that."

It showed a younger version of Tom Lee with a badge pinned to his breast, and it was captioned, *Tom Lee, Deputy Sheriff, New York County*.

"Tom Lee ain't no outlaw. He was the first Chinese law-and-order man. You put *that* in your paper."

I thanked him for his time. He had told me more than I could have hoped for. It was a one-sided account, but nevertheless, the vague outlines of the conflict were beginning to take shape: Tom Lee, the old hand, who once had the neighborhood in his grasp and the gambling parlors in his pocket. Mock Duck, the interloper, ready to break down the door in order to grab a slice of the action.

"You got everything you need, Observer? You want me to repeat it?"

I assured him that I was fine.

"Come back anytime, you hear? Tom Lee's always willin' to talk."

* * *

That evening, at our brownstone home on Eighteenth Street, I didn't discuss where I'd been or whom I'd spoken to with my husband. He was American, a physician, twelve years my senior. And although he had liberal ideas about many things in life and had broken with some of his relatives to be with me, he could also be cautious—particularly when it came to my safety.

Over a dinner of vegetables with curry sauce, roast chicken, and potatoes, we spoke about different subjects—his day at the city's Health Department, where he worked; the arrival of a new colleague; and how George B. McClellan, his one-time schoolmate and now Mayor of New York, wanted to promote the pasteurization of milk—and of course clean drinking water—for sanitary reasons. Dr. Morley was an enthusiastic proponent of both.

I listened as attentively as I could, but my thoughts were downtown, on Mott and Doyers Streets. The Hip Sing Tong had just gunned down four of Tom Lee's men. No doubt, the On Leong chief hadn't talked my ear off solely out of kindness.

He must be setting the stage for something—some form of retaliation.

Chapter Four

Before I could probe Tom Lee's thoughts any further, matters took an unexpected turn. Just eight days after the shooting, and the day after my visit, George B. McClellan summoned the press to City Hall. Built early in the previous century, the marble building, with its phalanx of French windows, central dome, two projecting wings, and brownstone rear, seemed modest in comparison to the ambitions of our mighty metropolis, which had, about a decade prior, swallowed the city of Brooklyn, the villages and farmlands of Queens, and picturesque Richmond County, and added them to Manhattan and the Bronx to form the most awe-inspiring city in America.

Flanked by his Health Commissioner, Fire Commissioner, Parks Commissioner, and the five borough presidents, Georgie B. stood on the front steps. Clean-shaven and vigorous, with words like "honest" and "upright" bandied about even when his enemies spoke of him, our mayor declared that districts like Chinatown were unworthy of New York, which would one day be the center of the world. As such, the city must combine the best of the Old World with that of the new.

What was needed were more schools, hospitals, and libraries. Greener promenades and more attractive public buildings. Improved gas and electrical lines, and of course, a new supply of fresh, clean water that would quench the enlarged municipality's thirst for generations.

The bigwigs applauded, heads bobbing up and down in unison.

Districts like Chinatown, the mayor thundered, his voice carrying to my window across the street on Newspaper Row, were districts of yesteryear.

"Chinatown is a slum, a hotbed of vice, not to mention a fire hazard. It is a blight on our metropolis. The time has come for us to take a stand. The time has come to say, 'no more.' The bloodthirsty act at the theater has only cemented my views on this matter. The tenements on Pell, Mott, and Doyers Streets must be demolished."

Chinatown would be replaced, he continued, to rousing cheers, with a public park and playground. "By so doing, we will kill two birds with one stone. No more slums, no more of these tong wars, and a new green lung for an overcrowded section of the city that desperately needs it."

The project would be no different than what had already been accomplished at nearby Mulberry Bend Park, he added.

"If it were solely up to me," Hizzoner went on, "I would bring in the wrecking balls immediately. But our laws being what they are, a public hearing must be held. To that end, we will convene a meeting of the Board of Improvement at once."

* * *

"Now, that's what I call progress." Dupont was delighted. Mulberry Bend Park, Central Park, they all required slums to be cleared to make space, and once the settlements were gone, no one missed them. "It's as if they never existed." He grinned with satisfaction.

He couldn't wait for the reporter he'd dispatched to City Hall to return. "Don't stare at me like some goatherd. Write it up, Mrs. M."

Twenty minutes or so later, I turned in the article.

He noticed me loitering. "What is it now?"

I tentatively inquired whether I might cover the hearing.

"Really, Mrs. Morley. What have I told you?"

"I know, I know. Women and politics don't mix, but the lads have their hands full." And they did, because, apart from the "Sob Sisters"—four female journalists with a penchant for purple prose—the judge on the Thaw case had banned all women reporters from the courtroom.

The editor scratched his pock-marked cheek. "Truth be told, I wasn't planning on sending anyone.… Then again, the fact that it is Chinatown might be of some interest." He sniffed, opened his logbook, and ran his index finger down a list. "Let's see. Holger—busy; Dixon—ditto. O'Malley—out for the week. A *week?* Is his mother *dying* of typhus?" He read off a few more names. They were all accounted for, and all men.

It hadn't been easy when I came on board the paper as a secretary. The lads had tried to figure me out, asking questions, teasing, and sometimes getting downright abusive. Fortunately, when they realized I wouldn't take the bait, that I kept my head down and concentrated on work, they lost interest. And while that meant I was isolated most of the time, I preferred that to the alternative.

"You really want to go?" Dupont stared at the ledger.

"Not if you don't want me to." I tried to sound nonchalant.

"Oh don't be coy. It's one thing to hire you for odds and ends. Another to allow you to cover hearings of the board." He looked up. "Fine. But no questions, nothing like that. Don't tell anyone you're from the *Observer.* Listen, take notes, type them up. All I need is a couple of inches. You think you can manage?"

* * *

I headed home, marveling at the age in which we lived. The eviction of an entire village from their homes only merited a paragraph or two, while the trial of a millionaire who shot his wife's paramour in public generated endless pages of reportage, analysis, and gossip.

Sure, Harry Thaw had shot Stanford White, the famous architect, on the rooftop of Madison Square Garden; and yes, Madison Square Garden had been among White's greatest creations; and of course, it was horrifying how the randy architect had taken advantage of Mrs. Evelyn Thaw, née Nesbit, when she was just a young, unmarried girl of sixteen. But months and months of unflagging attention? The public couldn't get enough, no matter how much drivel we fed them, but I, for one, had had my fill.

I spotted Mary Archer, a reporter from an Afro-American paper. She was on her way back to Brooklyn. We knew each other through a couple of stories that both our papers had covered.

I remarked how strange it was that no one seemed to care about anything except the Thaw case. "A hundred other things go on, and no one notices."

"Not us. We've barely printed a word about it. Then again, the general public doesn't care about our affairs either, so I suppose that's fitting."

She wasn't the slightest bit surprised to learn about Chinatown's impending fate. "It had to happen sooner or later. Frankly, I'm amazed that it's taken as long it has. But after that bloodbath at the theater, the mayor could hardly delay it any longer."

She went on to tell me about Seneca Village, a neighborhood of mainly Black, Irish, and a few German families that had been razed to make way for Central Park. Homes, a school, and a church had been demolished.

"Why do they always tear down our homes," she asked. "Why not raze Mr. Morgan's place"—she was referring to the banker J.P. Morgan—"and put a park there instead?"

* * *

Dupont received word that Thaw's wife, Evelyn, would be lunching at Pontin's, and so I almost missed the hearing. The editor wanted me to secure a table, or peer through the glass, and find out what she ordered, how she looked, whether she had an appetite or pushed the plate away untasted. By this point, even I felt sorry for the young woman whose past and present were being pawed over by the prosecution, defense, press, and public.

Of course, the place was swarmed, and I had to jostle and push for a position with a view, but fortunately, the young Mrs. Thaw's plans changed at the last minute, and she failed to make an appearance. *C'est la vie.*

I extricated myself as quickly as I could—there are crowds, and there are crowds; New York can't match Venice or the holy city of Benares—and hoofed it to one of the many nondescript buildings near City Hall, where the municipality rented rooms for official business. To this day, I maintain that the blandness of a committee's name often conceals the true scope of its responsibilities. So it should come as no surprise to learn that the "Board of Improvement" and the "Board of Estimate and Apportionment" were two of our city's most powerful entities.

Tom Lee had already arrived. He sat in the back row of the cramped hall alongside several of his countrymen. Leather shoes polished to a brilliant shine, trousers pressed with a sharp crease, gold fob of his pocket watch conspicuously visible, he looked the part of the district's wise and respected protector. To his right sat a giant with arms like tree trunks and a fierce scar running from ear to chin. Must be his nephew, Lee Toy, the one who had been shot in the jaw on New Year's Eve by the Hips, as Lee had said.

Satchel bumping against his side, Tom's grandnephew and Lee Toy's son, William, arrived out of breath. He had cut school for the important event. William looked over at his great-uncle, who stared resolutely toward the front, legs apart, hands resting on an ivory-handled cane, but his father pointed to an empty seat in the corner, and William slipped into it. If even a fraction of the reporters who hovered outside the Thaw courtroom had stopped in, the place would have been overflowing, but apart from a man sent over from the *World*, which had been baying for the district's destruction, I seemed to be the only reporter present. The rest of the room was filled with members of the public, both Asiatic and white.

I checked the time on the pocket watch that my father had given me before I set sail. He could never have imagined the path my life had taken since his and my mother's deaths shortly after I arrived in this country. We had planned that I should visit England, tour Italy and Greece, and then spend six months in America. He had wanted me to see the world and learn about American democracy, just like Pandita Ramabai. Although he worked for the British as a civil servant in India, he knew that one day we would be free and that it would be necessary to be prepared.

At about ten-thirty, six graybeards filed in one by one and took their seats at a long table. After brief introductory remarks, the chairman, a pedantic, elderly gent with a penchant for noisily shuffling papers, opened the floor for discussion. "Gentlemen, please keep this short and civilized," he instructed.

I scanned the room again but saw no sign of anyone resembling Mock

Duck. Since it was the Hips' actions that had brought matters to a head, his absence was revealing, and it also proved Tom Lee's point: the only thing the gangster cared about was himself.

Adolph Block, a Jewish property owner, began the proceedings by submitting a type-written document detailing 131 reasons why the neighborhood should not be replaced by a park. J.J. Hill, of the Metropolitan Parks Association, said he favored a playground in the general area, but believed that the large sum of money that would be required for its construction would be better spent elsewhere.

Resplendent in a red bowtie and shiny oxblood boots, lawyer Bartow S. Weeks made his way to the front of the room and introduced himself as the representative of several Chinese merchants. He proposed a modified plan that would open up the east side of Doyers Street for a playground and plaza but leave the rest of the neighborhood untouched. Tom Lee and his men nodded and clapped in agreement.

"There are no more law-abiding people than the Chinese," William Beecher of 170 Broadway declared. "I have acted as counsel to Chinamen for over twenty years, and there is no more vice in Chinatown than there is on the Bowery or in the Tenderloin. Mott, Pell, and Doyers Streets are exclusively business thoroughfares. And if the Chinese merchants are forced to move, they will sue the city for losses sustained by their various business enterprises."

A Concerned Citizen leapt to his feet. "The park would save the police and fire departments at least $200,000 annually. Ordinarily, the area has a Chinese population of eight or nine hundred. But on weekends, it swells to five thousand, engaged in every imaginable act of crime. The abolition of Chinatown is worth every dollar we must spend."

The room became hot as a gentleman who claimed to be a banker chimed in: "I would like to make it clear that any opposition to the park is the result of one simple fact: greed.

"Lots in Chinatown assessed for fourteen thousand dollars produce twice that amount annually in rents. Nowhere else in the city, not even on Fifth or Madison Avenue, is there property so productive of profit." He went on to explain that unscrupulous landlords made astronomical profits from the Chinese, who had few other choices.

Mr. Frazee, a moral crusader, dealt the final blow. "The Chinatown rookeries are not tenements in the legal sense of the term. To whit, Charles Bacigalupo, the undertaker, buries one-hundred and twenty-five white women each year from that part of the city."

A hush fell over the room. Allegations of white slavery trumped any other considerations.

A lone female voice pierced the silence.

"I want to defend the young Chinese men of this city." Mrs. Edith Maxwell, a grandmotherly figure from the Morningstar Baptist Church, stood to introduce herself. "Chinatown is open to our missionaries; we are free to come and go as we please, and I never had anyone say an out-of-the-way thing to me, although I have been among them for a good long time. The Chinese aren't to blame for Chinatown. It's the police. They've been collecting money from the Chinese for years, and they are still doing it. Why, one of my boys told me there was a raid the other day, and the sergeant let four fellows go for thirty dollars!"

Lawyer Weeks waved his hand. "I must also object on technical grounds. The Small Parks Act proposed by Mayor McClellan is not a tool for demolishing tenements or suppressing vice. Its sole purpose is the creation of parks and playgrounds."

Thus far, none of the Chinese had spoken. I glanced at Lee, who was listening intently. He cleared his throat, pushed down on his cane, and shuffled to the front of the hall.

"My name is Tom Lee," he said. "I have lived in Chinatown thirty years. Our people keep to ourselves, keep our troubles to ourselves. We don't bother no one. Some of us ain't never gonna go back to China. Many can't go back to China. We can't become American either"—because of the Chinese Exclusion Act. "We can't vote, or go home to see our families. But we work here, live here, our children are born here. We serve this country, and Chinatown's the only place we feel at home." He paused for a second. "If you make us leave, where will we go?"

William leapt up and cheered. Lee Toy nodded his head, and the Chinese in the back row, as well as Mrs. Maxwell and Lawyer Weeks applauded.

Not being able to vote meant that elected officials had little reason to fight for your interests. (I knew this as both a foreigner and a woman.) No wonder Lee worked so assiduously to cultivate political connections. He would have had to operate through those connections to get anything done. But the limits of his friendships must have already been reached because no official sprang to the community's defense.

The chairman thanked the attendees for their participation. The board had heard enough, he said, and now it was time to deliberate. The graybeards moved off the dais.

I stepped outside for a breath of fresh air. The city wasn't shy about tearing down neighborhoods. In fact, in ten years, I'd seen so many structures go up and come down that the entire island seemed to undulate. And once its plans were in motion, no one could stop the municipal juggernaut.

I pictured temple chariots to the god Jagannath. The British claimed that these vehicles crushed believers mercilessly beneath their stone wheels. Who knows whether or not that was true, but here in New York, the municipal juggernaut was alive and well and much more powerful than its divine counterpart. If the Board of Improvement voted yes, and the Board of Estimate agreed, it wouldn't be just one or two people in the way who were crushed. All of Chinatown would be history.

Sounds drifted from inside the hall, and I hurried back. The chairman had returned and requested everyone to be seated. It had been scarcely more than an hour and a half since the proceedings had begun, and he mumbled his verdict so softly that I couldn't be sure I had heard him. But Tom Lee's face fell, and the men accompanying him looked crestfallen, and William shoved his fist in his mouth to stop himself from crying out loud.

The chairman said a name and a mousey fellow with drooping mustaches and gloomy eyes stepped forward. Another board member introduced Engineer Webster and instructed him to prepare, as swiftly as possible, a set of detailed drawings for both the demolition of the quarter and the construction of a new park.

After this, only one step remained, and the member continued. The drawings and accompanying cost sheet would be submitted to the Board of Estimate for its vote.

That seemed to leave a little gap for some hope to squeak through. But since the board was composed of the mayor and a handful of others who had been part of the City Hall announcement in the first place, their approval was hardly in doubt.

Chapter Five

The On Leong chief berated his lawyer on the way back. "If I told you once, I told you fifty times. No one gives a damn about the Small Parks Act." He banged the sidewalk with his cane. "What the heck am I paying you for? You're supposed to save Chinatown, not act like a fool. What are we gonna do now? With the neighborhood gone, how am I gonna pay your bills?" And so on.

The lawyer hung his head. "I did the best I could, Mr. Lee, but their minds were made up. You saw how fast it went, they don't want to listen to reason. And what I said is correct. The Small Parks Act—"

"You say those words one more time, and you will never work for me again. You hear that, Weeks? Even that old lady, Mrs. Maxwell from the church, she could have done better."

The beleaguered lawyer peeled away a few blocks later, and not long afterward, Lee, leaning heavily on his cane, Lee Toy, and William disappeared into the tobacco store on Mott.

I had followed the crowd to see how the news would be received locally. It was one thing to report on the hearing and another to capture the human angle. I knew I was supposed to keep it simple, but Dupont was a big fan of the human angle—at least in some instances. We'd certainly given Harry Thaw and his family every possible angle, and some that I didn't even know existed.

But instead of demonstrations of consternation or outrage, what I noticed was the group that had gathered on Pell in front of the Hung Far Lowe Restaurant. At first, I thought it might be a protest or a political meeting, but on closer inspection, it turned out they were watching a wrestling match.

In the center of the ring of onlookers, two men had stripped to their trousers and were feinting, kicking, and parrying while the others shouted encouragement. Onlookers made wagers, and a couple of bookies went around collecting cash. The atmosphere was frenzied, a combination of excitement, fear, and pent-up anxiety. The men punched and kicked each other hard, sprays of sweat and blood flying.

Just as the contest reached fever pitch, and the faster of the two pugilists appeared ready to deliver his slower but bigger opponent a knockout blow, the commotion died down, and the crowd went silent. The fighters wiped the sweat from their brows, and the crowd parted to make way for a slim figure dressed in black, his eyes obscured by dark-purple-tinted glasses.

"Who's that?" I wanted to ask. But I didn't need to. I already knew the answer from the way he was being treated.

Mock Duck walked to the center of the ring as if he had all the time in the world. He held out his hand, and without demur, the bookies passed him their earnings. He didn't deign to examine the cash, just dropped it into his pocket and waited.

One by one the onlookers melted away. The bookies slunk off, as did the fighters, leaving the highbinder and a white lad with curly hair and freckles who stood a few paces behind him.

"You see," he told his companion in smooth, unhurried tones, "that's how we do it here."

His companion didn't reply, just stared at him in awe.

I knew I should vanish, slink away into the shadows. Instead, I spoke up. "Mr. Mock?" My voice trembled slightly.

He lowered his glasses and glanced at me over them. No interest. If anything, perhaps a hint of boredom.

The sun beat down. I felt hot; I felt faint. Those eyes. That face. I had seen him before. Yes, in the papers and on playing cards, but somewhere else too. In person.

"Mr. Mock"—my voice continued of its own accord—"I'm with the New York *Daily Observer*. I wonder—"

He yawned.

"I wonder," I repeated, "why you weren't at today's hearing?"

Mock turned to the freckled lad. "Go inside. I'll meet you in a minute."

He waited until his companion was out of earshot. "Now, what was your question? Oh, that's right, why wasn't I at the meeting? I wasn't there because there was nothing I could do. This neighborhood's fate was decided long before I came along."

"So you don't feel responsible?"

"Me?" A superior smile hovered at the corner of his lips. "You overestimate my abilities."

"The shooting at the theater—"

He held up his hand. "I've said it a thousand times. Not my doing."

"You really expect the public to believe that?"

"They can believe what they want. Now, if you will excuse me—"

"One last question, Mr. Mock. Are you saying that you are willing to allow Chinatown to perish, and you won't lift a finger to stop it?"

He paused. The hem of his tunic fluttered. He thought for a minute before he responded. "Life is like a river. Far be it from me to alter its course."

I stood there, dumbfounded, as he turned and strolled into the restaurant.

* * *

The questions kept intruding, even though Dupont kept me busy typing, filing, and chasing minor tidbits for the next several days. I had spoken to Mock Duck, one of the most feared gangsters in the land, and he had spouted some gibberish about life and waterways. But he couldn't be as unconcerned as he made out. If the Thaw trial was the *Observer's* bread and butter, Chinatown must be Mock's. He couldn't just stand by and watch it being destroyed. Because if Tom Lee was correct, and he really didn't give a damn, then he had to be a fool. And that didn't square with everything else I knew about him.

At the same time, something about the entire encounter felt false, as though he had staged his appearance at the fight for a purpose. That outstretched hand. The parting of the crowd. Was that how gangsters truly behaved, or was he putting on a performance? And if so, for whose benefit?

Shrimpy, one of the younger, greener lads at the *Observer*, and one of the few with whom I chatted, told me he'd gone by the neighborhood and heard that the children from the local school had put on a dance for the mayor's wife. But while Mrs. McClellan complimented their efforts, no amount of pleading would persuade her to ask her husband to reconsider.

"The mayor must make some decisions that seem unfair to a few, but are good for the many," she told them.

"Tom Lee even brought gifts," Shrimpy said, "but to no avail."

As much as I'd heard about Mulberry Bend, Central Park, and other places, Chinatown's death knell had come incredibly fast. And that Tom, with all his connections, couldn't do anything to slow it down—that didn't feel right at all.

But what did I really know about such things? Nothing. I'd had very little experience in these matters. In New York, it was what I had learned by reading and typing up stories for the *Observer,* and prior to that, I'd spent a few months attending classes on government at Barnard, and before that, just what I had studied on my own in India.

I went to Mulberry Bend Park to see if it sparked any insights. A broad swath of grass was punctuated by benches, and tenements surrounded a flat walkway around its perimeter. Recent arrivals—Jews, Irish, and Italians—strolled, snacked, and spoke to each other in their own languages. Probably, the park was better than the slums that once stood here, and the former residents had found other homes elsewhere. Who was I to say otherwise?

A familiar voice chortled, and I turned to see three girls. The youngest, dressed in yellow silk pajamas, looked familiar. It took a minute for me to place her: she was the child I'd seen at Chatham Square counting train cars with her father. And the man, the father, on whose shoulders she had been riding—could that have been Mock Duck? The same Mock Duck I had seen at the fight? It didn't seem possible. But, why not? I knew nothing about his private life. He could have a family. He could have children.

The two older girls were dressed in sturdy cotton outfits, and all three were supervised by a smooth-haired beauty in traditional Oriental dress.

"Little pig, little pig, let me come in," the eldest girl cried.

"Not by the hairs of my chinny-chin-chin," the other two yelled.

"Then I'll huff, and I'll puff, and I'll blow your house down."

The two little pigs ran off, yelling with glee while the wolf chased behind.

"Lily, May, Ha Oi," the woman called. She was beautiful enough to be a gangster's moll with her clear porcelain skin, heart-shaped face, and beautiful hands, each finger as delicately shaped as an okra. But something about her manner didn't fit. She had a crisp way about her, as though she was accustomed to being practical rather than decorative.

The older two girls responded to the summons at once, but the child in yellow took her time, and when she was reunited with the group, stomped her foot and evidently didn't appreciate being scolded.

The highbinder had taught her well, I thought. She certainly possessed his imperiousness.

I considered approaching the woman, but felt disheveled and sweaty in comparison, and hesitated. The moment passed.

The group turned toward Chinatown, and then I headed home myself.

* * *

The front door to the brownstone on Eighteenth Street creaked, and Dr. Morley's keys clinked into the bowl. He entered the living room, where I was sitting with my stockinged feet up on an ottoman, and dropped a kiss on my cheek.

"You really shouldn't," I said.

"Shouldn't what?"

"I've told you before. Show affection like that. It tempts the fates."

"And here I was thinking I'd married a modern woman."

"And here I was thinking I'd married a sensible man. I suppose we were both mistaken."

He laughed and settled his broad frame into a chair. He had good news and bad news.

The good news was that we'd been invited to the McClellans' for dinner the following evening. It was a last-minute invitation, since another guest had dropped out, but still an honor—and a first. Although they'd both attended the same boarding school as boys, my husband and the mayor had only recently become reacquainted. It wouldn't hurt for Dr. Morley to have a friend at the top.

"I suppose I will have to pull out one of my saris and my jewelry."

"I think you will."

"And the bad news is—?"

"Remember those plans you told me about Chinatown—how it's going to be demolished?"

"Yes." The hearing had taken place about a week ago.

"They've been put on hold."

"That can't be." I sat up straight. "The Board of Improvement approved. Engineer Webster is drawing up plans—"

"And he's the one who identified the problem."

Apparently, there was underground water beneath Doyers Street. The stream that had once run through it was indeed what had caused its bend. What with Collect Pond and Canal Street, that entire section of the city must have once been crisscrossed with waterways that were later filled in. So now, the engineer needed to investigate the terrain, and as a result, the entire process was projected to take longer, would likely be more complicated, and would certainly cost far more than planned.

"Indefinite delays" was the industry parlance. It could mean anything from maybe sometime…to never.

"At any rate," my husband went on, "Dr. Darlington"—the Health Commissioner, and his boss—"told me that Georgie B. is livid. He wants to get the Chinatown park done *tout de suite* in order to shore up support for his more ambitious projects. And now Webster's thrown a wrench in the works, and everything is going to become that much more difficult."

Mock Duck's remark about rivers came to mind. What had he said? Something about not being able to change their course. Was that why he seemed so unbothered? Had he known that this would be the outcome? Or was I succumbing to the myth of his omnipotence?

But if rivers do what they please, so did the story I was following, and it pulled me along.

When I got to work the next morning, fully intending to speak to the engineer, Dupont ordered me to clear my calendar. Vincent Pisarra, an agent of the Children's Society, was on his way to Mock's place, and I had to find out what in god's name was happening.

Chapter Six

The Society for the Prevention of Cruelty to Children, or the Gerry Society (after its founder, Elbridge Gerry), rescued children in distress. Children who were chained by their ankles to radiators, children who were beaten, starved, branded, or forced into lives of thievery, or much worse. I'd witnessed the Society's efforts, covered some of the agents' raids, even worked there briefly after my marriage, but the opportunities they offered women—essentially becoming a matron—didn't suit my temperament.

I thought at once about the three girls as I jumped in a cab and told the driver to hurry. But I'd seen mistreated children before, more than I wanted to, and all three girls from the park had appeared perfectly fine and healthy.

The traffic had crawled to a stop as we neared Chatham Square, so I paid and half ran, half walked to No. 10. It was about eight-thirty in the morning when I arrived. The neighborhood was waking up, and there were people waiting in line to use the public taps while five or six men brushed their teeth in the open.

A small crowd had gathered outside Mock's home. Dupont had offered for Shrimpy to accompany me for my safety. Although he didn't say so explicitly, I knew that was what he had intended, and he probably also thought it would be good for me to have backup. Only briefly regretting having turned down the offer, I elbowed my way through. In any case, Shrimpy would only have gotten in the way, and his build and mild manner hardly served as a deterrent.

I felt my way up a dark, rickety stairwell and followed voices coming from behind a door that had been left slightly ajar on the third-floor landing.

I mumbled a prayer, took a quick breath, and entered through a passageway kitchen. The last time the police raided the highbinder's home, they had uncovered a cache of weaponry: knives, pistols, blackjacks, knuckle-dusters, along with several suits of armor. In the kitchen, however, porridge bubbled on a stove, utensils hung neatly from hooks, and freshly chopped vegetables had been left on a wooden cutting board. A dreary sliver of sunlight squeaked through a rear window. I crossed the threshold into a larger living area that reeked of an unmistakable sweet, flowery fragrance.

Pisarra, a swarthy Italian with mutton-chop whiskers, was speaking to Mock, who looked like he had just awoken. He was barefoot, his eyes red and sleepy. A white muslin undershirt hung over his loose black trousers.

A short, sturdy woman stood beside him in a drab ochre robe belted at the waist. Thick gold rings circled her broad wrists and fingers, and gold discs shone from her ears. She couldn't have been older than twenty, and her nut-brown forehead was creased with concern.

Tall and skinny as a beanpole, a grizzled white woman wearing a beige apron and holding a wooden spoon in her hands hovered beside Mock and his companion.

But they weren't the only ones crammed into that room, neatly furnished with two beds, a bureau on which at least three different morning papers lay stacked, and a handsome beige and blue rug. Pisarra had brought along three others whom I later learned were Butts, his beefy, yellow-haired colleague; O'Connor, a uniformed roundsman; and a runty fellow from the *Times*, E.K. Hornby.

"This is ridiculous," Mock said to Pisarra. I would have recognized that bored, insolent voice anywhere. "What will it take for you to leave me alone? Just name your price."

"You think we do this for the money?" Pisarra took a step toward one of the beds, but with a speed and suddenness that made my head spin, Mock Duck stood between the glaring agent and the bundle I noticed beneath the covers, who, by some miracle, was still asleep. But now her eyes peeked out, and she leapt from her bed, straight into the gangster's arms.

"I know you want to lock me up." Cradling the girl, Mock turned to the roundsman. "But this is taking it too far. Don't punish my daughter for whatever it is you think I've done." His voice had an edge to it.

"Come now, Mock," the copper replied mildly. "The Gerrys here, they ain't got no choice. If what Mrs. Mock says is correct"—he looked up at the robed woman and added hastily— "and I'm sure it is—if Ha Oi really is your foster child, then the judge will send her back before you know it."

"You expect me to believe that?" The highbinder's voice rose an octave, and he held the girl tighter. "What do you think—I was born yesterday?"

"I'm sorry, Mock," the roundsman said. "But we've gotta do our jobs, so don't put up a fight. You'll only make it worse for her."

From the safety of Mock's arms, Ha Oi defiantly stuck out her tongue at the roundsman and the Gerry agents.

"This is bullshit," Mock spat. "Scaring a little girl. Terrifying her mother. And all because of some unsigned letter." He held out his hand. "Let me see it."

"We'll read it out in court," Pisarra said. "We're just following the rules." He didn't look like he would budge an inch, and I knew from experience that he wouldn't back down. Blood would be shed before Pisarra deviated from his appointed mission.

Mock must have sensed that, too, because he asked, "How long will this take?"

"Half an hour," the roundsman said, "an hour at most."

"And you promise no funny business?"

"Not from our end."

The gangster muttered under his breath, but he knew when he had no choice. "Her mother, Tai Yow, will go with her." He took a step back and whispered in the young woman's ear. Then he turned to the woman in the apron. "And Bedelia, our maid, will go along to translate."

"That's fine," Pisarra said, nodding. The girl's mother disappeared behind a beaded curtain, and the tension in the room lifted just a little bit.

I looked around for a moment. The place was spotlessly clean. No sign of weaponry or armor anywhere. I ran my finger against the wall. Not a speck of dust.

Ha Oi tugged at Mock's earlobe. He smiled and said something to her in a low voice. She wriggled from his arms and, before anyone could prevent her, ran to the bureau, opened the drawer, and handed him something.

"Now wait a minute—" Butts said.

But Mock had already begun rapidly winding the string around a top, which was fat and round like a turnip. He inserted his finger into the loop and whipped the wooden spindle into the air. It flew onto the flat of his open palm, where it spun and danced in a circle like a whirling dervish until it finally toppled on its side, exhausted. The child laughed and squealed with delight. The gangster burst into a smile so wide and warm that it completely transformed him. All of a sudden, he looked like a motion-picture star who could light up a screen. He tossed the top to Ha Oi, and she ran and hid it under her pillow.

In the meantime, Bedelia had fetched a fresh blouse and pair of pantaloons from the bureau. Mock crossed his arms over his chest, his face set, daring anyone to interfere as she dressed the little girl. Ha Oi shot furious looks at Pisarra and Butts while she raised her arms to have her blouse removed, and again when the clean tunic was pulled on, and as she waited patiently for the cloth buttons to be fastened.

Tai Yow rustled out, her squat form overpowered by a black silk gown with a bow at the neck, and mutton-chop sleeves. She wore an elaborate black hat like an upside-down mushroom to complete the ensemble, and didn't seem entirely comfortable in any of it.

Pisarra checked the time on his watch. Bedelia unsheathed a comb, brushed Ha Oi's hair, and caught it with gold ribbons into two bunches. Soft stray hairs poked out like a baby hedgehog. She brought out silk slippers and the child sighed like a long-suffering martyr, stuck out her foot, and allowed the tiny appendage to be coaxed and cajoled into its fussy covering.

Tai Yow reached for her daughter's hand and kissed it, but Butts had reached his limit. Without warning, he scooped up Hai Oi and began to move.

"No!" Mock yelled and stretched out his arms.

Ha Oi began to yell and pound on Butts's chest with her tiny fists, but the Gerry agent scarcely noticed. He kept going through the kitchen and out the door of the apartment. I started to follow him, but an anguished howl stopped me in my tracks.

I returned to the room. The gangster had fallen to his knees and buried his face in Ha Oi's pillow. He was weeping.

Chapter Seven

To keep the gods from getting jealous, some mothers in India don't claim their children as their own. When asked who a child's parents are, they might give the name of the nearest tree or stream or mountain. Others don't even count the number of their offspring for fear that one might be stolen. For me, seeing Ha Oi hauled away was like having that superstition come true. For Tai Yow, it must have been a horrifying, unfathomable experience.

On our way out, the Mocks' downstairs neighbor, Mrs. Woo, joined us, out of breath. She was the woman who had been with the children in the park. She told Bedelia to go back and attend to Mock Duck, that she would translate. And she spent the journey walking alongside Tai Yow, trying to comfort the distraught mother. Other neighbors came out onto the street, faces appeared at windows and on balconies, and people stopped what they were doing in order to watch the sorry procession go by.

The agents brought Ha Oi to Children's Court, a gloomy box on Third Avenue and Eleventh Street. How we made our way there with Ha Oi squirming in Butts's arms—she knew how to put up a fight and didn't get tired—Pissara all wound up, Tai Yow struggling to keep pace, and Hornby from the *Times* trying to ask questions, I'll never know.

Children's Court was a relatively new institution, and it was one which made our city proud of its benevolence. It allowed minors to be tried separately from adults, and in the days before *L'Affaire Thaw*, Dupont sent me there often. Now it had been at least a month since I'd last set foot inside.

Layers of peeling paint covered the walls, and colorful *bon mots* courtesy of dirty minds and mischievous hands had been carved into the rows of wooden benches. Butts dumped Ha Oi in the holding pen, and the little girl, so carefully dressed in silk, stopped struggling and gazed about her in wonder. Her baby fists clutched the bars, and as she stuck her face between them, she looked like a diminutive prisoner being held for a crime she couldn't comprehend. She didn't at all resemble the other children—all were white, many were waifs, ill-kempt, and shabbily clothed. When Ha Oi momentarily vanished behind another youngster, Tai Yow would sit up straight and tug urgently on Mrs. Woo's sleeve. She didn't relax until she spotted her daughter once more.

Memories of my own parting from my parents intruded. I was nineteen and leaving of my own accord, yet still my mother wept from the moment we arrived at the docks. I pushed the thoughts away.

Magistrate Mayo presided over the day's cases. Despite his unkempt beard and gruff manner, he was generally considered to be fair. He began by admonishing a misbehaving schoolboy, Robert Pasquale, for writing love letters to his teacher at Public School 70 and reading them out loud to his classmates. He'd been brought in by a janitor, but the teacher declined to press charges so the judge let him go with a stern warning to behave in the future. Next came fourteen-year-old Nellie Lahiff, who had run away from home and found herself a job as an assistant duster at the Waldorf Hotel. Her mother demanded that she return at once, but Nellie refused. She wanted to make it on her own, she told the magistrate. At home, she looked after her six siblings and wasn't paid a cent, while the hotel paid fourteen dollars a month! The judge sent her home. Parents, he said, knew what was best for their children.

As Butts and Pisarra approached the bench, a reedy fellow with bulging eyes and a pencil jutting from behind his ear loped in. He folded his lanky frame into a seat at the rear and cocked his head to listen. Now, there were three of us: Pike from the *Sun*, Hornby from the *Times,* and me. Not too bad, given the competition downtown.

Magistrate Mayo beckoned Ha Oi forward. The clerk, a ruddy-faced, middle-aged fellow, opened the gate to the pen. The six-year-old stepped out and, following his clipped directions, faced the smattering of spectators. Butts stood behind the girl, and the top of her head barely reached his waist. Nevertheless, a proud spark flickered in her eyes.

"What is your name?" the judge asked.

"Ha Oi," she replied clearly.

"Your Honor," Pisarra began, "based on information received by the Children's Society and the results of our foray into the home of the Celestial highbinder, Mock Duck, I would like to submit that this child, living at No. 10 Doyers Street, is not related by blood to either Mock Duck or his wife. And further, when we arrived on the premises, we found both adults under the influence."

Pisarra reached into his pocket and handed the judge a note. "This letter, which we received over the weekend, clearly states that the girl, Ha Oi, is neither Mock nor Mrs. Mock's offspring. Indeed, there is a possibility that she may not even be Oriental."

Mrs. Woo gasped. I shook my head in disbelief. The claim was absurd.

The judge frowned, unfolded the note, and began to read. He nodded, folded it back up, and returned it to the agent. Then he turned to Tai Yow. "What do you have to say?"

Mrs. Woo whispered a few words to her neighbor before she stood and introduced herself. "My name is Grace Woo, Your Honor. My husband, Mr. Woo, is a photographer. We live on Doyers Street with our two daughters. Our girls and Ha Oi are playmates. I studied at the mission school right here in Chinatown, and I help my husband with his business. I buy the photographic chemicals and speak to customers."

"Go on." The judge appeared intrigued.

"Mrs. Mock doesn't speak English, so I will translate for her. She says that this letter is a lie made up by enemies of Mock Duck, men who wish him ill."

"There must be many of those." The judge smirked.

Hornby from the *Times* tapped my arm with a pencil. "What's the bird's name again?"

"Grace Woo."

"Who?"

"Woo," I repeated.

"Ha. Good Look's more like it." He grinned like a cat who'd caught a pigeon.

Tai Yow pulled her neighbor's sleeve and spoke rapidly in her own language.

"You must tell Mrs. Mock not to interrupt," the judge said sharply.

"If I may, sir, Mrs. Mock would like you to know that Ha Oi is the daughter of her first husband—"

"*First* husband?" The magistrate jotted a note.

"Yes, sir. He was a jeweler by the name of Chin Mung and they lived in San Francisco."

"Go on."

"Chin had been married to an Irish girl, Lizzie Smith."

Hizzoner frowned. He may not have approved, but marriages between people from different countries happened more often than was generally acknowledged. Tom Lee and his wife, my husband and I, and all the Anglo-Indians I knew at home were proof of that.

"Lizzie died during childbirth," Mrs. Woo continued. "So Tai Yow raised Ha Oi from when she was an infant. When Chin Mung passed away during a trip to China, Tai Yow moved to New York and brought the little girl along with her. She met Mock Duck, they married and adopted Ha Oi for their own. They are very happy together."

The judge made a few more notes. "Irish mother…Oriental father… adoptive parents…" he murmured. "That's a lot of twists and turns for one so young."

"Ha Oi and Mrs. Mock have both suffered great losses, sir, but they have been fortunate in finding such a kind and generous provider in Mock. He denies his daughter nothing." In fact, the photographer's wife added, she and her husband often wished they could do as much for their own daughters.

Tai Yow, growing impatient, again whispered loudly to her neighbor.

"Mrs. Woo, please tell Mrs. Mock to wait her turn." The magistrate spoke sharply. The situation seemed to be spiraling away from the two women through no fault of their own. The very facts of Ha Oi's life were at odds with what the judge deemed right and proper.

Mrs. Woo explained that Mrs. Mock wanted the court to know that a year ago, teachers from the Morningstar Mission school had visited Mock Duck to request that he enroll Ha Oi, but Mock refused because he didn't want his daughter attending an ordinary school with ordinary classmates. Instead, he hired a private tutor to teach his daughter. Miss Elsie Wong came to their home three times a week. The lessons were expensive, but that didn't matter. "Mock Duck wants only the best for Ha Oi, and he can afford it."

"Anything else?"

"She is the apple of their eyes, sir. And her father *was* from the Orient. Mrs. Mock Duck, who knows the situation best, assures me of this."

Ha Oi had been facing the court the entire time. She clasped her hands behind her back, swung her leg back and forth, and blinked, trying to hold back tears as she stared at the ceiling.

The magistrate's demeanor softened. He questioned Pisarra about the child's living conditions, and the agent grudgingly allowed that Mock's home was spotless. "He keeps a servant, Your Honor, an Irish maid—"

"An Irish maid?" Mayo's eyebrows brushed up against his hairline.

"Yes, Your Honor. And as you can see, the child appears to be well-clothed and well-fed…. However, we did find an opium layout on the premises"—I hadn't seen one, but certainly smelled it—"and as I mentioned earlier, when we arrived, everyone, with the exception of the maid, was under the influence."

Mayo pursed his lips grimly. Then turned to Ha Oi. "Who are your parents?"

"Mock Duck and Tai Yow."

"Where do you want to live?"

Tai Yow said something, and Grace Woo spoke up. "Mrs. Mock would like to inform you—"

"Silence!" Mayo banged his gavel. "Permit the girl to answer."

Ha Oi took a deep breath. Her childish voice carried to the back of the chambers. "At my home. On Doyers Street."

"Very good." The judge nodded. "I am in possession of all the facts."

He paused for several seconds. "First, I must compliment Mrs. Woo on her command of the English language and her spirited defense of her countrywoman. Unlike Mrs. Duck, she appears to have taken the trouble to learn the customs of this country, our language, and the decorum required in a courtroom. If only there were more like her...."

He marshaled his thoughts. "The court has heard that the child in question has been well cared for by the gunslinger and his wife. However, her material comfort is not my primary concern. It is her moral upbringing that matters." He steepled his fingers in front of his lips. "Given the nature of the claims put forward by Agents Pisarra and Butts and the admission made by Mrs. Duck regarding the child's parentage, it appears that further investigation into her ancestry would be the prudent course. If she is white, she certainly cannot be allowed to remain in an Oriental home."

Mrs. Woo's hand flew to her mouth.

"It is the opinion of this court that she be remanded to the care of The Society for the Prevention of Cruelty to Children until her origins can be conclusively determined."

"No!" Grace Woo jumped to her feet, desperation crackling through her voice. "That can't be right, Your Honor. Ha Oi is so young. She and Mrs. Mock have never been separated. Mrs. Mock didn't mean to speak out of turn. Please, won't you show them some mercy?"

Ha Oi began to cry. Tears trickled down her cheeks. The little fighter was suffering, and her mother was desperate. From her bag, she pulled out a rag doll with button eyes and a checkered dress and held it out. The clerk checked with the judge, who indicated his approval. He ran over and handed the doll to Ha Oi.

"The steps we are taking are for the good of the child," the judge went on sharply. "For her benefit and the benefit of society. Please explain that to Mrs. Duck."

He gestured to the agents. Butts, who still had his hands clamped on Ha Oi's shoulders, began to lead the girl away.

"This case is adjourned for the next two days, by which time, I trust the Society will provide evidence that will enable the court to reach a final decision." He banged his gavel with conviction. "Next!"

Tai Yow froze. As Butts led her away, Ha Oi looked back. She didn't resist the agent, but the expression of reproach and bewilderment that flashed across her tiny face said it all.

Chapter Eight

I was hungry, tired, and shaken by what I had seen that morning, so I stopped by Foley Square for some nourishment. Oyster sellers, roasted peanut vendors, and tea and coffee purveyors conducted a brisk business. I bought a packet of peanuts and munched them down, followed by a cup of milky coffee with two heaping spoons of sugar. Somewhat fortified, I stood at the edge of the crowds and listened to George Washington Plunkitt, the Tammany bard, who had stepped onto his rostrum, an overturned fruit crate, at Graziano's bootblack stand, to deliver one of his popular sermons. If nothing else, Plunkitt was always good for a couple of laughs.

"Can anyone tell me the difference between honest and dishonest graft?" the former state senator and current Democratic Party operative thundered. "No? Well, allow Plunkitt to enlighten you. Say the Democracy's in power. It's in power, and it's going to undertake public improvements. Well, I'm tipped off, say, that they're going to lay out a new park, or a school or such, at a new location. So what do I do?

"I see my opportunity and I *grab* it." He made a grasping motion with his fist. "I go to that place and buy up all the land I can. Then The Board of This or The Board of That makes its plan public, and there's a rush to get my land, which nobody cared particularly for before. Ain't it perfectly honest to charge a good price and make a profit on my investment and foresight? Of course, it is. That's honest graft."

The peanut gallery roared their approval.

"Now dishonest graft—blackmailin' gamblers, saloon keepers, disorderly people, and such—that's a different business entirely. I've never gone in for it, and neither has any decent politician I know. There's better money in honest graft, and no penal code either!"

Plunkitt was incorrigible, but he also summed up the workings of Tammany Hall—as the local Democratic Party was called. Feeling a bit lighter after a jolt of Plunkitt's wisdom, I returned to the office. Along the way, I wondered whether anyone had bought land in Chinatown in anticipation of it becoming a park. Then I realized that land in the neighborhood must not be cheap since property there generated so much profit in rent. In fact, if the park ever went through, which seemed unlikely, landlords would lose a tidy sum.

Dupont looked up the instant I walked in. "What happened?" he demanded. "You've been gone long enough."

"Were you worried?"

He scoffed. "Hardly." But he wiped his forehead with a handkerchief and, if I'm not mistaken, exhaled deeply. He wanted a blow-by-blow, which I gave him. Then he told me to write up the day's events.

I submitted my story a couple of hours later and returned home in a blur—only to be reminded by my husband that we'd been invited to the McClellans' that evening for dinner.

Scarcely able to stand or think clearly, I splashed cold water on my face and drank another cup of coffee, combed my hair, and switched out of my trousers and into a peacock blue silk sari with an embroidered gold border. I slipped on gold bracelets and earrings. A traditional ensemble was my best disguise and quite useful in some situations. Like the reporter who wrote about me while I attended classes at Barnard, people only saw the "petite Hindoo Princess" in her "native garb." They would ooh and aah, ask the most obvious questions, marvel at my charming ways, and afterward, compliment me on my English.

And when it came to accepting my marriage, well, marrying a Hindoo princess, while an eccentric choice, wasn't entirely out of the question for someone like Philip Morley. A physician whose forebears had been sea captains and members of the Salem East India Marine Society, Dr. Morley might make decisions that others would not.

* * *

Georgie B. lived in a townhouse on Washington Square, and although it wasn't at all far from our place, Dr. Morley had hired a car for the occasion. I would have been fine with hailing a cab, but I preferred not to walk on the streets in my "native dress." That was what I had done for my first six months, before I switched to skirts and shirtwaists. And now, I had grown so accustomed to disappearing in trousers and a hat that passersby's stares made me uncomfortable.

The mayor didn't own an automobile, or his own home, for that matter. In fact, he sometimes complained in public that he had to rent a house that befitted his station and allowed him to entertain guests in a manner that did credit to the city. He went on to suggest that mayors ought to be given use of an official residence, residential telephone line, and automobile. Without these perquisites, the job could only be carried out only by men of wealth or scoundrels.

"And which one are you?" a cheeky journalist had asked.

"Neither," Hizzoner replied. "I happen to be one of those honest fools who spends a disproportionate amount of his salary on rent, just so I don't entertain official guests in a poky apartment."

Georgie B. was the son of the Civil War General by the same name. Yet, despite his pedigree, he was a salaried man. And even his rivals conceded that he kept his hands clean, and that his conduct in the matter of bribes, graft, and the usual quid pro quo of local politics, was beyond reproach.

My husband remarked that I was looking tired as we drove downtown.

"And I was trying to look exotic and glamorous." I told him about what had happened that morning without naming names.

He agreed that it was awful. "A child being kept from her parents for no reason at all?"

"They're saying she might be white. And, it turns out, she is adopted."

I recalled Ha Oi's face peering out between the bars at court and wondered how that child, who had been so doted on, would manage in the Society's nursery, surrounded by unfamiliar faces. She would be made to change out of her colorful clothes, served tasteless food, and would have to eat, sleep, wake and play at set times—none of which, I suspected, was the case at home.

Did she understand what was happening? Would the other children be kind? Tai Yow must be beside herself. She had left the courtroom leaning heavily on Mrs. Woo, who had tried and finally succeeded in flagging down a taxi. I ran over to help, but the Mocks' neighbor said she could manage. And as for Mock, did he wish he had pulled out a gun and refused to let his daughter go?

No. I told myself I was overreacting. It would just be a few days; the court would realize its mistake and send the child home.

We pulled up in front of the Washington Square Arch, another one of the murdered architect Stanford White's contributions to the island. White's taste and influence could be felt all across town.

A ragtag group of demonstrators in rough-and-ready clothes, their skin burned from working outdoors, stood beneath the arch, holding placards and chanting: "Our water ain't for sale. Stay away from the mountains. Stay away from the Catskills!"

"Better Georgie B. than me." Dr. Morley looked through the car window. "Never a dull moment, even over dinner."

Across the street, lights glowed in the picture window of a stately townhouse. A single policeman stood on guard outside, flanked by two glass lamps—the kind you see outside subway stations or precinct houses. Apart from that, you might have thought that the home belonged to any ordinary, albeit well-off, New Yorker.

My husband stepped out and offered me his hand. "Nervous?" he asked, smoothing his salt-and-pepper beard.

"Why should I be?" I said lightly.

"That's right." He smiled, and the corners of his eyes crinkled. "There's no reason."

My parents would have been proud. It wasn't the match they would have preferred—spanning continents, races, and religions. They would have worried about what would happen to us, how society would accept us, how we would raise our children. But they would have seen that we were happy together and that he was one in a million.

Chapter Nine

A uniformed butler opened the door before Dr. Morley had the chance to knock. He took my husband's coat, I held onto my light shawl, and he led us into the living room, where a chandelier burned brightly.

The mayor and his wife stood to greet us. I'd only ever seen Hizzoner at a distance, mostly through the office window, and I was struck by how small he was in person—about five foot six, nearly half a foot shorter than my husband. But he was fit, and with his clean-cut features, he exuded youthful energy. Rumor had it that he was someone to look out for, someone who would go far... maybe even all the way to 1600 Pennsylvania Avenue.

Mrs. Georgiana McClellan—yes, it's true, George and Georgiana, two peas in a pod—wore a cameo brooch pinned to her dove-gray gown. Her brown hair was sleekly brushed away from her forehead.

She complimented my sari. "What fine workmanship! I do so love fabrics from India." She glanced at my shawl. "Cashmere?"

"Shatoosh. It's made from the wool from the necks and chins of Tibetan antelopes."

"How wonderful." She offered me a seat and a glass of fruit punch.

We were the first to arrive, and the men began to reminisce about their schooldays and how young Phillip Morley had rescued George from the clutches of school bullies.

"I didn't know that," I said.

"It's a bit of an overstatement," Dr. Morley replied.

"You are too modest." Mrs. McClellan smiled.

It turned out that the mayor had been a sickly boy, like Teddy Roosevelt, the current president. The boys at school called him a "Copperhead" and teased him mercilessly on account of his father, Little Mac—as General George B. McClellan, a Democrat who served under President Lincoln, was known.

The mayor looked up at a portrait of the general in full military regalia that hung above the marble mantel. His warm brown hair swept off his forehead, his chin held high, one hand resting on the scabbard at his hips, Little Mac stared into the distance.

"The boys laughed because I couldn't fight," he said. "So Phillip stepped in. But my father was the bravest man I've ever known, and his troops worshiped him."

His men would have followed him to the corners of the earth, even to the doors of the White House, if he'd given the word, Georgiana McClellan added. General McClellan's tragedy, she went on, was that he never received his due. Despite his troops' valiant showing at the Battle of Antietam—the bloodiest battle of the entire war—President Lincoln accused him of not having done enough, of not having pursued the enemy further. And then he released the general from his duties. Still, Little Mac never spoke an ill word about his commander-in-chief or the wasps who poured poison into the president's ears.

"It's unfortunate that the two men never saw eye-to-eye," Hizzoner said. "They were both on the same side, both devoted to their country.... But we must put all that behind us now."

"It isn't behind us, my dear," Lady Mac said in her quiet yet certain voice. "Just the other day, *Munsey's* ran a story, inquiring whether, despite the mayor's abundant virtues, his honesty, and his openness, he had—in addition to the general's great name and talent for organization—also inherited his father's tendency to vacillate and temporize."

"Mrs. Morley is a member of the press, Georgiana," her husband said with a smile. "We must be careful."

"Oh, I know. And I hope you don't mind me saying, Mrs. Morley, that you remind me of the ladies in those lovely Indian miniature paintings. When

I heard you are a reporter, I imagined someone quite different. Someone loud and strident.

"I'm glad I don't disappoint."

"Not in the slightest."

Other guests began to arrive—a banker, a lawyer, an urban planner, an architect, and their spouses. The room quickly filled with chatter. The men naturally gravitated toward one another, the women either knew or knew of each other and begun to talk amongst themselves.

I was accustomed to being the odd one out, so I adopted a pleasant expression and sipped my drink, hoping to convey an impression of contentment. But I watched as I always did, observing how Lady Mac moved about unobtrusively, greeting her guests one by one, asking a question or two. She expertly indicated her interest in others' affairs—how was little so-and-so, had so-and-so begun college or married.

Every now and then, voices of the Catskills protesters filtered through.

"Does the opposition to the aqueduct bother you?" someone asked the mayor.

"It's a small price to pay," he replied. "Fresh, clean water pouring out of every tap in all five boroughs. No need for filtration. Enough to drink, enough to bathe in, enough to prevent diseases and drought. If we don't take action now, the city will grind to a standstill. It won't happen tomorrow, nor the day after, but soon enough."

"I hear the reservoir will submerge villages in the mountains?"

"No more than half a dozen. And, naturally, the inhabitants will be relocated to higher ground. I'm sure it will cause them difficulties at first, but it's a small price to pay for progress."

Mrs. McClellan turned to me once all her guests were settled. "Since this is your first time here, Mrs. Morley, would you like a tour?"

I nodded gratefully, and we stepped into the hallway together. She pointed to the sketches of Roman monuments hanging in frames. The mayor was something of an expert on Italian history, she said, and before he took office, they traveled to Europe nearly every year to visit historical sites and museums. He had written a book, *The Oligarchies of Venice.* Had I heard of it?

"I believe I might have." I had not.

"If Max was a private citizen, we'd have chosen a smaller place, and traveled more," she explained. "The thing is, everyone believes that thanks to his family's name and my uncle's fortune, we've never had to lift a finger. It simply isn't true. My husband has always had to work for a living. In fact, he started as a journalist.… I believe you write for the *Observer*?"

"I do."

"You must enjoy it. I enjoy my work as well—I've devoted all my energies to my husband's career." She opened the door to the mayor's study. The walls were covered from floor to ceiling with books in English, French, Italian, and German.

"The mayor appears to be quite the reader," I remarked.

"Everyone was amazed when he was first elected—a literate chief in City Hall! And when they discovered he'd written a book—about the history of Venice, no less—you could have knocked them down with a feather."

We proceeded to the dining room, where a long table had been set with linen, crystal, and silver. Elaborate floral arrangements spilled over the sides of low vases. French doors opened onto a patio and a small garden where fireflies flickered in the darkness.

Lady Mac's cheeks glowed. She made up her mind. "You must be wondering why I pulled you away from the other guests, Mrs. Morley. I hope I can count on your discretion.…" I felt the weight of her fingers on my arm. "My husband says that Dr. Morley has been a good friend to him. And I'm sure you are aware that the mayor is under siege. He has great plans for our city, but like all visionaries, he has his detractors. People who would like to see him brought down several notches. For instance, Mr. Murphy, the leader of Tammany Hall.

"Now, I know you are a person of conscience. You must be, and I do not mean to influence you in the slightest. But may I suggest an interview with my husband or perhaps a feature on his New Vision for New York City? If you believe in his aqueduct and schools and good government… Every little bit that we can do to nudge the public's opinion helps."

"You want *me* to write about the mayor?"

"That's right."

"I don't usually cover City Hall."

"Perhaps you can make an exception this time," she said sweetly. "This wouldn't be a political story at all. Just a piece about the man, his ideas, his honesty, his virtues. I could have someone call your editor, make the arrangements."

I didn't know what to say. I could hardly be rude on account of Dr. Morley, so I told her I would check, but that I couldn't promise anything.

She smiled benignly. "That's all I can ask.... Now let's join everyone else, shall we, or they'll think we got lost!"

Back in the living room, the mayor was displaying his self-deprecating sense of humor. "It is one of the chief pleasures of the American citizen to abuse any man he's elected to public office and denounce him as a rascal. Far be it from me to deprive him of his amusements." Up close, and at ease, Georgie B. appeared effortless.

Dr. Morley shot me a quizzical glance, and I nodded, hoping to reassure him that everything was all right.

At dinner, I was seated between the banker and the planner. They didn't know what to make of me, so they asked a few perfunctory questions, then spoke over me for the rest of the meal. I ate my *vol-au-vents* in silence. Afterward, the men went off to smoke while the women retired to the drawing room. They put aside any awkwardness and peppered me with questions.

Yes, I replied, I'd lived in New York for over a decade. My English was good because I had learned it as a child. And I didn't have much of an accent because I had a good ear for languages. No, I was not familiar with Mr. Choudhary, even though he was a successful barrister in Calcutta. Nor Mr. Desai either. But yes, I was familiar with Pandita Ramabai (so called because her mastery of Vedic texts made her a "lady pundit"), who had journeyed from India to America nearly twenty years ago and lectured extensively on the plight of Hindu child widows and child brides. And yes, she was beautiful, but also so intelligent. In fact, I owned a book that she had written during her travels: *Conditions of Life in America.* Oh yes, she had written a book—not in English, however. And yes, it was fascinating, particularly the sections in which she explained to her readers why native Americans were called Indians, I said with a smile.

I had been struck by many of the same things as Ramabai when I arrived: how Americans drunk copious amounts of iced water in any kind of weather. How it wasn't polite to walk around the house in bare feet; how Black and Native Americans, as well as the Chinese, were treated as second-class citizens, or worse. And yet, like her, I also admired the relative freedom that many women enjoyed. They could travel, speak in public, study in college, run their own businesses, become doctors and lawyers.

And (I didn't mention this either), it was the fact that both Pandita Ramabai and Dr. Anandibai—who studied at the women's medical college in Philadelphia—had made the journey on their own before me that gave my father the confidence that I would be able to manage.

Fortunately, no one asked whether I had visited the Himalayas or ridden on an elephant. If they had, the answer would have been yes to both. But we did briefly touch upon Swami Vivekananda and his address to the Parliament of the World's Religions. One of the ladies had met the Indian philosopher on his second visit to America and had been deeply moved by his teachings. Before she could ask further questions about the swami, Mrs. McClellan came to my rescue by passing around a plate of bonbons.

By the time the evening drew to a close, I was completely exhausted.

My husband and I climbed into the waiting car while the McClellans thanked their guests and waved goodbye. The protesters had left, abandoning their signs along with discarded sandwich papers.

"What did you think?" Dr. Morley asked.

I replied that they seemed perfectly pleasant. In fact, quite down to earth, given who they were. (In addition to being the mayor's wife, Georgiana McClellan was the niece of a well-known financier.)

"Georgie B. has big plans," my husband said. "And the more I speak to him, the more convinced I am. He's changed since his schooldays—become bolder, developed elbows. He's the kind of man who, if he wants to, could lead this country into the future."

"Lady Mac wants me to write a piece on him."

"*Lady* Mac? Really, Archie. Sometimes, your jokes…" Dr. Morley groaned, but I could tell he didn't mind. "Is that why she took you aside?"

"I thought they wouldn't approve of my work, but I guess being a reporter comes in handy."

He wanted to know what answer I gave Mrs. McClellan.

"I told her that I'd need to speak to Dupont. I don't want to create any problems for you."

He brushed away my concerns. "Unless you write something truly damning, I'll be fine. And how about the ladies? Did they ask about India?"

I filled him in on the conversation.

Light from streetlamps flashed across his face, and lights from inside apartments briefly illuminated scenes of everyday life: a mother and son clearing up after dinner, an old man asleep on his rocking chair, someone practicing the piano. And I felt a sudden pang for a girl who had been ripped from everything familiar.

As the car rumbled through the streets, I resolved to do whatever it took to find out who wrote that letter.

Chapter Ten

Dupont printed my story under the headline: *CHILD SEIZED AT MOCK DUCK'S. HER RACE A MYSTERY. GANGSTER BEREFT.* "Find out more if you can, Mrs. Morley," he said. "The mood on the street, etcetera. And plan on attending part two." Not too bad for a piece he'd shoe-horned somewhere on page five.

I had bought copies of the *Times* and the *Sun* from a bright-eyed newsboy at the corner of Broadway and Chambers. Normally, I didn't feel the need to check the competition, but in this case, I was curious about how they had explained the events we all witnessed.

It turned out that they barely explained at all. Hornby's account in the *Times* verged on insulting and ridiculous. Titled *CRUELTY SOUGHT AT MOCK DUCK'S,* it began:

> *Mock Duck, the Chinese leader of the Hip Sing Tong, was peacefully resting in his smoking bunk at his residence at 10 Doyers Street yesterday morning, and all the little ducks were floundering in a Pell Street pond. Bedelia, the house servant, had turned them out at 6 o'clock so that she could prepare a chop suey breakfast.*
>
> *Into this domestic scene butted a Roundsman from the Elizabeth Street Station, the patrolman on the beat, and two agents from the Society for the Prevention of Cruelty to Children.*
>
> *"Butts, is he in?" Pizarro asked.*
>
> *"If he butts in," responded a voice from within, "I'll scauld him wid hot water."*

"We want to see one of the Ducks," shouted the policeman, catching on to the joke.

"Y're a pretty fresh rooster yerself," replied the voice of Bedelia.

And so on and so forth. Bedelia became "Barrier Bedelia," the roundsman referred to Ha Oi as "Hiawatha," and Grace Woo indeed became "Good Look." The story ended with a scene from the nursery in which Ha Oi spoke in "pure Chinese" and informed the other tykes that she would "dearly like to own a live teddy bear." It sounded as though Hornby himself had been smoking something when he wrote the article.

Pike's version, *MOCK DUCK BEREFT OF HIS JOY*, struck a more somber tone.

All day and late into the night, you could hear the sound of Chinamen mounting the creaking stairs to Mock's home in Doyers Street. They came to convey how sorry they were, but there were among them Chinamen who had long been Mock's enemies, and Mock knew their sorrow was for Ha Oi and not for him. The visitors bored Mock with their expressions of sympathy and invitations to smoke pen yen and forget for the present; he wanted to be alone, and he waved them away, saying he would have fought the agents to death, except that he had promised the district attorney to behave himself.

In all the gambling houses, restaurants and stores in Chinatown, the gamblers who had missed Ha Oi's cheery face in the window cursed their luck, and in the opium dens the smokers looked into the flickering flame of the lamps and saw the little girl calling. Later, the gangster stole quietly from his house and knelt before the joss on the top floor of the Mott Street tenement and fervently prayed that his little Ha Oi would be restored to him.

It was moving and certainly more believable than what Hornby had written, but was it based on facts, or had Pike taken a kernel of truth, something he heard, and then embroidered it as he saw fit?

Over the years, I've learned that although reporting is supposed to be objective, that doesn't always happen. What people want to see combines with what they think and hope to see, and just like that, the truth becomes malleable.

* * *

Dupont gave me his blessings to return to Chinatown that afternoon because he knew I was on to something. Say what you will about the man, he was shrewd, and he had a nose for a story. He sensed that if he didn't dispatch me, I'd find my way there regardless. At least now, he could maintain some control and guide the situation.

Despite everything the neighborhood had been through in the past few weeks—from the shooting to the hearing to Ha Oi's removal—Pell, Mott, and Doyers Streets seemed back in business. Maybe a pall hung over the streets, maybe locals could sense Mock grieving and fretting at his window, but nevertheless, they hurried about, putting one foot in front of the other and getting on with their tasks. If you really think about it, what choice did they have?

When my parents passed away from the plague in 1897, I mourned for some time, then made my decisions. I wouldn't return to India, where I couldn't be as free as I was in New York; I would stay on, at least for a few more months. The funeral had long passed, and my friend Cyrus and his family would take care of our home and possessions. My hostess in New York, Miss Natalya Osiroff, a genteel spinster, urged me to remain as long as I liked and treat her home in the "Village" as my own. I met Dr. Morley some months later through a mutual friend; one thing led to another, and now here I was.

Tom Lee greeted me warmly from behind a fog of cigar fumes. It was only my second visit to the store, but already, its hanging bunches of leaves and heady aroma had begun to feel familiar.

"You think I'm behind this, dont'cha?" the On Leong chief said. His assistant puttered about, and William crouched in the corner doing schoolwork.

"But Tom Lee ain't no fool. I wish a thousand misfortunes on Mock Duck, but not this. Never this. Tom knows what it is to be a father."

"Any ideas about who wrote that letter—the one that the Gerry Society received about the girl?" If the On Leong chief wanted to retaliate for the shootings without firing a single bullet, I could see no better way to do it than to pen that note.

He laughed. "Walk around the neighborhood and take your pick. Could've been anyone, but he gotta be some idiot. Mock won't do nothin' to no one now that they have her. But when she's back? It won't be pretty. Whoever did it, better watch out."

He turned pensive. "You know, one time, his fellas, they got hold of a laundryman, one of my boys. They tied him down on his ironing board and chopped him up with a cleaver."

"That can't be true." I shuddered with revulsion.

"Oh, you better believe it. That Mock, he's a savage."

Under different circumstances, I probably would have walked away, or at least thought twice about continuing my investigations. But now, regardless of Mock's brutality, a child's future hung in the balance.

"Did you hear"—Lee changed the topic—"that Engineer Webster saved us? This business about those streams." He shook his head in amazement. "Never had no idea we were walkin' on water. They say there's water everywhere— you can't see it, but you can feel it. Makes the ground real soft. Seems firm enough to me.

"Tell you the truth, I thought we were finished. Even went across the bridge to check out land in Williamsburg. Glad we've been spared. Tom's too old to start again… and Williamsburg's too far from the Bronx."

"The Bronx?" I was confused.

"Oh, sure. I live there. Take the train down every day."

"Not here?" I had assumed he lived above the store.

"Nah." He waved a hand as if the idea was absurd. "This ain't no place to raise a family. You see for yourself how dangerous it is."

Reeling at Lee's dismissal of the place of which he was considered the de facto mayor, I took myself to the nearest precinct house in search of the roundsman who had accompanied the agents to No. 10.

* * *

The duty officer in charge glared at me suspiciously when I told him I was with the *Observer*.

"Who are they hirin' these days? Monkeys?" But then he let me know that I could probably find the copper wetting his beak at the Readypenny a few doors down.

I noted his words and let them slide off me. If I allowed every insult to stick, I'd become so heavy I wouldn't be able to lift a finger, let alone walk. As promised, O'Connor was at the inn, dressed in mufti, nursing a pint.

I introduced myself in case he didn't remember me. "As if I could forget." He had promised the highbinder that his daughter would be returned "before he knew it."

We spoke for a few minutes. O'Connor insisted that Ha Oi would be sent home after the upcoming hearing. "Sometimes they've gotta show they're taking the allegations seriously. These things just take a little while." He had no idea who wrote the letter to the Children's Society. Like Tom Lee, he thought it could be anyone. "But," he added, "we've got coppers out and about makin' sure there's no trouble."

I hadn't seen evidence of that, but didn't argue.

"You know, these fellas," he said all of a sudden, "when they ain't up to no good, they're workin' hard. Ten, twelve hours a day in laundries, restaurants, haulin' supplies, whatever. Live in dormitories—dozen or more to a room.... You ever seen one?"

I hadn't.

He wiped the foam from his mustache. "I'll show ya. Least I can do," he said, when I paid his tab.

"I feel sorry for the girl," he added once we were outside. "She ain't done nothing wrong. Neither has her mother. She's just a wee one."

"You've dealt with Mock before?"

"Sure."

"What's he like?"

The copper scrunched up his face. "Hard to say…. He's a slippery one, really."

It felt strange to be walking through the district in the company of a roundsman. The few locals who were out gave him a wide berth, but a couple of them met his eyes, and he nodded briefly in acknowledgement.

"You always swan around in that getup?" He shot me a sideways glance.

"You have your uniform, I have mine. It gives me some protection."

"Hmm." He didn't sound convinced. "I'd be careful, if I were you."

And I was. As careful as I could be without spending my life behind locked doors. My father would say: "If something bad is going to happen, it can happen anywhere, Archana. All I ask is that you keep your wits about you. After that, it's out of your hands."

The copper and I paused in front of a tenement with a cobbler's shop out front. We walked inside, stepped over a strip of leather that had been marked with chalk and laid out to cut, and exited into a dingy courtyard puddled with greasy, rancid water. From there, another rickety door led to the stairs of a rear tenement, which opened onto a pitch-dark landing.

"The dormitory's in there?"

"On the fourth floor."

"I don't need to go."

"C'mon," he cajoled. "You write for the papers. You need to see this and tell everyone about it."

I studied his face. He seemed trustworthy enough.

"You scared?"

"No."

"Well then, don't worry. I don't bite." The copper held his handkerchief to his nose and pushed open a door. The pungent odor of wet laundry, cooking, charcoal, and who knows what else overpowered me as I stepped inside. Holding on to the little pocketknife I carried in my jacket for protection, I followed him up the stairs. Who knew what he really had in mind?

The stifling, fetid chamber he brought me to couldn't have been more than eight feet by six. A tiny window looked out onto a brick wall and the edge of another blind window. There was nowhere to cook, nowhere to wash, no furnace for heat, and it was impossible to breathe.

A row of worn hammocks stretched between poles. They sagged so low they nearly touched the floor, and there was barely enough room to walk between them. Six men lay fast asleep in the fabric beds—one hammock held two, stretched head to foot. A row of threadbare slippers waited just inside the threshold.

Bone tired, the sleepers were dead to the world and didn't stir when we entered. I felt guilty for standing there without their knowledge, but the sight of the slumbering Hips affected me more than I expected. Living like this…it was no wonder they sometimes went berserk and started shooting.

Chapter Eleven

The bartender at The Pelham Cafe hemmed and hawed, but he too fell back on "could be anyone" when I asked about the letter writer. "It's gotta be someone who takes what Mock has done personally," he added.

Again, that hardly narrowed the field. And my inability to communicate with Mock and Tom's men didn't make things any easier. Not that they were likely to have confided in me, even if I was able to speak their language. They kept to themselves, as Tom had said at the hearing.

I spent the next day at the *Observer's* morgue looking over past stories and came up with a list of names of people who might have a grudge against Mock that was long enough to fill a Lothario's diary. But an unusual detail stood out. Daniel O'Reilly, who currently served on Harry Thaw's legal team, had previously represented Mock on a legal matter. Apparently, Mock Duck had approached two policemen and offered them money if they would release his cousin and a friend who were about to be taken into custody. Not only were the two men not released, Mock was thrown into jail on charges of bribery. O'Reilly defended Mock, saying that no crime had been committed.

And when the judge asked whether the lawyer thought bribery wasn't a crime, O'Reilly responded, "Not for the Chinese. They don't think it's wrong." His defense wasn't successful, and Mock languished in jail until an associate bailed him out.

It could still be, however, that O'Reilly, a New York City character and man about town, might have some valuable insights.

* * *

The following morning, I made my way to Foley Square, where everyone in the know, and anyone who wanted to be in the know, congregated. Even at ten to eight, the piazza was buzzing. Coffee had been drunk, deals had been struck, and information had traded hands many times over. George Washington Plunkitt was back at Graziano's bootblack stand in the center of the square. He paced back and forth as he prepared to dispense his daily dose of wisdom.

Stepping onto his rostrum, he called out: "Who can tell me the difference between an anarchist and a patriot?"

No takers.

Someone yelled back, "Why don't you tell us, George-ay."

The philosopher obliged. "A patriot is an ordinary citizen with the promise of a government job."

"And what about the anarchist?"

"An anarchist is a *former patriot* who has been *denied* a job because he can't pass the civil service reformers' wretched examinations!"

Wild laughter.

"The thing about jobs is that they are the key to everything," Plunkitt continued. "The reason the Irishman is more honest in politics than many Sons of the Revolution is because his one thought is to serve the city which gave him a home. He has this thought even before he lands in New York, for his friends here often have a good place in one of the city departments picked out for him while he is still in the old country. Is it any wonder that he has a tender spot in his heart for old New York when he is on its salary list the mornin'after he lands?"

Feet stamped in approval.

I kept checking the crowd for O'Reilly, who was known to spend the early hours here, but couldn't spot him. I wasn't able to wait forever, either. Ha Oi's hearing would begin soon, so after giving it a while, I headed uptown.

I wondered whether Mock would attend this time. He must be distraught, plotting, aching for his daughter. No one I'd spoken to in the neighborhood knew what he had been doing since the Gerry agents raided his home.

And the little girl? They would release her, no doubt about that. They'd taught him a lesson. He'd been shown that anytime the courts pleased, he could be hurt in a way that meant more than losing money or status.

Poor child. I imagined her running over to her mother, clinging to her tightly. Flinging her arms around Mock's neck. Blowing a kiss to Bedelia. Telling them how awful the nursery was, how she hated the food, how scared she'd been, but how she hadn't cried, and weren't they proud of her?

"Beg your pardon." A nimble figure swerved past me.

"Lawyer O'Reilly!" What a coincidence. "Do you have a minute, sir?" I quickened my pace to keep up. "This has nothing to do with the Thaw Trial."

O'Reilly was so used to being hounded by members of the press that he didn't stop, just nodded, and kept walking.

"I'd like to talk to you about Mock Duck. I believe you once represented him on bribery charges."

He glanced at me. "Haven't you heard of attorney-client confidentiality, young man? I make it a point never to breathe a word about my clients without their express permission."

"Have you heard about this business about his child, sir? Any thoughts on how he should win her back? And apart from Tom Lee, who else would want to see Mock daughter gone? I'm with the *Observer*."

"I have more than thoughts, young fellow. I have a plan! Tell your readers that."

"A plan, Mr. O'Reilly?"

"Haven't you heard? The Thaw trial's been adjourned for the week, so I will be representing Mock and his family this morning."

I hadn't heard, or maybe I had, but hadn't paid attention. In any case, it didn't matter. Mock had one of the city's most in-demand attorneys on his side. He meant to make sure his daughter would be released.

"The Thaws don't mind?" I asked.

"Mrs. Thaw"—Harry's mother—"pays well enough, but she doesn't own me."

"How do you intend to get the child back?"

"You will have to see me in action to find out."

"Any thoughts on who wrote the letter that got her taken away in the first place?"

The lawyer didn't slow down for a second. "Haven't the faintest."

* * *

Mock Duck waited in the shadow of the court, arms clasped around his chest, lips pinched, eyes obscured by the purple-tinted glasses. He wore his usual ensemble of black high-collared tunic and loose black trousers. They say he gave up his western suits and started dressing like an ordinary Chinese worker to make it harder to pick him out in a lineup.

"You're late, O'Reilly," the highbinder growled.

"Traffic, Mock, traffic," O'Reilly apologized.

I loitered a few paces behind so I could hear.

"You came across on the bridge?"

"Oh sure."

Mock glanced at the lawyer's gleaming footwear. "So you get your shoes shined in Brooklyn now?"

"Forget about the shoes, Mock. I'm here to bring your daughter home."

"Boo!" A voice said in my ear.

I jumped. "Hornby!"

"Thought I'd find you here." The *Times* man laughed.

Behind his purple glasses, Mock's face hardened. "She better come home today," he said to the lawyer. "My wife won't survive another minute without her. And frankly, neither will I."

Tai Yow and Bedelia stood behind him, and a group of Chinatown locals made their way into the building.

"We better hurry," Hornby remarked. "Looks like the entire chop-suey belt is in attendance."

I fixed him with a withering look and followed Mock and his attorney inside. They had just about reached the door to the courtroom when a clerk raced down the length of the corridor.

"Mr. O'Reilly," he panted, coming to a halt. His eyes darted nervously between the two men.

"Spit it out," O'Reilly ordered.

"They have the child waiting upstairs in the judge's anteroom, sir, but they won't bring her down."

"How is she? Is she all right?" Mock demanded. Then he turned to his attorney. "Take me upstairs. I have to see her."

"They won't allow anyone in, Mr. Mock." The clerk sounded wretched. "All I heard is that she's wearing a white dress, playing with her dolly, and eating an apple."

"What? Must be another child. Ha Oi hates apples. She wouldn't touch them." The highbinder removed his glasses.

"Let's get this over with, Mock." O'Reilly put his hand on his client's arm.

The gangster shook him off. "One hour, they told me. One hour. It's been three goddamn days."

"Let's go finish this charade."

O'Reilly, Mock, Tai Yow, and Bedelia filed into the courtroom, which was packed to bursting. Mrs. Woo and her two daughters, red bows in their hair, sat behind the family in the second row. Residents of Chinatown filled most of the seats that remained. I recognized a clerk from a store, Mrs. Maxwell, and a couple of her students. Tom Lee's grandnephew, William, sat in the back, scribbling in his notebook.

Hornby and I joined Pike from the *Sun*. Pike leaned against a wall off to one side, head bent and hands in his pockets.

Magistrate Mayo presided once again, but that day, instead of Pisarra, Superintendent Jenkins, the head of the Children's Society, spoke on behalf of the organization.

His head as round and bald as an egg, Jenkins raised one small hand, swore to tell the truth, the whole truth, and nothing but the truth. He began by reviewing the circumstances that led the society to Mock Duck's home. Then he went on, "Your Honor, under normal circumstances, I would allow Agent Pisarra to address the court, but the matter at hand is so grave, and the results so shocking, that I felt it was my duty to share our findings with you."

Mayo nodded somberly. A chill passed across my arms.

"It is my responsibility to inform you that after a mere three days in the Society's care, we have come to the conclusion that a gross deception has been perpetuated on the public. The child known to all as Ha Oi is not Oriental in the slightest. No matter what Mock and Mrs. Duck claim, this little girl is the child of white parents."

My legs went weak. A murmur coursed through the courtroom. "Stark, raving mad!" Bedelia yelled as Mock jumped up. O'Reilly yanked his client back into his seat. Mrs. Woo leaned forward and whispered in Tai Yow's ear.

"Quiet!" Mayo roared. "Quiet."

"Allow me to explain," Superintendent Jenkins continued, unperturbed. His tone remained flat and emotionless; his thin lips barely moved as he spoke. If you didn't follow his words, you might have imagined he was reciting from a car repair manual. "Born in San Francisco's Chinatown, and knowing no other people than those of the Orient, the little girl was so transformed until the Celestials themselves, who did not know her past, believed that she was one of them."

The skies began to rumble. The windows darkened, and fat raindrops smacked against the panes. The gods were furious.

"We admit the Mocks have treated the child well," Jenkins said, "and that she does not lack for creature comforts. When she first arrived at the Society, she wore silk pantaloons and a blouse. Her hair had been done up in pigtails. But her feet were cramped in Chinese slippers, and her small face was pale. She was rarely allowed out of doors. At first glance, she might have been taken for a half-breed, although her features bore not the slightest trace of Oriental characteristics."

Tai Yow hung her head while O'Reilly continued to rest his hand on Mock's shoulder. Water poured in streams down the panes, dissolving any view of the outside world. And the world outside hardly seemed to matter. Everything that was important, everything worthwhile, had been concentrated on the events unfolding in that courtroom.

"It was the way the child was presented," the superintendent went on, "the clothes she wore, the way she spoke, and how her hair was arranged that led even the Celestials to believe—as they had been repeatedly told—that her father was one of them. Yesterday, I invited a reporter from the *Sun* to the Society's nursery, and he witnessed the transformation for himself."

I turned to Pike, but he looked away, refusing to meet my eyes. Never mind, I would corner him later.

"Twenty or more children were playing ring around the rosy and laughing," Jenkins said. "Ha Oi was among them. 'Now, pick her out of this group,' I told the reporter. The children stopped their game and stood in a row while he walked from one to another and carefully scrutinized each face. The only child he found with any resemblance to a little Chinese girl was an Italian with jet-black hair and deep brown eyes. Then I called Ha Oi's name, and a pretty child with great round eyes of blue, soft flaxen hair that hung down to her shoulders, and a bright blue dress stepped forward and inquired in pigeon-English what was wanted."

The courtroom gasped. I thought I must be going mad. I couldn't believe what I had just heard. We weren't in some remote village that believed in shapeshifters or ghost stories. We were in New York City. In 1907. A mixed-race girl couldn't transform into a blonde, blue-eyed child simply because the authorities said so.

"Show me this Ha Oi!" Mock shouted. "Let me see for myself! Bring her down!"

"Mr. O'Reilly, calm your client, or he will be ejected for good."

"I beg your pardon, Your Honor." O'Reilly whispered urgently to the highbinder.

Hornby whistled softly and raised his eyebrows. Pike studiously looked away.

The superintendent waited for a moment and then resumed his narrative. "The child showed her disappointment with the interruption of the game but consented to come forward and talk to the reporter, whom she told how happy she was with her new playmates. In the excitement of the games, she would yell out her delight in Chinese, but that was all that betrayed that she had been born and brought up in the foreign environment of Doyers Street.

"Although she has been away from Chinatown for only three days, she has made remarkable progress in learning the tongue of her playmates, and yesterday, she was able to ask and answer several questions in English."

Mock spoke forcefully to O'Reilly, and the lawyer sprang up. "I object, Your Honor. My client paid a teacher to teach his daughter the language. He speaks English to her himself. It is a language in which he, as an American, is fluent. She didn't just pick it up out of thin air."

"Mr. O'Reilly, you will have your chance to present your case," Mayo admonished the lawyer.

"She has been playing with her dolly and with the other children in our care," the superintendent continued, "and has rejected all offers of rice and noodles." He picked up steam. "The truth—I regret to inform everyone—is that your own eyes have deceived you. This child is no half-breed. She is a full-blooded American. But it is not only your eyes—human hands have played a part in the mischief.

"When the matrons washed Ha Oi's hair the first night she was with us"—he paused for a breath—"a dark residue ran into the drain, revealing the flaxen locks beneath."

Mrs. Woo whispered in Tai Yow's ear, and the mother vigorously shook her head. The accusation made its way through the room, and the Chinese erupted in protest.

The judge banged his gavel several times. The policeman on duty began to patrol the aisles, brandishing his nightstick.

The superintendent waited for the hubbub to die down. "We are so certain that this girl is pure white," he went on, quite calmly, "that we have dispatched two likenesses of her, one in Oriental garb and the other as she appears today, to our counterparts in California. Although many of their records burned after the terrible earthquake, we hope to receive proof positive that her father was American. We believe he may have been a lobbygow, a regular in the Chinese quarter of 'Frisco. And since the child was born while Lizzie Smith and the merchant Chin Mung lived under the same roof, the Celestial must have been deceived into believing the infant was his own offspring."

I couldn't imagine what Tai Yow and Mock Duck must be feeling, hearing their daughter's parentage being torn to shreds by scurrilous conjecture. And not a glimpse of Ha Oi herself. I'd seen Anglo-Indian girls who were so light-skinned that people mistook their mothers for their maids. If Tai Yow had darkened her daughter's locks in order to avoid cruel remarks, then so be it. Plenty of mothers might have done the same. As for the blue eyes, that was strange. Her eyes hadn't looked blue to me. Maybe the superintendent was deceiving himself, or maybe he was lying outright. But he certainly seemed to believe what he was saying.

Jenkins removed a photograph from his jacket. "Don't take my word for it. See for yourselves."

From a distance, all I could make out was a blur of brightness: light background, light dress, palish hair.

The clerk retrieved the photograph and passed it to Mock, who took a look and handed it back. "I can't make it out. This could be anyone."

Tai Yow leaned forward, head in her hands. Mock conferred urgently with his lawyer.

Jenkins left the stand and returned to his seat. He wiped his glistening pate with a handkerchief.

Finally, it came to O'Reilly's turn. Mock's lawyer stood, held the lapels of his jacket, and puffed out his chest.

"Well, that is quite a story, Your Honor," he began. "Quite the Cinderella story, one might say. I wonder where we will find the pumpkins or a fairy godmother."

He approached the bench. "Now, we all know of the man sitting here, Your Honor." He pivoted and pointed to Mock. "The papers tell us that he is a highbinder, a lawbreaker, the leader of the infamous Hip Sing Tong. But the truth of the matter is"—the lawyer's voice turned weighty—"that we have never known Mock Duck, the businessman and devoted father. We have not felt the deep bond he shares with his child. But here are the facts." He ticked them off on his fingers.

"Private tutor for English lessons. Silk pantaloons and tunics. A maid, whose duty consists of cooking, cleaning, and caring for the family, and

Mr. Mock's enlistment of my services. As Your Honor is aware, they do not come cheap."

That drew a laugh.

"All this goes to show how much Mr. Mock dotes on Ha Oi and the lengths to which he is willing to go to ensure that she returns home as swiftly as possible."

The highbinder nodded.

"When Ha Oi's father, the jeweler Chin Mung, died, there were rumors that the little girl would be sold into bondage to some wealthy mandarin in China. It was Tai Yow who intervened. It is her selfless love that saved the little girl, Your Honor. It is only thanks to Mrs. Mock's devotion that Ha Oi is here with us today. We do not deprive even our most depraved criminals of their offspring. So why should we do such a thing to Mock Duck and his wife? Is it because he has committed the crime of being Chinese? And as for Mrs. Mock, she has committed no crimes at all, unless"—he lowered his voice, waited—"it is a crime to look after and treat as one's own a helpless orphan.

"As for this business about her hair and appearance, Superintendent Jenkins ought to know better. He says the Chinese were fooled because of the way Ha Oi spoke, looked, and was dressed. I say the Society has been fooled for similar reasons." He thrust his hand into the air for emphasis. "That is the essence of a half-breed—they straddle two worlds. Dress the child in silk, and she appears Oriental; put her in gingham, and you will swear that she's American.

"It is possible that Mrs. Mock used a substance to clean the girl's locks that deposited a residue over the strands. The residue may have built up over the years to the point where the color changed, and perhaps Mrs. Mock herself didn't notice. Or perhaps she believed that the hair had darkened of its own accord. That is not uncommon, even among American children.

"My own white shirts become less white over time, and it is not because my laundryman is a cheat. No, Flanagan is an honest, hardworking fellow, the best of the lot, but the cleaning agents"—O'Reilly shrugged—"he has no control over them. Just as Mrs. Mock has no control of the soap she uses for her daughter."

The lawyer spoke fluently and without a pause. He paced the floor when needed, gestured broadly with his hands; fixed the judge with a keen stare to drive home his point and then turned to his audience.

"When the matrons at the society washed Ha Oi's hair, they may have removed some of the residue, and possibly, in comparison to what they observed earlier, the strands now appear to be of a lighter shade. To assert that this alters Ha Oi's origins, that it makes her a completely different child—well, Your Honor, that is patently absurd. The truth of the matter is simple." He pointed an index finger at Jenkins. "It is *this* man who has known Ha Oi for a mere three days who has made the error! Not the denizens of Chinatown who have known her for years. Not her mother, and not my client!"

He returned to his seat. "I rest my case."

Magistrate Mayo scratched his nose, rubbed his hands. "How long will it take to receive a reply from San Francisco, Mr. Jenkins?"

"About a week, Your Honor. In the meantime, may I request that the girl remain with the other children at the nursery? It would do her more harm than good to be shuttled back and forth."

O'Reilly objected. "Your Honor, Mr. and Mrs. Mock have already borne the loss of Ha Oi for longer than they can tolerate. Mrs. Mock's health has taken a violent turn for the worse. Surely, Ha Oi may return home until the Society receives the relevant information from San Francisco. The child is just six years old. I am sure she misses her mother and father terribly and wonders why they have forsaken her—which they most certainly haven't."

"Your Honor, her rapid transformation demands that she remain with us," Jenkins countered. "She has already made so much progress. She is well-fed and happy. It will only cause her grief to return to the pestholes of Doyers."

Mock pushed himself upright. His face was ashen, and his voice reverberated with feeling. "Before you make your decision, Your Honor, my wife and I would like to see our daughter. Just for a few minutes."

Bedelia's lips moved in silent prayer. Magistrate Mayo folded his hands and closed his eyes while he deliberated.

The sound of the rain had stopped. A light drizzle slipped across the panes.

The magistrate looked up. "I will give you exactly seven more days to make your case, Superintendent. In the meantime, the child will remain with the Society for her own sake. If you are wrong, and she is a half-breed, she will be returned at once to Mock Duck and his wife. If you are correct, we will have spared her additional upheaval."

Still on his feet, the highbinder wavered like a tree in strong winds. Then he reached out his hand and Tai Yow rose. They didn't look left or right; just held their heads high as they departed the courtroom.

Chapter Twelve

The sky was still overcast, but the rain had stopped. A shaft of light pierced the billowing clouds and brightened the steps outside the court. The downpour had been brief yet fierce, and garbage mixed with horse manure and dog shit swirled through the gutters.

Mock stood on the top step and with only barely contained fury, addressed the gathered crowd, first in his native language, then in English. Dressed in black, he transformed into a preacher, belting out fire and brimstone. "These lies have nothing to do with me, my wife, or my daughter," he thundered. "They're doing this to scare you and hurt me. They think that by taking Ha Oi, they will frighten all of us. But you know me better than that. My wife and I will move heaven and earth to bring Ha Oi home. And I won't rest until she is back with us."

I confronted Pike before he could skulk away. "Was it you the superintendent was talking about in there? The Gerrys allowed you inside?"

The reporter from the *Sun* examined his shoes. "What's it to you?"

"Did you really see a blonde-haired, blue-eyed child?"

The reporter shrugged.

"I didn't hear you."

"I didn't say anything."

"Is she the same girl you saw in court three days ago?"

"Fuck you. I don't owe you anything." And he stormed off.

I hurried back inside, where a couple of down-on-their-luck lawyers handed out calling cards and hustled for business. Notices affixed within glass-fronted cases advertised courses on religious instruction and vocational training. In Magistrate Mayo's anteroom, a bored young man slumped over a legal volume. His eyes fell shut as I entered and the bread roll he held slipped from his grip.

"Excuse me?"

He jerked awake and wiped the crumbs from his mouth.

"Was a little girl just here?"

"And who are you?"

I told him I'd come to inquire about the child in the Mock Duck case.

"Well, you're too late. They took her away half an hour ago."

"Did you happen to see her?"

No, he hadn't. He'd been asked to leave. They told him the child should remain alone with the matron. "They made me wait in the hallway for the duration of the hearing. Of course, I can do it. I'm physically capable." His voice rose an octave. "But this is my office. Not much to look at, but it's mine. Not the cloakroom of some godforsaken railway station."

In the waste bin I spotted a half-eaten apple, tiny toothmarks scarring its dappled green skin. That was the only sign of the child who had been brought here.

Had she only eaten half because she hated apples, as Mock said? Or had she eaten half because she'd changed so much that now she loved them?

* * *

Over the weekend, the *Times* printed *FIGHTING TO KEEP YELLOW-HAIRED HA OI*, a piece riddled with errors and inaccuracies. Tai Yow became Tie Yu, Lizzie Smith turned into Annie Smith. The article described Mock and Tai's trip to the Supreme Court in response to their writ of habeas corpus. I never heard of such a visit, and Hornby told me he didn't go himself, but that the paper had received word from someone who was present. The story said that the child appeared at the Supreme Court with masses of yellow hair, a pink and oval face, and "big round eyes that grew rounder and rounder as each new thing was presented to her."

It seemed that Ha Oi was becoming whiter and whiter by the minute.

* * *

I went to the Society to see what was happening, but the matron on duty at the nursery, a small but formidable character, informed me in no uncertain terms that the children were asleep and that I couldn't enter. In his office, Pisarra hemmed and hawed so much that finally, unable to contain myself any longer, I burst out, "You're pulling a fast one, aren't you? She hasn't changed one bit."

"How can you suggest such a thing, Mrs. Morley!" The agent sounded aggrieved. "You know I consider this my calling." A simple wooden crucifix hung on the wall behind his desk, along with a colored print of the Savior. His folders were arranged in two neat trays, one marked "In Progress" and the other "Finalized."

"The child has changed." He laced his fingers together. "And that is all I will say about it."

"Why can't I see her then?"

"She is in our care now. We must protect her privacy."

"You allowed Pike in."

"Enough." He pushed back his chair. "I must ask you to leave, or I will escort you out myself."

Something inside me snapped. The stories of her transformation were unbelievable, and even if she was white—which I didn't believe was the case, did that mean she loved Mock and Tai Yow any less? The image of Ha Oi counting trains with Mock, stomping her foot with Mrs. Woo, even the glare she tossed her mother as she was led away—these were signs of a child who knew she was cherished.

I thanked Pisarra for nothing and left the Society's headquarters near Madison Square Park. The golden statue of a naked Diana the Huntress that graced the tower of Stanford White's Madison Square Garden glinted in the distance. She soared above the city, once the tallest object for miles around. People said she was visible all the way from Connecticut to New Jersey. Her nudity had caused an uproar, but over time, the public grew accustomed to her, and the moral brigade gave up its crusade and moved on to other causes. No one paid her much notice anymore. She was just another landmark, helpful if you needed to find your bearings.

If the public could grow accustomed to that statue (said to be modeled on one of White's many paramours), surely they could grow accustomed to anything—even a mixed-race child being adopted by a gangster and his wife.

As the thought occurred to me, I realized how unlikely it was. When it came to the changes in Ha Oi's appearance, forces more powerful than me, more powerful than any one individual, were at play. The outside world was creating the child they wanted her to be, not the child she thought she was.

And maybe that was what prompted my resolve to do more than just report the story as it unfolded in the courts. I would take the extra step. I would tell it from Mock and Tai Yow's point of view, and perhaps that would help bring home their daughter.

Chapter Thirteen

While not exactly charming, Mulberry Bend Park was cool and spacious, a welcome change from the tenements around it and an unobjectionable place to spend a quarter of an hour. I sat on a bench, enjoying the breeze against my cheeks while I waited for Mrs. Woo, and watched a group of scruffy children, who spoke half a dozen European languages, kick a rag ball between them.

I had first visited the park shortly after it opened in the summer of '97. At that time, I was staying with Miss Osiroff, a tireless writer and member of the Theosophical Society. She and my father maintained a brisk correspondence that grew out of an article she had published in a journal of metaphysics. He wrote to tell her how much he admired it, and she promptly wrote back. When she heard I wanted to visit America, she insisted I should be her guest.

Miss Osiroff lived alone in the "Village," and her door was always open to a variety of artists, thinkers, and reformers. One of them, Mr. Jacob Riis, took us on my first tour of the notorious Five Points. The poverty and squalor of the district matched the worst I'd seen back home. Old men and women from every corner of Europe sat aimlessly on street corners. Wild-eyed children with distended bellies rummaged through ash heaps. Mothers begged for coins with babies in their arms as toddlers played around them.

Mr. Riis showed us Bottle Alley, where the rag-pickers lived, and Blind-Man's Alley, where a colony of blind beggars eked out a rudimentary living. He brought us to "stale-beer dives," where those on the lowest rungs swilled the dregs from spent beer barrels for two cents a cup while rats scurried around their feet. But in the midst of the degradation, we saw signs of industry: buttons made, ties sewn, cigars rolled, socks knit, and stories woven like the one told to us by old Mrs. Benoir, a native Indian, who wore her hair in braids and smoked a clay pipe in a room that wasn't much larger than the rickety bed she occupied.

Mr. Riis's photographic exposé, *How the Other Half Lives,* prompted a public outcry and resulted in the demolition of a section of the tenements.

The layout of the park that took their place didn't delight the eyes or allow those who would use it to wander. Instead, sturdy benches, a flat expanse of lawn, and trees in metal cages placed along the perimeter delivered a clear message: stick to the assigned paths, and no funny business. The unobstructed lines of sight made it easy for coppers to keep watch and discouraged the possibility of mischief.

Mulberry Bend Park was a far cry from the undulating meadows, shimmering lake, and the poetic woodland Ramble of Central Park farther uptown. Its sole mission was to bring the poor out into the open, provide them with opportunities for wholesome recreation, and introduce them to American norms. From time to time, volunteers from the Playground Association of America would hand out pamphlets with titles like "Play as Training in Citizenship" and "The Social Value of Playgrounds in Crowded Districts."

As for the residents who had been displaced, no one knew what had happened to them. They were either absorbed into the surrounding tenements, as some said, or maybe Mrs. Benoir and her clay pipe just vanished into the ether.

* * *

Mrs. Woo arrived with her daughters in tow. She handed each girl a small cake and sent them off to play. The older girl counted to three, then charged ahead; her younger sibling chased behind her.

Grace Woo flicked a speck from the high-collared tunic that reached her knees and sat as far from me as the space on the bench would allow. She trained her attention on her daughters and apologized for bringing me here, but said it was for the best. Her husband didn't like her talking to strangers, especially reporters, and there was no need for others to gossip, which is why she didn't invite me in when I knocked.

I took the opportunity to ask what she thought of the proceedings in the courtroom.

Mrs. Woo looked distraught. "This business about her being white? She never looked the slightest bit white to me, even though I knew her mother was Irish."

"Everything that has happened must have hit your daughters hard." The last time I saw her here, she had all three girls at her side.

Mrs. Woo nodded. "They're always together, either at my place, or upstairs, or here. Most of the time upstairs though, because Tai Yow doesn't like Ha Oi to go anywhere without her. And now Lily and May are terrified. Ever since Ha Oi's been gone, they wake up in a panic, dreaming that the Gerry men will also come for them."

She twisted her handkerchief between her fingers. "At home, every five minutes, they look into the mirror to check whether the color of their hair or skin or eyes is changing. I tell them that isn't possible, but they don't believe me. They worry if it can happen to Ha Oi—it can happen to anyone. And then they will be taken away too.

"What am I supposed to say? If those men could come for Mock's child, and *he* couldn't protect her, how can Mr. Woo and I do anything to stop them?"

I told her that I'd like to try to help her. That I wanted to write a story about what was happening to Ha Oi from Mock Duck and Tai Yow's perspective. The public deserved to know about it.

"The public doesn't care," Grace Woo said bitterly. "All they want is to get rid of us."

"The more that people know—" I began, but she held up her hand.

"Nothing ever changes."

"Harry Thaw's mother paid for an entire moving picture to be made to sway the public's opinion." It was called *The Unwritten Law* and billed as "a thrilling drama based on the Thaw-White case." Dupont had made us all watch it.

"That might work for the likes of Thaw, but it doesn't work for us. Don't tell me I'm wrong. I've lived here my entire life, and I know what people think." She put the handkerchief in her lap. "So you want to write about Mock, Tai Yow, and Ha Oi." She looked me in the eyes. "What do you get out of it?" She was nothing if not direct.

"Mrs. Woo, I don't have children, so I can't know exactly what they're going through, but I'm a long way from home myself."

The last glimpse I'd had of my parents was from the deck of the steamer. My father waving, my proud mother with her head bent. Had I known it was the last time I'd see them, the last time I'd see the world they represented, more than likely, I would never have left.

"No children because you didn't want to, or couldn't?" Grace Woo asked. She really did get down to personal matters. Maybe she should have become a reporter herself.

"A bit of both, I suppose." Dr. Morley and I had lost one child in the early stages of pregnancy, and after that, we decided that we couldn't ask our offspring to pay the price for our unusual marriage. Although I sometimes questioned our decision, most of the time, I felt we had done what was right. Our children would have been adrift in the world, and it would have been impossible for me to work—which was what I really wanted.

In the distance, Mrs. Woo's daughter tripped and fell. Grace Woo jumped up but sat down again when she saw the child lean on her younger sister's shoulder and limp back toward us like an injured soldier. The two planted themselves in front of us, and the eldest showed her mother her knee. Mrs. Woo wet her handkerchief with spit and wiped away a trickle of blood.

"Why do you wear trousers?" the younger girl asked, looking at me.

I laughed.

"May!" her mother scolded.

"It's all right. I wear trousers because it makes it easier for me to do my job."

"But you're a lady…?" She sounded skeptical.

"May!" her mother repeated.

"Where do you go to school?" I asked.

"Morningstar Mission School, but next year, we'll go to PS 23 with the Italian children."

"You're good friends with Ha Oi?"

They both nodded.

"You must miss her."

Nods again.

"May is older than Ha Oi," Lily, the elder sibling, said, "but Ha Oi is stronger."

"She is not," May responded.

"She beat you in tug of war."

"She was cheating."

"You cheated."

"Go and play for a few minutes," their mother instructed.

The two girls ran off, still arguing.

"Will you help?" I turned to Mrs. Woo. "All I need is for you to speak to Mock or Tai Yow. Ask if they will talk to me."

"I don't know…" She sounded uncertain. "I shouldn't get involved. I don't think Mr. Woo will like it."

"You said in court that you help Mr. Woo with his business?"

"That's right. He doesn't speak English, so I buy all the supplies and talk to the customers when they're tourists."

"You enjoy it?"

"I love to watch the pictures come to life in the chemical bath. It's like magic." She looked wistful. "In a different life, I might have been the photographer."

"Have you ever taken any photographs?"

"Once or twice." A quick intake of breath. "When my husband was sick, I took one of the girls."

"You're like me." I knew I was going out on a limb. "A working woman. I disagree with my husband sometimes too…but, for Ha Oi's sake, please consider my request."

Mrs. Woo stood, pocketed her handkerchief. "It's getting late. I should go." She called to her daughters.

"You'll think about what I said?"

"Um-hm." She didn't look at me as she reached for daughters' hands, and the three set off, Grace Woo in the middle, the two smaller figures on either side. They became smaller and smaller until they turned a corner and vanished.

Chapter Fourteen

"Hello, hello." A theatrical personage wearing an eyepatch, tall boots, and a white silk shirt strolled over as I prepared to leave Mulberry Bend. "You from the *Observer*? I've seen you around." His complexion was tawny, and a halo of frizzy hair encircled his face. He held out his hand, and I caught a whiff of musky cologne.

"They call me the Corsair. I've held down my corner on Chatham Square for ages. I hear you have questions. If so, I have answers." He sauntered along beside me. "Tourists, I charge by the quarter of an hour for my knowledge and a flat rate for a one-hour tour—but for a mention in your publication, I'd be happy to disclose the contents of this"—he tapped his forehead—"*gratis.*"

"That's generous." I noticed the shiny gold ring wrapped around his index finger.

"It was my grandfather's. Given to him by his grandfather who bought it at a market in Algiers."

"You're from North Africa?"

"Aden. You know it?"

"The ship stopped there on my journey from India." It was a bustling port, with traders and travelers from everywhere en route to the Red Sea. "And now you're a lobbygow." That was what they called the hangers-on in Chinatown, men who earned their living by doing odd jobs or leading tourists around, or a bit of both. Like the lobbygow in San Francisco, whom the Gerry Society claimed had fathered little Ha Oi.

"I hate that word," the Corsair scoffed. "So insulting. I prefer to think of myself as a chronicler. A storyteller in the manner of the great Scheherazade.

But one who tells the truth, with just a little extra added"—he brought his thumb and forefinger together to form a pinch—"to give some zest.

"But when it comes to Mock Duck—that is who interests you, am I right?" He didn't wait for me to reply. "I find that spice isn't necessary. When it comes to Mock Duck, the truth, the whole truth, and nothing but the truth suffices."

We had veered away from the park, and as though it was the only direction in which we could go, drifted back toward Chinatown through a narrow maze of alleys.

"I bet you haven't heard this one." The Corsair's soothing voice and practiced patter drew me in as he launched into a tale about the gangster as a boy. He painted a picture of the Chinese quarter in 'Frisco, similar to the one in New York, but with more people, more secret nooks and passageways, twists and turns. It was here that Mock had roamed about as a child, skinny legs poking from ballooning khaki shorts, attending the local mission school whenever he could or would—he had been a star student, apparently. Could have been a doctor or a preacher if he wanted, but instead, he spent most of his time stealing, smoking, or begging for scraps. His father was a drunk, his mother may or may not have been a prostitute, and both parents died by the time Mock was four or five.

"Is this the truth?"

The Corsair took offense. "If you've heard enough, I can stop."

I apologized. "Please go on."

Mock lived in a lean-to with a dozen other waifs, my guide said. He was so poor that he owned nothing save for one item, his prized possession: a wooden top, shiny from the grease of his fingertips and smooth to the touch. It was one of those tops that you could buy for a few cents at the market. Mock could make that top dance; he could skip it from surface to surface, get it to jump and spin so fast that it made onlookers dizzy. It was the envy of all the urchins, and they begged him to teach them how to do it, but he always refused. Sometimes, he was able to earn a penny or two by performing a trick with the top for strangers.

I recalled Mock spinning the toy on his palm as Ha Oi watched with delight.

"Does he still have it?"

"Please, be patient." Days and years passed, the Corsair went on. Mock turned twelve, and one day, a gang of older boys cornered him. "Full Pant," they cried. "Full Pant"—they called him that precisely because his pants ended at his knees. "Show us something new. Something that will amaze us."

Mock knew the boys well enough to understand that it wouldn't be wise to refuse. He demonstrated his latest move.

"Not bad," the ringleader conceded when he finished. "Now, to thank us for watching, give us a reward."

Mock's grip on the spinner tightened. He knew what was coming next.

Another boy noticed the clenched fist. "You want to keep that thing?"

Little Mock nodded.

"Give us something else then."

But Mock had nothing else to give. Nothing but the clothes on his puny, undeveloped body.

The group closed in on him, eyeing him up and down. "Give us your belt. Your belt." A palm stretched out. "Hand it over."

"Belt, Full-Pant. Belt," they chanted as they circled round and round.

Mock began to feel dizzy. He wasn't wearing a belt, he wore a length of cord tied around his waist, but it served its purpose. The taunting group inched closer. He could hear the threat in their voices. Mock began to panic, but he knew he had no choice, and with fingers slippery from sweat, he clumsily unknotted the length of rope, and pulled it from the makeshift loops.

As he released the cord, his shorts dropped to his ankles.

The boys began to guffaw and point. "Tiny peas and baby carrot! So small you can barely see them!" Mock stood there, red-faced and unable to move. Their cries echoed in his ears long after they left, twirling the rope overhead like a lasso.

Afterwards, the Corsair said, Mock made a decision that would forever change the course of his life. He decided that he would never again allow anyone to humiliate him. "He would become hard. He would become cold. He would become the man we know now, the man who would bend others to his will, and not the other way around. And that's how it was—until the day that Ha Oi came along.

"She reminded him of his sister, you see. He had a sister who died when she was two or three years old. The same age as Ha Oi when he met her."

"And that's the truth?" It sounded a little too good.

"You don't believe me? Fine." He shrugged. "Your loss."

"All right, Corsair. If you know so much about Mock Duck, can you tell me this? Was he behind the shootings at the theater?"

"He says he wasn't."

"I know what he says. What do you say?"

"I say Mock moves in mysterious ways, and it's not for us to judge."

"And what about the murder they tried him for? Do you think he committed that?" An On Leong tailor visiting from New Jersey had been shot and killed, and both Mock and a friend had been seen chasing the man through Chinatown with their guns blazing.

"They accused him of masterminding the crime... But everyone knows he didn't pull the trigger."

Mock Duck had been tried twice for the murder, but on both occasions, the jury wasn't able to convict him. That was when the chief witness against him jumped from the balcony above the burning restaurant.

"Mock is special," the Corsair said, after a pause. "Did you know the On Leongs shot him three times in the stomach?"

I hadn't heard that.

"Three bullets straight to the belly. Guts, blood everywhere. It would have killed any other man. Even the doctors said he wouldn't make it. But he came back three or four months later, stronger and fiercer than ever. You'll print that in your paper, won't you? And put my name with it."

We came to Chatham Square as a train rumbled through.

"Let me know if I can be of any help. You can find me here." The lobbygow pointed to a crate off to one side.

I pictured Mock with Ha Oi riding on his shoulders, his hands holding on to her chubby legs. They began to walk toward me. And as I tried to muddle through what kind of man he really was, father and daughter started laughing.

Chapter Fifteen

Dupont kept me busy for the next two days while I waited anxiously for word from Mrs. Woo. Would she speak to the Mocks, or had she decided against it? Maybe her husband had prevented her; maybe she was scared. I would go by her place and find out what had happened if I didn't hear from her soon. But first, an article about Evelyn Nesbit's latest outfits, and then a trip to a quack doctor on Thirty-Fourth Street who was rumored to perform illegal eye surgeries. I pretended to be a patient and, in return for a hefty fee, the doctor said he would put me under the knife the following morning. Dupont notified the police, who surrounded the clinic, and when I arrived, cash in hand, they arrested the doctor and his accomplice. But not before his assistant clocked me in the jaw, and the physician hurled several choice abuses my way. The editor would no doubt print his insults verbatim and accompany the story with suitably harrowing illustrations.

I caught a glimpse of my reflection in a store window. I looked worn out, my hair was disheveled, and my jaw was ballooning. I was getting too old for this, I thought, as I staggered back to the office. My mother would have been appalled. I could hear her: *What are you doing with yourself, Archana? Try to be more sensible.* And to my father: *How can you let her go? What will become of her?*

* * *

My jaw continued to throb despite Dr. Morley's pills and ointments, and

I woke up the next morning feeling lousy. I had told my husband that I'd tripped and fallen on the stairs, but he didn't believe it. "You've got to stop working at some point, you know that, don't you, Archie?" he'd said. "This can't go on forever."

Despite the ache, my face looked better than it did the night before. I took a lukewarm shower—much better than ladling water out of a bucket like we did at home—dressed for work, drank a cup of tea, and ate a slice of toast with butter.

Our maid, Clement, came to ask what she should make for dinner, but I couldn't think clearly, so I told her to prepare whatever she liked. It would invariably be meat for Dr. Morley, a piece of fish or an omelet for me, and overcooked vegetables.

My husband had already left for work, but I reflected on what he had said. He was probably correct. I couldn't go on like this indefinitely. I didn't see myself eating omelets and boiled vegetables to my dying day, and apart from him and the paper, there wasn't much tying me to New York. Kindly Miss Osiroff had passed away a few years previously, and without her presence and Bohemian circle, my own world had grown smaller. For obvious reasons, Dr. Morley and I didn't entertain very often. And apart from my friends from Barnard, most of whom were married and busy with their children, and a handful of Dr. Morley's bachelor friends from medical college, we didn't socialize much.

At the *Observer,* Dupont greeted me with some wisecrack about my appearance and then informed me that I seemed to be in high demand. "An Oriental bird came looking for you. She left this note." He dangled a piece of paper in front of my nose but wouldn't let me take it. "And Hizzoner's wife telephoned. She'd like you to interview her husband. I offered to send one of the lads, but she insisted on you. 'A woman's perspective on our city and its leader,' or some such thing." The editor cupped one hand to his mouth and called out, "Hear that, boys? Mrs. M. knows how to lean on her connections. You should take a page from her book."

I groaned inwardly—there was no need for Dupont to stir the pot. Best to leave it alone, lest it spilled over and I was scalded. But sometimes, he just couldn't resist. And he wouldn't give me Mrs. Woo's note until I wrote up a piece on Evelyn Nesbit's schoolgirl diary, which the District Attorney produced in court. In the entry he focused on, Evelyn wrote that she didn't want to become a wife and mother when she grew up; she wanted to become an actress. The attorney cited the entry to prove that that Mrs. Thaw hadn't been an innocent child when Stanford White seduced her and that she knew what she was doing all along.

What any of this had to do with Harry's decision to shoot White, unprovoked, years after the architect's liaison with Evelyn, was anybody's guess. I did as I was asked as quickly as I could so that I could get back to what I considered my real work.

* * *

Gusts of wind blew the rain nearly sideways, and pellet-like drops hammered against the panes, creating a roar within the Blackboy, which took up the basement of a wedge-shaped building that one could still sometimes find on the rare, irregular-shaped lot in New York City. A cast-iron silhouette of a frizzy-haired child graced the entrance to its otherwise unmarked doorway.

If you could put up with Haitian Jim's ever-present scowl and paid your bill promptly you would be welcome, no questions asked, so the place was usually packed with an assortment of characters.

That day, because of the weather, the tavern was uncharacteristically quiet. A group of old codgers stared at pieces on a chessboard, elbows resting on the table, chins cupped in their hands, and a bespectacled socialist paged forlornly through a stack of pamphlets with titles like "Workers of America, Unite!" Jim fixed a leak in the ceiling—a bucket had been placed below to catch the drops, and Mrs. Jim was mopping the floor when the door blew open, and Bedelia bolted inside, struggling to close an umbrella that had been twisted inside-out by the gale.

"What a day, what a day. I'm glad to be out of it." A brown waxed cloak hung over her patterned dress. She reached into her pocket, wiped her damp face and hair with a kerchief, propped the umbrella by the door, and slapped a few coins on the counter. Mrs. Jim wordlessly poured her a pint.

Mock's maid joined me at my table at the back. "Good to see yeh, Mrs. Morley. Thought yeh'd never show because of the storm." She noticed my face. "What happened to yeh?"

I touched my jaw. "Just a fall."

"Yeh best be careful. Little falls lead to big ones. Me mam fell and broke her hip. A month later, she was six feet under."

"I'm sorry to hear that."

"I'm sorry too. But such is life…one minute we're upright, not a care in the world. Next thing yeh know, the worms have started gnawing." She took a sip of her drink and sighed. "Mrs. Woo spoke to me. She says yeh wants to talk to Mr. Mock and Tai Yow. Write somethin' about them for your paper—but I have a question: What's your interest in us and the little rascal?"

I replied that our readers would want to know how a hardened highbinder and his wife came to care so deeply for a girl who wasn't their own. They would want to see the human side of the gangster, as it were. And if the truth came out, it might help Ha Oi's case.

"Yeh thinks so? They shouldn't never have taken her in the first place."

I told the maid I agreed, but that it was time to move forward. And that everyone understood the importance of the right kind of publicity these days. If Harry Thaw's ma thought it was worthwhile to pay for a motion picture to tell her son's side of the story, then a sympathetic article in the paper would certainly do Mock and Tai Yow no harm, and might even benefit them. And unlike the other reporters, I added, I was willing to give the Mocks a fair shake.

Mock's maid pursed her lips. "They should lock him up, that Thaw fella. Everyone saw what he did. But because he's rich, they'll let him go free, and our Mr. Mock, who ain't never hurt no one, they'll take his daughter from him."

"Never hurt anyone?" I couldn't keep the skepticism from my voice.

The maid nodded. "In all these years, he ain't never raised his hand nor his voice to me, or Tai Yow, or the kiddie. He reads, he writes, he's well spoken. He's devoted to that child. When he ain't workin', they're always playin' together. 'You'll spoil her,' Mr. Mock, I say, and he replies that that ain't possible because she ain't no cup of milk."

In answer to my question about how long she'd worked for Tai Yow, Bedelia replied that it was since Tai Yow, Chin Mung, and Ha Oi arrived in New York. Tai Yow had become like a daughter to her; Ha Oi, a granddaughter. And Chin Mung had been a generous man, just like Mr. Mock. Tai Yow had been lucky with both her husbands, which was good, considering all the hardships the young woman had faced. They never fussed about how Bedelia spent her time, and Tai Yow allowed Bedelia to buy whatever she wanted at the market. At Mock's, things were better, naturally. Bedelia ate what the family ate; she didn't need to ration her supplies of tea or sugar or soap, and she didn't sleep on a mattress on the floor. On Doyers Street, Bedelia slept in her own bed.

After Chin Mung died, the maid said, things became difficult for Tai and the little girl. Ha Oi's mother had been ready to give up the rented room on Bayard and move into a smaller room farther away, when she met Mock Duck.

"When was that?"

Bedelia smoothed a strand of gray hair with her fingers. She remembered it like it was yesterday. Mock had just been released from Bellevue, and the Hips held a banquet to celebrate. Everyone who wasn't an On Leong had been invited. Tai Yow went, dressed in her best outfit, and brought three-year-old Ha Oi along. Later that night, she told Bedelia what happened.

Mock looked pale but fit and sat at a table in the corner, chatting with his friends. As evening turned into night and his friends flew sky-high on rice wine, the highbinder, who'd barely touched a drop, noticed a small child careening around the tables. He beckoned her over, and when she stood in front of him, he pulled a one-cent piece from her ear. Then he found a scrap of paper and folded a little bird whose wings flapped when you pulled the tail. Ha Oi ran to show the bird to her mother, then she brought her mother to meet the guest of honor... and that was how it began. "If yeh asks me," Bedelia said, "our Mr. Mock didn't have no holes in his stomach—he had a hole in his heart, and our rascal filled it."

Every day, Bedelia cleaned, cooked, and bathed the child. Dressed her in fresh silk outfits.

"That business about the hair dye that they said in court? It ain't true. Me or Tai Yow put dye in our rascal's lovely hair? Why would we make such mischief? Me mam always said, 'Bedelia, folks see what they want to see, they believe what they want to believe.' If that child's all white, then I'm Mongolian." She pounded her fist so hard against the table that the glasses rattled.

"What's going on?" the proprietor looked up from his labors.

"It's been long enough since the rascal's been away." Bedelia lowered her voice. "And now they're tellin' us that the hearin's been delayed again."

"I hadn't heard that."

"It's on account of 'em havin' difficulties findin' her papers in San Francisco. Because of that fire, the earthquake, and such. I'll tell yeh why they're havin' difficulties. Because there ain't no papers to be found. Chin Mung was Ha Oi's father. That's all there is to it. To hear 'em say that it was one of 'em lobbygows…?" She made a face. The very idea revolted her.

"This is what the public needs to hear, Bedelia. But they need to hear it from Mock Duck himself. Will he speak to me?"

"Not so fast, lassie." The maid snapped back to attention. "First things first. Reporters ain't never been fair to Mr. Mock, what makes yeh any different?"

I told her what I'd told Mrs. Woo, and then some more: that I knew what it was like not to have people understand who you are, or where you come from. I knew what it was like to always have to prove myself. And I had seen Ha Oi and heard what the roundsman promised. The girl whom the Society described didn't match the child who'd been taken from Doyers. I had my questions and was still looking for answers.

Bedelia's expression gave nothing away. She asked. "And where d'yeh live?"

I frowned. It was a strange question.

"Yeh know all about us," she said. "You've been to our home."

I didn't like to, but I gave her my address.

"In one of 'em nice houses?" the maid exclaimed. "I used to work for some English there. Folks think I've come down in the world, but they don't know what it's like to work for the Celestials. Tai Yow treats me better than any English ever did."

I veered the conversation back to the subject at hand. "You'll tell Mock what we discussed?"

She nodded.

"Maybe he should read what I've written about the case."

A melancholy look stole across the maid's eyes. She had never learned her letters, she said, and Ha Oi had been trying to teach her the alphabet. "'Bedelia,' she scolds me, 'yeh ain't tryin' hard enough. Here's how yeh makes an 'a' and here's how yeh makes a 'b.''And I reply, 'Ha Oi, the letters they dance in front of my eyes. I ain't sharp like yeh.' And she says, 'Don't worry, Bedelia.'" The maid's voice cracked with emotion. "'I'll teach yeh.'"

Bedelia finished her pint. "Yeh's a good listener, I'll give yeh that. Some people, they talk, talk, talk. Yeh can't get a word in.… Yeh know who sent me here?"

I shook my head.

"Tai Yow. Mr. Mock says we can't trust scribblers. But Ha Oi's mam says she knows yeh has a mother's heart—even if yeh dresses like a gent.… Grace Woo told me you don't have kiddies of yeh's own?"

"No."

"Ain't nothin' wrong with that. I don't either." She stood and grimaced. "These old bones, they creak in the rain."

I asked how old she was. She had no idea.

I asked whether she had ever been married.

"Ain't never had the time… nor the inclination. Well, I should be on my way." She shrugged on her coat, which was still wet, and wove her way between the tables. Then she reached for her umbrella in the stand, stood for a moment in the doorway to gather herself, and pushed on into the darkness, although it was still pouring and the wind howled outside.

Chapter Sixteen

I kept myself from constantly speculating about the outcome of my conversation with Bedelia by preparing for my upcoming interview with Hizzoner. "This is a step up for you," Dupont said, as though I needed reminding. It was also a balancing act. I didn't want to anger the McClellans, but I didn't want to write a puff piece either. "Make sure you've done your research," the editor advised. "You need to be prepared. We can't have you letting down the paper." In all my years at the *Observer*, I'd never interviewed a city official.

Given Georgie B.'s interests, I pored through articles about the City Beautiful movement, which maintained that a city's design and social improvement went hand in hand. Then there was the New York City Improvement Commission, which detailed plans that would "anticipate the future growth of the city for many years to come."

I scanned through the news of Georgie B.'s marriage to Georgiana Heckscher in Newport in 1889. Georgiana's mother was Cornelia Whitney, and her father was a prominent member of New York Society, who served under Gen. McClellan in the Union Army. That probably explained how she and Georgie B. met and her fierce devotion to the memory of her late father-in-law. One of the stories said that she was the mayor's chief advisor and that she possessed "a knowledge of politics equaled by few men."

My next stop was at a lending library, where the sprightly librarian dusted off a copy of Hizzoner's *Oligarchies of Venice,* written before he became mayor. The book was dedicated to his wife, and the chapters bore daunting headings like "The First Coup d'État," "The Querini-Tiepolo Conspiracy," and "The War of Chioggia." It seemed strange that the same man who had written a scholarly account of Italian history also consorted with Tammany leadership, served as Congressman from New York for several terms, and then ran for mayor. Had his intellectual pursuits prepared him for political office, or did they make him unfit for government? So far, he seemed to be doing a good job.

I also unearthed a copy of the article from *Munsey's* that Lady Mac had mentioned when we met. It was titled "George Brinton McClellan, Son and Namesake of the Famous General, His Personality, Political Success, and Rise to Prominence as a Figure of National Interest."

The story noted that when McClellan was nominated for his first term as mayor, he was a mere thirty-eight years old, and when he was renominated to a second term at forty, it was "difficult to find anyone to run against him." Looking ahead, he was the logical Democratic candidate for governor, and a possible presidency loomed in the background.

Then came the section that Georgiana referred to: In addition to his name, the article said that Georgie B. had "inherited his father's great capacity for organization and system. It is natural for people to fear that the general's tendency to temporize and vacillate, which marred his career, might also have descended to his son. That is for time to prove."

And finally, there was chatter about Georgie B.'s rift with "Silent Charlie" Murphy, the Tammany Hall leader. They had a falling out because the mayor refused to appoint Murphy's cronies to high-level government jobs. As the leader of the Democratic Party in New York City, Murphy was the man who would orchestrate elections in Georgie B.'s favor. Now, McClellan would have to fight and win them on his own. But his pledge to raze Chinatown had stalled indefinitely, and his plan to build a mighty aqueduct from the mountains was on course but meeting opposition.

No wonder Lady Mac thought he could use a boost.

* * *

Georgie B. maintained a punctual schedule, the general outlines of which were known to the public. He walked to work each morning—a good way to gauge the mood of the city and get in a bit of exercise. He started work at about a quarter past nine with a review of his correspondence and appointments. Next, he met his department heads and attended all the official meetings that he could, never failing to attend the monthly meeting of the almighty Board of Estimate and Apportionment, whose eight members determined the city's future by deciding what would be built, what would be torn down, and who would be granted licenses, all behind closed doors, and with the stroke of a pen.

The mayor took lunch at noon, usually in the company of a member or two of his cabinet, at the nearby Hardware Club, where a table was always reserved for him.

From one to two, he discussed business matters with bankers from Wall Street and titans of industry, but at two o'clock sharp—a matter of pride—he held his "daily scrum." This was a no-prior-appointment-required, no-special-favors-necessary gathering, during which ordinary New Yorkers could tell the mayor exactly what was on their minds.

Dressed in a smart skirt and neat hat, I crossed the street to City Hall at two-thirty, passing the gaggle of bureaucrats, favor seekers, gossips, and pigeon-feeders who loitered in the park outside, when suddenly it occurred to me that maybe Georgie B. or his wife had initiated the proceedings against Mock's child in order to teach the gangster, and the entire neighborhood, a lesson. If they couldn't raze the district, they could at least force its residents to behave. The thought stopped me in my tracks.

Would our aristocratic, scholarly mayor do such a thing? Would he stoop so low? Followed immediately by, why not? He had to win elections. And why should he care what happened to a gangster's child? If she turned out to be white, so much the better. Punish Mock and save a white waif. The letter that alerted the Children's Society could have been written by anyone. All they needed to know was that Ha Oi existed—and Lady Mac, who visited schools in the neighborhood, seemed to know a lot about everyone.

In a fog, I floated beneath the portico, along the floors of gray-veined marble to the pair of curved marble staircases that rose up unsupported and conveyed visitors to a pillared rotunda.

The sound of voices from the scrum echoed in my ears. I was supposed to speak to the mayor about his plans for the city, not his plans for Mock's daughter. I was supposed to represent the *Observer*, not embarrass my husband, nor ruffle any feathers.

The tall wooden door to the reception room swung open. "Please, go ahead." The petitioner, who was exiting, waited for me to enter.

Decades of neglect and budgetary shortfalls showed in the pink wallpaper that was peeling from the walls and the threadbare upholstery on the chairs in the high-ceilinged reception hall. Electric light bulbs emitted a constant low hum, a suitable background to the chorus of "Mr. Mayor! Mr. Mayor!" The room burned hot with the hopes, dreams and grievances of several dozen citizens.

"Please wait your turn, ladies and gentlemen! Everyone will be heard," a smart-looking aide ordered.

"Your first time?" A lady who clutched a notebook to her chest like a shield inquired.

"That's right."

"I attend every week to present the mayor with a list of ash cans that have not been emptied by ten each morning."

"You personally inspect every ash can in the city?"

"A team of dedicated volunteers assists me in my endeavors." She sniffed. "Well, don't be shy. Press on, press on."

At the center of the hubbub and flanked by a personable secretary on either side, Georgie B. mingled amongst the crowd. He bent his head, listened attentively to complaints about fire codes, promised to consider extra funding for Bellevue, and agreed that motion pictures were a menace that led youngsters and the more susceptible classes astray.

He heard out a proposal to solve the traffic problems on the lower part of the island: open a new thoroughfare from Eighth Street to Wall Street, reserved exclusively for gentlemen driving their own traps. The proposer (who naturally owned his own trap) had taken the liberty of hiring an engineer to draw up the plans, which he submitted to the mayor in the hopes that it would speed up construction.

"New York City's roads have always been open to all members of the public," Georgie B. replied without missing a beat, "and although I doubt that will change anytime in the near future, my aides will be happy to take a look. Thank you for your trouble."

Better him than me. I couldn't have put up with all the clamor, and responded to all those questions, even the daft ones, with such good humor and forbearance.

A bell rang at three o'clock sharp, and an aide discreetly whispered into Hizzoner's ear. Someone apologized on the mayor's behalf, and assured those who hadn't had a chance to speak to him that they would be given precedence the following afternoon. A few grumbles, and then the petitioners dispersed.

A voice called, and a hand beckoned. "Mrs. Morley? This way, please."

I followed the ramrod-stiff figure toward the mayor's private rooms. A desk the size of a steamship backed onto floor-to-ceiling curtained French windows—through which the offices on Newspaper Row were clearly visible. Given a pair of binoculars, Hizzoner could probably have read what we were typing.

Three visitors' chairs were placed in front of the desk, and a couch and armchairs arranged around a plush Oriental rug created a separate seating area. A photograph of Lady Mac on her wedding day leaned on a bookshelf in a geometric marquetry frame—her delicate features and figure accentuated by a marble stand and a vase filled with white flowers.

Images of the mayor in action hung above the photograph of his wife: operating the city's first subway line; cutting a ribbon for a memorial to the *General Slocum* victims with President Roosevelt; shaking hands with various dignitaries, including the banker J.P. Morgan, and Presidents McKinley and Cleveland.

Georgie B. caught me looking. "I drove the subway myself. You should have seen the engineers' faces. Didn't stop until we emerged into the light at 116th. Ha! All the bankers had to hold on to their hats throughout the journey!"

He offered me a seat, while he rotated his right arm in its socket a couple of times. "All this hand-shaking makes me sore. Now, if only I possessed Mrs. Cleveland's talent: Our former first lady was one of the best shakers of hands in the business. The great thing about her was that she really looked as if she meant the warm clasp she gave you."

"And did she?"

He grinned, putting me at ease. "That is an excellent question."

When Georgie B. first took office, everyone thought he was nothing more than a Tammany stooge. One of the papers had printed a full-page cartoon that showed him standing in this very room, gazing steadily ahead while the unsmiling, sphinxlike Tammany leader, Charlie Murphy, pulled the puppeteer's string from above. The caption simply read: *NEW YORK CITY'S REAL BOSS.*

McClellan's break with Murphy in his second term signaled otherwise. But now, the mayor needed to show the public what he was worth. Hence, the push for favorable publicity from any and every source—including someone like me writing for a two-bit rag like the *Observer.*

I opened my notebook, and George B. took a seat. His suit hung easily from his compact, athletic frame, his trousers creased just so at the ankles, and his shoes looked well-made and elegant. "I realize this interview might put you in an awkward position, but please know that I was a journalist once, and I understand that you must feel free to use your own judgment."

Easier said than done, but I appreciated the sentiment—and his skill as a politician. Showing sympathy won him a friend and cost nothing.

An aide brought in a jug of water and two glasses on a metal tray and placed them on the table between us.

We continued the light chit-chat—his years in Washington and how much both he and Georgiana missed the camaraderie of Congress. We returned to the subject of presidents—the late President McKinley, whom Georgie B. admired and had dined with on numerous occasions, and President Roosevelt, our current commander-in-chief—who, the mayor said, perhaps a little too politely, seemed to be faring well for one so young.

I could tell that I was being warmed up, lulled into the sense that this would be an easy conversation, and I was almost ready to let down my journalistic guard. There would have been no shame in it, except that Dupont had sent me off with some questions, and I had prepared a few of my own.

I redirected the conversation, and he took it well, making it all appear effortless.

"My wife tells me I tend to ramble. Please, fire away."

I began with an easy one: Which of the many projects in his "New Vision" was he most excited about?

"I'm so glad you asked." He gestured to an aide who handed me a pamphlet titled, "The Catskills Waterworks: Fresh, Clean Water for Every New Yorker. Quenching New York's Thirst for Future Generations."

The mayor leaned forward, elbows resting on his thighs, looked me in the eye, and explained that, in order for New York to fulfill its destiny, a constant supply of clean water was absolutely required. No one had prepared for the city to grow in such leaps and bounds. Our current water supply was patched together from various sources, and it was woefully inadequate. Although the New Croton Dam had been completed just the previous year, demand for clean water had already outstripped what the new dam could provide.

The jump in population, thanks to the consolidation of the five boroughs, plus record immigration, year after year, all combined to create conditions ripe for a public health crisis. And that's what we would have if we continued on our current path. Buildings where water didn't reach above the fourth or fifth floor; more outbreaks of typhus and cholera; children, adults, especially those who lived in tenements, falling ill and dying in massive numbers.

The Catskills Aqueduct, however, would change everything. It was the most ambitious engineering, planning, and political feat ever undertaken by a municipality. Tunnels would be dug deep beneath the earth's surface and would carry clean, pure drinking water all the way from the mountains to the city—a distance of over *one hundred miles*—powered entirely by the force of gravity. No pumping or turbines, no mechanical aids or filtration necessary. The aqueduct would be a twentieth century marvel on par with the Panama Canal—which, mind you, had been organized by the federal government. New York City's aqueduct would be longer than any built by the Romans.

He motioned to the glasses on the table between us. "Have a taste."

I took a sip.

"What do you think?"

"It's wonderful!" I exclaimed. "Clean. Fresh." None of the usual tang, no mysterious sediments, no aroma.

"It is the cleanest, freshest water you will ever drink. And when we are finished, this is what will flow out of each and every New Yorker's tap."

"Then the public will salute you." I couldn't help but be impressed.

"I hope so. But the public's memory is troublingly short. This project will take ten years to complete. People will be happy when it's over, delighted with the results, but I doubt they will remember who made it possible. Voters only think in the short term."

"So why bother?"

"Because it's the right thing to do. It is absolutely necessary for our city's survival."

"I've heard about your other projects." I listed a few: improvements of the roads and pavements, numbering of houses, Staten Island ferry service. "And any developments on the Chinatown park?" I slipped it in casually.

"Oh, the people love the idea. It's a surefire vote-getter, and it's right for the city. It's a shame it's stalled.… Between you and me, Mrs. Morley—may I count on your discretion? This is off the record."

"Absolutely."

"Between you and me, I think there's something fishy about it. Someone must have pressured the engineer. Underground streams creating so much disruption? We've dealt with underground water before. It's not insurmountable."

"Any idea who it could be?"

"Haven't a clue. Could be a business owner. Could be one of my enemies. Could be one of the locals. They hire all sorts of people to do their dirty work for them. But it's not over. That park will be built. I've given New Yorkers my word."

I made a note to look into the delay. Then I added: "Have you heard what recently occurred in the district?"

"More violence?"

Studying his expression carefully, I told him about what happened to Mock's child.

He seemed only slightly troubled, if that. "It's unfortunate. But I have full faith in the Gerry Society. They will make sure she goes to the correct home—whether an American one, or back to Chinatown."

In for a penny, in for a pound. "Do you have any idea, sir, why Mock's child would be the target of such an action?"

"Absolutely none." He sounded firm. "To be honest, I am surprised by your interest in this Celestial hoodlum. Now, do you have any further questions that I *can* answer?" He tried to conceal his annoyance.

I returned to the script. "This one is from my editor, sir. Our readers will want to know how you plan to win elections without Charlie Murphy and Tammany Hall's support."

"Here's the thing, Mrs. Morley." He was back in his element. "Charles F. Murphy is one man, and while many believe it is impossible for a Democratic mayor to remain in office or get anything done without Tammany's blessing, I intend to prove that belief wrong. If the wrong men too often control our government, it is only because the right men too often refuse to do their duty. I will always act according to the dictates of my conscience and put the welfare of this city and its residents above all other considerations."

"Thank you, Mr. Mayor. And one final question from our readers." Actually, it was mine. "You bear your illustrious father's name. You have written a book on Italian history. Why did you take up politics and decide not to become a scholar, for instance?"

He stared into the distance, and again, I thought I might have offended him.

But then he said, "My father taught me to believe in service. In the principle of *noblesse oblige*: For those to whom much is given, much is required."

"My father taught me the same thing."

He blinked, perhaps surprised by the thought that someone like me should feel the same sense of privilege and responsibility that he did.

An aide whispered in his ear.

"Well, I'm sure we'll have more to discuss, Mrs. Morley." He stood and shook my hand warmly.

"Was that a Cleveland special?"

He laughed. "I am a mere shadow of the original."

His aide opened the door, and before I knew it, I'd been escorted out of that rarified chamber and was back on the streets breathing ordinary air along with every other New Yorker. And I realized I didn't have a handle on what I'd learned, or where I stood, despite our lengthy conversation.

Chapter Seventeen

"Not bad, Mrs. M. Not bad at all…." Dupont flicked at the sections of my article that he approved of the way he did when he was pleased. "Nice comparison of his aqueduct to the Romans…. And that bit about Murphy"—he chuckled—"looks like we're gearing up for a brawl. Hey, maybe we ought to put you on the City Hall beat. What do you think about that, boys?" He yelled to the back of the room for the second time in what felt like as many days. "Mrs. Morley as our new politics correspondent?"

"Very funny," Shrimpy said.

"You'll have a walkout, Mr. Dupont," someone called.

"Why do you taunt them?" I asked under my breath.

Dupont grinned. "Keeps 'em on their toes."

"At my expense," I muttered.

"What did you say?"

"Nothing."

"So what's next for you, Mrs. M? Hmm. Back to courtroom gossip? We haven't written anything about Thaw's sisters lately."

I told him I had something else in mind.

"Care to inform me?"

"If it works out."

He sighed dramatically. "Why I indulge you is anyone's guess." He was clearly in a good mood. "But make it quick. Before I change my mind."

* * *

The trellised birdcage shuddered up toward the sixth floor of a building on Broadway. I stepped from the elevator to find myself in a hall packed with an army of men engrossed in dusty maps and busy with charts, rulers, and other instruments of torture. The city's engineer corps, ready to mow down or build up whatever was ordered.

I looked around but couldn't spot Webster among that thicket of white shirts, bent heads, pencils, and protractors.

In response to my question, one of the fellows reluctantly tore himself away from his task and pointed me to the back of the hall. "Thataway."

I skirted between rows of desks until I finally reached the mousey engineer who held the keys to Chinatown's future.

Georgie B. suspected that someone had gotten to him, maybe one of the Chinese, through an intermediary. My thoughts had flown to Bartow S. Weeks, Tom Lee's bow-tied lawyer, the fellow with the penchant for the nitty-gritty—*the Small Parks Act cannot be used to clear tenements*. It could have been Dan O'Reilly, but he seemed more likely to traffic with snake-oil salesmen than men of science. Or maybe, just maybe, Mock Duck himself— but that didn't sit right. I couldn't picture him strong-arming an engineer.

Webster brushed his hair from his eyes, coughed a couple of times, and squeaked, "To whom do I have the pleasure?"

I introduced myself and went straight to the point—I told him I'd heard about the subterranean streams possibly running beneath Chinatown and, hence, causing delays.

"Yee-ss?" He wrapped his arms across his chest in self-defense.

"Isn't underground water an obstacle that can easily be overcome?"

"Not at all. Our investigations are only beginning. As you may or may not be aware, hundreds of streams and creeks have been buried beneath the streets of New York over the centuries. Excavation can disturb them, and then they burble up to the surface and cause all sorts of trouble.

"If, as I suspect, there may be fluids moving through the substrate, then it behooves us to proceed cautiously. Once I sign my name to the drawings for this park, that is a guarantee that the park will stand for generations. Unlike other structures you may have heard of—the Tombs jail being the most notorious example—I will not permit any project bearing my name to start to sink the moment construction begins. The city deserves better, and it is a matter of professional pride."

"If there's a stream running beneath Doyers, how are the current tenements still upright?"

"But are they, madam? Have you ever wondered why they tilt toward each other? No. I didn't think so. Yes, they are poorly built, but I suspect that the foundations are also unstable. The reasons for this must be thoroughly investigated. Which is why I have informed the mayor that plans for the park are likely to take much longer than anticipated, they will be more complicated than previously foreseen, and they will certainly cost more." It sounded like a mantra.

"I know the public is all in favor of a swift demolition," he continued. "But the public cannot always have what it wants. We must take all factors into consideration. We must be thorough. We are engineers, not politicians."

I'd reached a dead end. Webster was sticking to his story, and I couldn't push him further without, at best, accusing him of not knowing his own business, and at worst, being corrupt. And notwithstanding Georgie B.'s suspicions, I had no reason to believe either.

My eyes fell on a photograph of an awkward youth with untamed hair on Webster's desk. He looked familiar. "What a handsome young man. He takes after you."

"My son, Timothy." The engineer flushed.

"Is he an engineer, too? Just like his pa?" I struggled to recall where I'd seen him.

"He could have been." The engineer's shoulders sagged. "Certainly, he possesses the talent.... But recently, he's had his troubles...too much time at the races."

"Young people these days."

"They think they know everything, never listen. But what am I to do? He's all I have left since his mother passed. A gem of a woman, Mrs. Webster. Enchanted by the natural world. In fact, it was she who alerted me to the plethora of streams that once flowed through Manahatta." He used a native word for the island as he sighed over the memory of his departed spouse.

I murmured words a few words of sympathy and extricated myself, zigzagged through the labyrinth of desks, and pressed the button for the elevator. Where had I seen Timothy Webster before? I wracked my memory and cast my mind back to the crowds outside Harry Thaw's trial, to the Chinatown hearing, and even to the eye doctor's clinic…but drew a blank.

The elevator carriage arrived with a clang, and I stepped inside. The contraption shuddered downward, I saw my distorted reflection in the brass plate enclosing the buttons, and it came to me. I'd seen Webster Junior with Mock Duck outside the Hung Far Low Restaurant on Pell Street.

Right after the hearing at which his father had been put in charge of Chinatown's demolition.

*　*　*

Four days since I had spoken to Bedelia, and still no word from the highbinder. I was going crazy. I wondered whether the maid had reported unfavorably about me to her employer, or maybe the gangster simply had no interest in speaking to reporters. The realization that Mock had been consorting with Timothy Webster moments after the Board of Improvement hearing ended, that the fight which Mock had interrupted so theatrically might have been put on for the boy's benefit, and that Webster's son gambled and probably was in debt, all brought me to the same improbable conclusion: that Mock had known what was going to occur at the hearing and took steps to derail the result—all before anyone else realized what was happening.

I berated myself: here I was again, attributing actions to Mock that any normal human being would be unlikely to think of, let alone accomplish.

"Do you think it's true," I asked Dr. Morley as we strolled through the neighborhood after dinner, "that society creates the conditions for crime, lays the groundwork, and criminals are just the means for carrying it out?"

"I'm not sure I follow."

"I've been wondering about Mock Duck…for someone as intelligent as him—"

"Intelligent?" my husband interrupted.

"I think so… Anyway, for someone with his abilities, and given the limited opportunities he had to choose from, do you think his path as a criminal was in some sense laid out for him?"

"That's nonsense, Archie. We all make choices." He turned to me. "What's this fascination with Mock Duck anyhow? Has his daughter been sent home?"

"Not yet."

"By the way, the mayor was pleased with your piece."

"He told you so?"

Fireflies flitted between trees, and an automobile roared past as we turned a corner.

"I heard it from Dr. Darlington."

"Well, I'm pleased."

He took my hand. "Well done. I'm proud of you."

We walked on in silence for a few minutes, enjoying the evening. During our earliest meetings, we'd stroll along the parapet of the Forty-Second Street reservoir. We would talk about my home, my family, his work and family—he only had a few elderly cousins, the ones who later disapproved of our marriage. He would tell me stories about his seafaring ancestors, who sailed around the Cape of Good Hope and on to China. They braved all kinds of adventures and brought back treasures—porcelain, carved chests, silk hangings, many of which we still owned.

He'd say he wanted to see the world too, and would come with me to India. I'd reply that I preferred to stay in New York. After my parents passed, there was nothing left for me at home, and I had also begun to enjoy my newfound freedom in America. I took the trolley, rode in cabs, and met new kinds of people. I was also aware that I had barely begun to do what my father had sent me to the United States for, and I owed it to him to learn as much as I could.

The reservoir, like so much else, was long gone, but Dr. Morley's and my habit of walking and talking continued. Sometimes, we would start a conversation during our walks after dinner and keep going through the twilight and into the darkness.

Finally, I broke it to him: I'd been trying to arrange an interview with Mock Duck. It wasn't likely to happen, I added.

He turned to face me. "Have you lost your marbles, Archie? The man is dangerous. A murderer. Don't romanticize him."

He knew me too well. "Mock won't try anything, not while the Society has his child."

"And what makes you the authority on that? Promise me, please, that you won't do it."

But I couldn't. "There's no need to worry. Nothing's been fixed."

He and I both knew that was hardly an answer. We walked a few blocks farther and then turned back with a foot of space between us.

Once inside, Dr. Morley headed straight upstairs, while I glanced at the bureau in the foyer. There was an envelope on it with my name in front but no postmark, nor name the name of the sender.

Instead of calling to her, I went into the kitchen and asked Clément when it had arrived.

"While you were out, Mrs. Morley. Someone slid it under the door."

I composed myself before I slit open the envelope and pulled out a plain sheet of white paper. *Tomorrow at noon. No. 10 Doyers St.*

Mock Duck now knew where I lived.

My husband was upstairs, and the portraits of my parents in the foyer seemed to watch me. My mother in her red sari with the heavy gold border and her firm, square jaw; my father with his gentle eyes, silk *topee*, and handlebar mustache.

I turned away and slipped the note in my pocket.

Chapter Eighteen

Then came the practicalities, like getting Hervé Dupont to sign on. I thought he'd be pleased when I gave him the news, but instead, he was enraged. "That two-bit lowlife doesn't get to lord it over me. Mock Duck can't summon you when and how he likes. If I'm to print the interview, it's going to happen when I want and with the reporter of my choice."

"So what should I tell him?"

"You won't tell him anything until I say so."

"He won't speak to just anyone, you know."

"Oh, so now it's not only our mayor, you also have a special relationship with Chinatown's Most Wanted? Don't get too big for your boots, Mrs. Morley. You know what happens to tall poppies." He made a slicing motion across his neck.

For a moment, I considered heading straight to Chinatown—Dupont, and everyone else be damned. I felt like the Little Red Hen who'd done all the work and was being asked to share her bread with others.

Then I cooled down a bit and realized that it would be better to have the editor on my side—if only because no one else was.

I tried to distract myself by leafing through a stack of letters and sorting them by subject.

When I finished, Dupont looked me in the eye and said simply, "Tomorrow."

"I beg your pardon?"

"You can go tomorrow."

"But Mock wants to see me today."

"Fine. We'll make it the day after."

"But—" I protested.

The editor raised his hand. "It's either that or nothing. Let him sweat. It will only make him hungrier."

But it was I who sweated for two whole days, worrying that I'd lost the story of a lifetime. At several moments, I almost headed off to Doyers, but something held me back. Maybe concerns for my own safety, maybe the sense that after years in the business, Dupont knew a few things I didn't.

I was more than ready when the day finally rolled around. I'd studied every scrap about Mock that we had in the morgue, which, in the end, boiled down to much the same as the information I'd already gathered. Mock had arrived in New York in his late teens, and on the pretense of wanting to help "clean up the district," he'd managed to cut down Tom Lee's gaming protection business and set himself up as a force to be reckoned with. At first, the papers referred to him as the "Celestial choirboy" because of his clean-cut appearance, western clothes, and mastery of English; over time, his reputation altered, and his now-familiar image—sullen, slippery, with the insolent stare, Chinese garb, and canvas slippers—seemed to accompany every story.

He'd been tried twice for the murder of the On Leong tailor from New Jersey, and on both occasions, the jury was hung. Violence and death seemed to follow Mock wherever he went, yet he steadfastly maintained his innocence. What struck me, however, was that the brutality of Mock and the Hips was more than matched by Tom Lee's On Leongs. A Hip Sing footman had his head crushed by a mid-sized boulder, and the story that Tom told me about the laundryman who was hacked to bits on his own ironing board? If the papers were to be believed, it wasn't Mock's accomplices who had done the deed. It was Tom's. In fact, it was Lee Toy, Tom's nephew and little William's father, who was believed to be responsible.

Traffic roared across the Brooklyn Bridge, sunlight dazzling my eyes when I finally set out. It was my lucky day—but when the wave crests, the only place for it to go afterward is down.

I sensed I was walking into danger. And worse still, I had kept my meeting with Mock from my husband. Since the day we'd met, at the home of his friend whose sister attended Barnard, I'd never explicitly gone against Dr. Morley's wishes, and we'd never kept secrets from each other. There was already so much going against us that we knew we had to trust each other completely, if we were to survive.

City Hall flashed past, then the Tweed Courthouse, Foley Square, and the usual hubbub at Graziano's. I turned onto the Bowery and strode through the bands of dark and light while the elevated train clattered overhead. Crowds descended from the staircase at Chatham Square. I looked around for the Corsair, but he must have still been asleep after a night of exertions. My footsteps pulled me to Doyers, moving with an urgency that was astounding.

But moments from my destination, my confidence faltered. What if Dupont had made a mistake? What if Mock was furious and was no longer willing to see me? What if he simply wasn't at home?

The Woo Photography sign eyed me warily as I pushed my way into No. 10. I hadn't been inside since the Gerry men had carried Ha Oi away, yelling, protesting, and fighting down the stairwell.

I held on to the banister and felt my way up. The stairs creaked and dipped in the center from years of use. The child's cries still echoed through the darkness.

The door to Mock's place was cracked open. I stepped over a sleeping body on the landing. Bedelia must have heard the sound of my footsteps, because she looked out.

"What took yeh so long? We thought yeh'd be here days ago. C'mon in." She beckoned. "Mr. Mock's been waiting."

I passed through the kitchen, noticing again how spotless it was. Utensils hung from hooks, bowls were stacked, and vegetables lay cut, ready to be cooked later. Clément could take a few lessons from Mock Duck's maid.

Over the threshold and in the adjacent chamber, Tai Yow sat cross-legged on one of the beds. She wore the same drab robe in which I had first seen her, but an exquisite filigreed dragon pendant hung from her neck. She was surrounded by piles of diminutive tunics and pajamas in shades of yellow, red, and pink. She picked up a pair of pajamas, shook them out, inspected them minutely for invisible blemishes, smoothed out imaginary wrinkles, and then folded them into a new stack.

She glanced at me when I entered, but her expression didn't change. She simply bent her head and continued her task.

Something about Mock's wife reminded me of my mother. Neither woman spoke English, yet nothing seemed to get by them. My mother couldn't follow the specifics of my father's conversations with his guests or with me, but somehow or other, she managed to piece together the gist of what was being discussed. I had that sense with Tai Yow as well. While she may not have understood the individual words spoken around her, she grasped their significance.

Mock Duck sat on Ha Oi's cot by the window in a white singlet and black trousers. A pair of spectacles balanced on his nose as he studied a hefty volume—it appeared to be a legal text, judging from the minute, densely packed type. A calendar from the Hockett Soap Company showed a rosy-cheeked girl in a pink checkered dress pinning laundry to dry from lines against a bright blue sky. Each day that Ha Oi had been gone was marked with a cross, and there were more than a dozen of them. Copies of the *Sun*, the *Times*, and the *Observer* lay scattered on the mattress.

I felt unsure of myself, as though I was intruding on a private moment, and yet, I'd been summoned.

Mock jotted a note on a separate sheet, inserted a pencil to mark his spot, and removed his glasses. His wife continued with her task. "Mrs. Morley." The highbinder's voice sounded icy. "Do you not understand the meaning of 'tomorrow'?"

I apologized and explained that my editor wouldn't allow me to come by sooner.

"I see. Beggars can't be choosers. He wants to show me who's boss."

"Not exactly."

"You don't need to sugarcoat things for me. I can take it."

"May I?" I gestured toward a stack of folding chairs leaning by the side of the bureau to buy myself some time.

"Go ahead."

I unfolded a chair and set it up opposite him. Took out my pencil and notepad, looked around the room. In addition to the beds and chest, there was a red-roofed cuckoo clock that I hadn't noticed before, its pendulum swaying back and forth, and a shelf displaying statuary and an incense holder.

"My maid tells me," Mock said, "that this story will help secure my daughter's return."

"Of course, I can't guarantee that—"

"Of course, you can't."

"But I know it can't hurt. It will help if people know your and your wife's side of the story. It should be on the record."

"As if I care about such things. But there is one person I know it will help." He looked at me with appraising, hard eyes. "An interview with Mock Duck, Chinatown's most feared villain. You know I never give interviews."

"And I appreciate you giving me the chance." He often spoke to the press but usually only to assert his innocence.

Bedelia came in with tea, milk, and sugar and set the tray on a low table.

"First things first." He was all business. "Let's get some facts straight. My daughter isn't white. Her father was Chin Mung, a Chinese merchant; and her mother was Lizzie Smith, an Irish lass. She belongs only at one place: here. No. 10 Doyers Street, with her mother and me.

"Now I've been accused of every crime in the book, but if I'm guilty, you tell me how the charges have never stuck.… See? You don't have an answer. So either your *law*"—he pronounced the word with a hint of disdain—"is broken. Or I'm innocent."

His words sounded rehearsed, as though he'd spoken them many times before.

Dupont had told me to ask Mock anything, the more wide-ranging the questions, the better. And I believed that the more I was able to present him as a fully fleshed out human being, the better his chances of being reunited with his daughter.

"If you don't mind, our readers would like to hear about your childhood, Mr. Mock. You were born in San Francisco?"

He scoffed. "My childhood? What does that have to do with anything?"

"It will help them see you more fully, understand who you are. That helps create sympathy."

He looked away. "They will never understand… better not to try."

"Why don't you tell me about Tai Yow, then?"

His wife looked up when she heard me say her name. "She's one of six children. Four girls, two boys. She's the youngest. And when famine struck their village, her parents sold her to a trader, who sold her to a merchant who brought goods and workers from China to the United States. She was lucky that she met Chin Mung sooner rather than later. She was lucky that Chin hired her as a maid for his Irish wife and their daughter, and maybe she was even lucky that Ha Oi's mother, Lizzie, died. Because from that day onward, Tai Yow took care of the baby as if she was her own."

I scribbled away feverishly.

"You met them at a banquet?"

"To celebrate my recovery from a shooting." He lifted the edge of his singlet to reveal a fierce red scar crawling across his pale stomach. "Almost didn't make it."

"Why does this little girl mean so much to you? You're a young man. You could have a family of your own."

He bristled. "What kind of a question is that? She is my own." He stared at his hands with their clean, neatly trimmed fingernails.

"Have you always wanted children?" I imagined the headline, *MOCK DUCK—SECRET FAMILY MAN!*

"No. But Ha Oi's special. She's fearless, knows her own mind. Did you see how she fought those assholes? She reminds me of myself when I was young. Biggest mistake I made was letting her go. Believing that idiot roundsman."

"You didn't have much choice."

He took a deep breath and shut the legal tome.

"You must have been fearless when you were young too."

"I'd do anything if I was dared." The shadow of a smile passed across his lips. "Tarred and feathered another boy once. Held my hand in icy water for so long that my fingers turned blue, and they thought they might need to cut them off."

"And now?"

"I'm only fearless in business."

"And what kind of business do you do exactly?"

"A little of this, a little of that. I own a store on Fifth Avenue."

I made a note.

"You don't believe me? You can go there if you want, and ask."

A knock sounded at the door, and a few seconds later, two weatherbeaten fellows looked in.

The newcomers didn't sit, just asked Mock a question that got them into a back-and-forth. Mock said a few sharp words and one of the men recoiled. He turned pale, seemed to apologize, then both men left. At no point did they come farther inside than the threshold between the room and the kitchen.

"May I ask what that was about?"

"Stupid questions don't deserve an answer." Mock waved his hand dismissively.

I couldn't be sure whether he was referring to the question that his countrymen had asked, or mine.

He thought for a few minutes. "I was one of the best students in my class at the Mission School. They thought I'd be a teacher or a preacher." He laughed. I pictured young Mock as a star pupil. "Then I fell in with some boys…they turned out to be Hips. And we soon discovered I had a gift"—he seemed to choose his words carefully—"for making things happen. They wouldn't leave me alone after that. Kept pestering me to do things for them and with them. Eventually, I had enough. I needed a change and came to New York."

"That's when you met Reverend Parkhurst?"

"That was a lark." Mock grinned like a mischievous child. "It was worth it for the look on Old Man Lee's face."

"The two of you don't see eye to eye."

"That's an understatement. But it's Tom Lee who can't stop thinking about me." He shrugged his narrow shoulders. "Thinks he's the mayor of Chinatown. Doesn't like it when people don't bow to him. Wants everyone to stand in line and wait their turn. But I don't give a damn. I do what I need and don't ask permission—just like any other man in business."

"So everything that they write about you—"

"Untrue. Untrue. Untrue. I've been in the wrong place at the wrong time. You've seen Chinatown. It's no bigger than a handkerchief. Trouble is never far away. And they say I'm the leader of the Hips, but I am not."

I was about to object, but he continued without a break. "The Hips listen to me. They come to me for advice because I think, I can read and I can write, but no. I am not their leader. Never have been."

"So the Opera House—"

"I told you already. It wasn't me. Why would I start a fight where everyone's shooting out in the open? Where does that lead? To trouble. You think trouble does me any good? All I want is to be left in peace, but every day, the cops find some excuse to come get me. Anything goes wrong, something's stolen, someone's shot, a pin drops for Chrissakes, they come hunting for me. And why? Because I had the audacity to speak to Parkhurst, because I ratted out some two-bit gaming parlors, because I have the guts to fight them on their own terms.

"You know, some of those lobbygows, they bring tourists to see all the places where I'm supposed to have committed crimes, and then they bring them here, to No. 10, and they all stand outside my window gawping like idiots."

Just as I had done once. "Why don't you leave?"

"Why don't you leave your home?" he retorted.

Tai Yow had finished re-folding the clothes, and now she put them away in the bureau. Then she adjusted the tiny pairs of soft, silk slippers lined up beneath the drawers.

"This is what she does," Mock said. "Folds and refolds Ha Oi's clothes, so that they'll be ready for her. Buys her favorite food each day—sweet buns from the bakery—and then throws them out because they have to be fresh.

"She's spent hours outside the Children's Society, hoping for a glimpse of our rascal, and Bedelia's tried to go inside and ask questions, but they just shoo her away. Then they told Tai Yow that she was disturbing the peace, so she went and stood across the street, and they told her that she couldn't stand there either." For a moment, his brow furrowed.

"Tai Yow is young, but she isn't strong. Me? It seems like nothing anyone does can kill me. But my wife has been through so much already, and the shock of this—the torture that the Gerry Society is making us suffer through—has become too much for her." His words petered out.

Tai Yow opened the door to the bureau and pulled out a silver bell attached to an ivory teether. Then, a notebook and a photograph, both of which she silently handed to me.

She waited by my shoulder while I opened the book. It contained childish attempts at a house, clouds, flowers and a tree. A series of capital letters. Simple three-letter words.

"That's Ha Oi's writing," Mock Duck said.

An Oriental couple posed together in the photograph. They were both elaborately dressed in traditional robes, she in a headdress with tassels and jewelry, while he stood behind her.

"Look closely," Mock said as his wife pointed at the woman.

"Lizzie Smith?" I said finally.

Tai Yow nodded and pointed to the man. "Chin Mung." Then she took the photograph and notebook and put them away.

"Are we done?" Mock said. In the window behind him, a neighbor watered plants growing from tins attached to the fire escape. "Do you have enough? I need to get back to things." His finger ran down the edge of the book he'd been studying.

I flipped through my notes. I needed something more, something to give the story some heart, some flesh.

"I saw you and Ha Oi at Chatham Square."

"We must have been watching the trains." His expression softened briefly. "She loves to go there.... It's the first thing we'll do when she's back."

"And afterward?"

"Eat buns. Buy some ice cream. She likes me to tell her stories while her mother combs her hair."

Tai Yow, who'd been standing quietly by the bureau, now went to the back room, which was separated from the front by a beaded curtain.

"I was going to ask whether there was anything she wanted to tell me."

"She's tired. She tires easily these days."

I understood. For months after I lost my parents, I was exhausted.

"One last question, Mr. Mock."

"All right." He reached for his glasses.

"Do you know Timothy Webster?"

"Who?" His face went blank.

"Engineer Webster's son."

"Never heard of him."

"I think you have, and I think you persuaded the engineer to—"

"I don't know what you're talking about." He cut me off. "But since you're casting around, let me tell you this. It's something your readers don't know and probably have never thought about." A pause.

"Yes?"

"Mock Duck doesn't exist."

"Excuse me?"

"There is no such person. He's a myth made up by those who need someone to believe in. Men who work all day and into the night just so they can save a few dollars to send home to their families. Men, who when they're outside Chinatown—and sometimes in it too—are abused, get beaten up, spat on, and hauled into jail for no reason.

"So when someone comes along, someone who isn't afraid, someone who understands how things work and uses that knowledge for his own gain… well, they begin to look up to him. Soon, they put him up on a pedestal, and his story takes on a life of its own. And then he's no longer recognizable, not even to himself. So if you ever meet this Mock Duck fella, let me know, because I'd like to meet him as well."

And Mock wasn't done yet. "Do you know my real name?"

"It isn't Mock Duck?"

"It's Mock Sai Wing. And I'm just an ordinary guy, a guy who lives on Doyers Street and tries to get by while he minds his own business."

Then he put on his glasses and reached for the book. The conversation was over.

Chapter Nineteen

"He's got you, Mrs. M. He's got you good." Dupont's finger moved over my draft. He laughed until the tears rolled down his pockmarked cheeks. "A teacher or a preacher…" He wiped the tears from his eyes, licked his thumb, and turned the page.

"And what's this?" The guffaw turned back on a few seconds later. "Mock Duck doesn't exist?" He looked up at me, eyebrows grazing his pomaded thatch. "He's Mock Sai Wing? Tell me another one. Hey lads," he called, "what are we going to do with Mrs. M.? Looks like that Asiatic thug has got her hook, line, and sinker."

"Time for her to go!" someone yelled.

"Kick her out!" another voice shouted.

"Give it a rest," I responded as firmly as I could. And to the editor, "Just stop. You're not making it any easier."

"Don't take it so hard, Mrs. M." Dupont grinned. "The boys are only kidding. But I can't print this." He stabbed at the interview. "It's not going to fly. Our readers want to see an ogre who eats babes for breakfast. Not someone who's thoughtful and can string together a sentence."

"So you want me to rewrite it."

He winked. "Clever girl. I knew I hired you for a reason."

I stopped myself from reaching over and ripping out his tongue. At this point you're probably wondering—why did I put up with the insults, and how had I managed to make it for so long without incident?

I don't have a clear answer to the second, but I knew that I'd been lucky—and that luck doesn't last forever. The longer I remained in the business, the longer I continued doing things my way, the greater the chance that I would come up against a wall that I couldn't get around. As for the taunts, like Mock when it came to relinquishing Ha Oi, I had no choice. If I wanted to be out and about in New York, if I wanted to see the city and write about it freely, then I had to put up with the consequences. Most of the time, it was minor. My prickly exterior, the scowl I keep plastered on my face might have helped, also the general perception that I was in Dupont's good graces. But if someone really wanted to hurt me—well, I don't weigh much more than a hundred pounds. One day, the protecting spirit who watched over me would turn away, or be distracted, and then, I'd better be careful.

In the meantime, I wouldn't back down. "If my piece doesn't work for you, Mr. Dupont, I can take it elsewhere. Maybe to the *Sun* or the *Tribune*."

He sat back in his chair. "You wouldn't."

"Try me."

"You're a goddamn piece of work, you know that, Mrs. Morley? And to think that when I first hired you, I thought you'd be a pushover." He held out his palm. "Hand it over."

"Word for word. No changes."

"We'll see what we can do."

I passed him the papers and grabbed my hat. My heart beat wildly.

No matter what I did, no matter how hard I worked, no matter how good my story, I'd always be on the precipice. Always one the edge—one remark, one slip away from disaster.

* * *

Dupont printed the interview under the headline, *HIGHBINDER CLAIMS HE'S NO LONGER MOCK DUCK. ALSO CLAIMS INNOCENCE ON ALL CHARGES.* He hadn't completely mauled it—there were no descriptions of "Mock the Ogre"—but he'd also soft-pedaled some of the language that I put in about how much the couple were suffering and had made the highbinder appear less sharp than he was. I couldn't expect much better and hoped that Mock and his wife would understand and that, at the very least, the perspective I had put forward would make some difference to the outcome.

Meanwhile, the Thaw trial was drawing to a close, and the city was seized by its own version of *Dementia Americana*—Harry Thaw's defense that an American man whose honor was violated was entitled to go temporarily mad and take revenge. (Of course, that defense could only apply to someone like Harry. If Mock Duck or Tom Lee shot someone out in the open, in front of dozens of witnesses as Thaw had done, honor or no honor, they would already be on their way to the electric chair.)

New Yorkers began to behave erratically as the tension mounted, and bizarre incidents took place. A nursemaid on Seventy-Eighth Street gathered her skirts and turned her perambulator into a missile, injuring a delivery boy who whistled at her one time too many. Fortunately, the infant remained unscathed. A Madison Avenue *patissier* beat a wealthy customer about the head with a baguette, showering him with crumbs and subjecting him "to the grossest abuses." A mother drowned herself and her infant in three feet of water. And the ghost of Stanford White was spotted lurking about and making louche remarks all over the city.

Everyone was in a state of heightened agitation, and I was too, ready to snap at the slightest provocation as I wandered the streets, wondering how the Thaw jury would vote and what decision the judge in Ha Oi's case would make. It seemed as though any semblance of reason and decency had gone out the window.

Dupont ordered me to canvass the busloads of tourists who rolled into town for the grand finale. They came from all over: Des Moines, San Diego, Omaha. Mothers clutched their scrapbooks filled with newspaper clippings; young men wore likenesses of Harry pinned to their lapels. They spent their mornings waiting on tenterhooks for any nuggets from the court and their afternoons making pilgrimages to key locations: Harry's home, Delmonico's, and the other restaurants he loved to frequent. They visited Stanford's love nest in the tower abutting the Garden and the cheap downtown lodgings that Evelyn and her mother had once rented.

Later, the editor added me to the *Observer's* team of six—four regulars plus two freelancers—responsible for covering every last minute. The papers continued to feed the frenzy: *THE TRIAL OF THE CENTURY! THE SCANDAL THAT SHOOK THE WORLD! HARRY'S LAST STAND!*

The story was rehearsed, reviewed, and retold gasp by gasp and breath by breath, ostensibly for the benefit of the few hermits who'd somehow managed to miss it, but really for the delectation of the masses who already knew all the ins and outs by heart.

Finally, the closing arguments on both sides were made, and Mama Thaw as well as Harry's doughty sisters, Lady Yarmouth and Mrs. Carnegie, waited tensely while the jurors deliberated. The strain proved too much for Evelyn and she went home to rest.

Sequestered in a windowless chamber, the jurors thrashed out their disagreements for fifty-six agonizing hours and had barely closed their eyes for the second straight night when they were marched to the Broadway Central Hotel under armed guard for breakfast. One of their police escorts broke down en route.

A hearty meal of eggs, meat, juice, and coffee revived the jurists, and they continued their discussions at a table in front of a plateglass window. The ogling crowd included lip readers, who did their best to decipher the outcome.

Ten to two, the rumors flew. "Ten to two," the bookies yelled. Ten to two for guilty.

Dan O'Reilly reported from outside the Tombs that Harry had rejected his meal of steak and a glass of claret, served as usual by Delmonico's staff on starched white linens in his cell. Instead, the Pittsburgh millionaire paced up and down and then penned a statement to the effect that he "despised those who carried concealed weapons" and had only done so himself on the day of White's death because he had heard from "professional sources" that his own life was in danger.

Thousands planted themselves on White and Franklin Streets for a glimpse of Evelyn, or Harry's sisters, or, failing them, the elder Mrs. Thaw. Inspector McCluskey had been assigned fifty men to hold the hordes in check.

More police blockaded the downtown courts. Justice Fitzgerald again stipulated that given the sensitive nature of the case, no female reporters, apart from the four "Sob Sisters," would be allowed inside the courtroom. News bulletins were dispatched from within, and newshounds waited outside so they could relay the latest as soon as it became available.

The final verdict came in on Friday at half-past four, not a minute too late: A hung jury!

Our metropolis exploded. District Attorney Jerome enjoined the crowd to remain peaceful and told the press he would retry the case but not immediately. Several other homicide cases were pending on his desk. He estimated that a retrial would have to wait until October at the very earliest. In the meantime, Mr. Thaw would remain in the Tombs—and as for bail, "I should consider it my duty to oppose such an application."

But I wasn't part of the throng when the verdict was delivered, I missed the commotion that followed, and the district attorney's speech.

At about two o'clock that afternoon, I overheard a scruffy newsboy, who'd been told by a pal of his, who'd heard from a copper working in the district, that a judge had finally decided it was time to determine Ha Oi's future and all of Chinatown was on the move.

Chapter Twenty

y the time I arrived, the chamber was packed, standing room only. I recognized several familiar faces from the district—shopkeepers and restauranteurs, Mrs. Maxwell and the Corsair, even the two pugilists from Doyers, who now seemed reconciled because they were sitting together quite amicably. I didn't care that Dupont probably would have preferred that I remain downtown—five reporters from the *Observer* were more than enough to cover the circus. Even as a child, the stories that interested me most were the ones that no one wanted to tell.

And as for Ha Oi's final hearing occurring on the same day as Harry's verdict, yes, it was a strange coincidence, but I'm not suggesting that anyone had planned it. There were too many different elements at play—the deliberations of the jury in the Thaw case, for instance. And no one needed to plan anything. One way or the other, Ha Oi's hearing would have been overshadowed. Even if only in the offhand manner in which it was covered. Because here's what hit me during my investigations: the future of a girl from Chinatown could never matter. It would always be an afterthought.

Yet somewhere deep down, a few people must have realized its significance, because although they had an excellent reason to overlook the proceedings entirely, four papers sent reporters: the *Times, Sun, Tribune,* and the *Observer.* (Although, to be strictly accurate, I sent myself.)

Hornby arrived in a foul mood. "What the hell am I doing here? Who cares what happens to the kid? The only thing that matters is what's happening downtown." He thumped the fist of one hand into the palm of the other. "What a colossal waste."

Mrs. Woo and her daughters had already taken their places. Lily poked May, May flinched, and their mother spoke to them firmly.

All heads turned when Mock, supporting Tai Yow by the arm, entered from the back of the room, walked the entire length of the central aisle, and lowered his wife into her seat.

"Always the showman," Hornby said.

Bedelia followed them. Tai Yow's skin had lost its luster, her face was lined and drawn, and the black gown, once so assertive and proud, now drooped from her diminished figure. But Mock appeared outwardly unaltered. He walked tall, head held high, uncreased tunic hanging easily from his shoulders. No doubt, that would be another strike held against him. If he harbored some doubts, some fear that he might lose his daughter for good, it was imperceptible.

Could he pull this off? Could he, as he had on so many previous occasions, pull off another miracle, a sleight of hand that would leave everyone gasping and further burnish his legend? I didn't put it past him. He'd outsmarted the law so many times, and this time, he had right on his side. Surely, the girl would go home.

Mock's lawyer swooped in. Not O'Reilly this time—Lawyer Dan clearly had more pressing engagements that day. Instead, an attorney by the name of Gerald Posner leaned one hefty hand on the back of the highbinder's bench, bent his thick mane, and whispered to his client. Mock nodded.

"Mock Duck doesn't appear the slightest bit worried," a tadpole from the *Tribune*, the newcomer to our trio, remarked to Pike, who was already seated.

"Any more visits to the Society?" Hornby asked the reporter from the *Sun*. "Any news about the child—have you seen her again?"

Pike wouldn't answer.

Judge Zeller presided over the courtroom. Younger than Mayo and with the build and face of a cherub—small, tubby, with apple cheeks—Zeller blinked his small blue eyes, and when he smiled, revealed tiny, shining, rounded teeth.

And if O'Reilly was sleek and quick like an otter, Posner moved slowly and spoke with the confident growl of a lion.

"He costs a packet, don't you know," Hornby murmured, jiggling his leg. "How much money does this Mock Duck actually make?"

Posner began by summoning Mrs. Edwin Wardell, wife of Roundsman Wardell—who, until recently, had been stationed at Elizabeth Street. She made her way to the stand sporting a plaid coat over a pleated skirt, and a parasol that she used as a walking stick. Her lips were as tightly pursed as the reticule that hung from the crook of her arm, and in her other hand, she carried a large brown portfolio.

Roundsman Wardell retired a month ago, Mrs. Wardell told Hizzoner, and her husband's constant presence at home had taken a toll on her well-being. "It's been good for the old man, yes, sir, but not so good for the missus."

Posner asked Mrs. Wardell to share what she did in her spare time with the court. A proud, controlled smile escaped the taut features: the roundsman's wife was an artist. She sketched portraits of those she met, as well as likenesses of criminal types from the rogue's gallery. Her husband's line of work had proved most useful in this regard. And she had assembled all her works in an album with a view to eventual publication. "If I say so myself, Your Honor, they make for fine viewin'."

"And have you met my client?" Posner asked.

"Indeed, sir. On more than one occasion. I even visited Mock Duck at his place of residence."

"Have you brought your album along?"

"Indeed I have." She unbuckled the folder, and the lawyer instructed her to show the court a few examples of her work. She began with a sketch of Doyers Street with its jumble of tenements, shops, signs, fire escape, and laundry lines. Some of those in attendance clapped.

"Keep it moving, Mr. Posner," Zeller ordered, evidently accustomed to the lawyer's theatrics.

The lawyer leaned forward and whispered to Mrs. Wardell, who protested for a few moments, then held up a sketch of Mock Duck, which was met with a chorus of admiration. She'd captured the highbinder's likeness perfectly— angled jawline, high cheekbones, full lips. He emerged from the sooty background full of intelligence and menace. I hadn't expected such talent from the artist.

The roundsman's spouse produced a different page. This time, a pensive Tai Yow gazed out of a window, chin resting on her fist, a single rose growing in a pot on the sill. A petal that had dropped from the bloom hung in mid-air like a tear.

"And did you happen to see the girl, Ha Oi?" Posner asked.

Mrs. Wardell nodded. "Did indeed."

"And you sketched her?"

"Most certainly—at Mock Duck's request."

"May we take a look?"

Mrs. Wardell displayed a portrait of an unmistakably Oriental child with rosy cheeks grinning impishly. She had dimples on her cheeks, and around her neck, she wore her mother's filigreed dragon pendant. Bedelia's hand flew to her mouth. Tai Yow reached her arms toward the image.

Posner held it up triumphantly. "And is this exactly what she looked like, Mrs. Wardell?"

"Realism is my forte, Mr. Posner." She sounded offended. "My instructors say that the truth never escapes me."

"Your Honor, please take note of the date."

"I sign and date all my pictures," Mrs. Wardell added with grim satisfaction.

Zeller leaned forward for a closer look. He nodded, clearly impressed.

Mrs. Wardell sniffed. "I always draw those I meet from life. It ain't just the outlines of the sitter's features that I aim to capture. A true artist observes what's happenin' inside and brings it to life on the paper."

"So you had occasion to observe Ha Oi closely."

"Each portrait takes at least half an hour to complete, sometimes longer. The sitter sits in front of me."

"And did it appear that Mock or Mrs. Mock were trying to hide anything about the child? Her ancestry, for instance?"

"That child has Oriental blood runnin' through her veins." The roundsman's wife bobbed her head up and down. "I'd stake my reputation on it. You can't fool an artist. These eyes see the truth. They drill right down to the core."

"Thank you, Mrs. Wardell," Posner said. "One final question. Can you comment on the condition of Mock Duck's home?"

"Oh, it was spic 'n' span, Mr. Posner, sir. Spic 'n' span. So clean you could eat right off the floor. Of course, they keep a maid. My own home would be spotless, too, if we could afford a girl, but that ain't possible on Roundsman Wardell's wages. So I cook and clean, watch over the kiddies, and make time for my sketchin'. But as I was sayin', the home was a delight, and the child, so well behaved, so well cared for…. Now, maybe she don't get out as much as she ought to. I believe that all children need fresh air and sunshine—"

"Thank you, Mrs. Wardell." Posner held up his hand and stretched his lips into a smile. "That will be all."

"If you will allow me, sir—"

"We must move on to our next witness, Mrs. Wardell," the lawyer said firmly. With a humph of displeasure, she put away her drawings and took her time straightening up before she returned to her seat.

Slickly attired in a bottle-green suit and blue bow tie, John Find, a Chinese importer, approached the bench next.

In addition to his establishment on Pell Street, Posner said, Mr. Find owned a fifty-percent stake in a Lexington Avenue antique store. He was a reputable and wealthy merchant. The lawyer inquired how long Find had known Mock.

"Several years," the importer replied. When Mock first came to New York, he worked at Find's store for two months. He spoke such excellent English and handled the customers so well that sales went up dramatically. Find quickly realized that Mock wouldn't remain his employee for long. "He has a way with all types. He knows what to say and how to say it to make people listen."

Since then, Mock's fortunes had risen but Find's former employee never acted snooty, and the two men had remained in touch.

"You meet him often?"

"Once or twice each month."

"Have you visited his home?"

"Oh, many times. But when *I* visit, I eat from a plate," he added hastily.

The judge and other reporters chuckled.

"And what do you think of the Mocks as a family?" the lawyer continued, undeterred.

"Mock Duck is an excellent businessman, Mr. Posner, a leader respected by the Chinese. And Tai Yow is kind and honorable. She don't gossip like the American ladies."

Mrs. Wardell jumped up. "I object, Your Honor!"

"Be seated, madam," the judge ordered.

Posner thanked the importer and summoned his final witness. The court stenographer paused, the policeman on duty stood at attention, and even Zeller wiped his forehead as Mock rose and made his way to the stand.

"Everyone knows who you are, but no one really knows you, Mock. Tell us about yourself, help the people understand," Posner urged his client.

The judge, lawyer, spectators, walls, everything vanished. Like an actor with the spotlight trained only on him, no one except for the storied highbinder seemed to exist in that cavernous space. There he was, a simple figure clad in black. Who was he outside of all the noise? This was our chance to find out.

Mock placed his hands on the railing and faced the judge. "I was born in San Francisco, Your Honor. My father was a laundryman; my mother, a seamstress." Now he was telling the world this? Would it have killed him to tell me when I asked? Of course, he could be making it all up and telling the judge what he thought he wanted to hear. I would have done the same in his situation.

"They believed in the importance of education," Mock went on, "and sent me to the mission school. I was an excellent student. My father passed of illness when I was eight, my mother followed when I was twelve.

"A member of the Hips took me in. The Hips gave me food, they helped me find work, and they allowed me to sleep in their dormitory. When I came to New York, naturally, I turned to them again for assistance. I may have made some foolish decisions and got caught up in matters that I had no business being involved in, but I have learned from my mistakes, Your Honor." Mock didn't seem to enjoy saying those words, but he plowed on.

"And I'm a changed man."

Back on surer ground, he continued, "Being a father, taking care of my wife and Ha Oi has changed me. I don't need the Hips anymore. I will never go back to them."

"Tell us, Mock, are you rich these days?" his lawyer asked.

"Not like before. All my money has been spent on court cases."

"My client's many—and may I add, wrongful—arrests have impoverished him," Posner explained. "And yet, here he is, fighting, struggling, giving every ounce of what he has left for his child. If Mock is a criminal, then the fitting punishment for him is jail. But, Your Honor, his only crime is that of being of an alien race. And for that reason, and that reason alone"—Posner's booming voice carried to the back of the chamber—"his daughter has been unlawfully snatched from his home. A great injustice has been done to my client and his wife—the only mother Ha Oi has known."

Zeller studied the papers on his bench and addressed Mock directly. "You deny that you have a criminal past. Yet you have been charged with every crime in the book: murder, assault, swindling, gambling, you name it. Even as we speak, there is a charge of bribery hanging over you. What have you to say in your defense?"

Mock replied with conviction. "I have never been guilty of violence, Your Honor. My hands are clean. And what some call bribery, I call encouragement. If I have unknowingly made a mistake and broken the law, I am willing to pay my dues. But don't separate my daughter from her mother because you think ill of me." His tone grew urgent. "Keep your feelings about her and me apart."

He took a deep breath, paused, and finally said, "If you wish, Your Honor, I am willing to leave New York City."

Sharp exclamations crackled through the courtroom. Mock Duck offering to leave town of his own volition? That was exactly what everyone—the district attorney, the police, the mayor—wanted.

"All I ask is that you permit me to bring my wife and daughter along. We'll move to the Middle West. Start a new life. You'll never hear from us again."

The offer seemed too good to refuse. The city could rid itself of Mock

Duck once and for all. All it had to do was return the little girl to her parents.

Zeller cupped his hands in front of his mouth and blew into them. He was going to make the highbinder beg.

"Or if you prefer," Mock went on, "I am willing to pay for Ha Oi to attend a boarding school of your choice." His voice crackled with desperation.

Zeller frowned, picked up his pen. "These are tantalizing choices, I must say." He scribbled on a piece of paper. "Quit New York for good. Boarding school of court's choosing."

"Name the school, the town, whatever you want, Your Honor, and I will do it."

Zeller motioned to his clerk, who nodded to a peon, who raced down the aisle to the back of the courtroom.

The doors swung open. There stood Pisarra and Superintendent Jenkins with a tiny figure sandwiched between them. The crowd surged to its feet, standing on tiptoes, craning necks, climbing on benches to get a better look. And although I climbed on a bench too, I could only catch fleeting glimpses. A light gray hood bobbed between the Gerry agents. Leather shoes squeaked. A dolly's limp arm dragged across the floorboards, and then all three stood in front of the judge.

Mock hadn't left the witness stand. His face turned pale; his mouth cracked open as he stared at the small figure in amazement. "Ha Oi," he called, but she was tightly blocked by Pisarra and the superintendent and didn't respond. He lunged toward her, but two coppers, who materialized out of nowhere, grabbed him by the arms and held him in place.

Tai Yow cried her daughter's name and tried to run to her, but Posner held her back. Pisarra and the superintendent closed ranks like sentries in tight formation.

"One step closer, one move out of line, and neither of you will ever lay eyes on this child again," Zeller warned. That did the trick. The parents stopped struggling.

"All right now." The judge turned to the Gerry agents. "Let's take a look at the little girl. Pull back her hood."

"Can you see her?" I asked Hornby, who, like everyone else, bobbed and weaved from side to side, hoping to get a good look.

"No—but I'm trying!"

"What's your name, little girl?" The judge cupped a hand behind his ear and leaned forward. "Louder. I didn't hear you."

Her answer was no more audible the second time around.

"Where do you live?" Zeller asked. "Does the Society treat you kindly?"

This time, the crowd quietened, and I heard a soft whisper, but I couldn't decipher the words she pronounced.

"All right," the judge went on. "I have everything I need."

A door to the side of him opened, and before anyone had time to react, Pisarra and the superintendent, along with their charge, walked through it.

"No!" Mock yelled as the spectators roared. Zeller banged his gavel several times, louder and louder, as the commotion reached a crescendo. "Order! Order!"

The court slowly went quiet. The judge paused for a minute before he spoke. "Since the records of her birth were destroyed in San Francisco's fires, and the Children's Society has not yet been able to prove the ancestry of the child known as Ha Oi with any degree of certainty, the court must make that determination itself." He breathed deeply. "After taking all the evidence brought before me into consideration, it is my firm belief that the girl brought before me today is fully Caucasian, and not a single drop of Asiatic blood runs through her body."

Still standing, Mock Duck swayed.

"Even if that were not the case," Zeller went on, "Mock Duck is no fit guardian for a young person, be she either of Mongolian or Caucasian descent. He has twice been tried for murder and many times languished in prison. Henceforth"—Zeller flipped through a stack of papers to find another document—"the girl once living on No. 10 Doyers Street in the home of Mock Duck and his wife, will go by the name 'Helen Francis.' We have been told that 'Helen' is the Christian name to which she responds at the Society, and 'Francis' has been chosen for San Francisco, the city of her birth."

Helen Francis. His words floated in the ether.

"Miss Francis will be remanded to the custody of the Society for the Prevention of Cruelty to Children, which in turn will place her in a home where she will be taught to forget her six years amongst the Chinese and be educated in American ways. I believe that several applications for her adoption have already been received, and I have no doubt that she will soon find a suitable family with whom to begin her new life."

Mock addressed the judge in a voice thick with grief and pain that came from somewhere deep within. "Your Honor, I am not the criminal. Today, it is you who have committed the crime."

Then he brushed aside the coppers who stood in his path and gently helped his wife, who rose unsteadily, to her feet. Her face a mask, she leaned against his shoulder for support, and together, the two exited the courtroom.

Chapter Twenty-One

Shattered, distressed, and roiling internally, I stopped by the Blackboy for a shot of something strong and a few minutes of quiet before I hoofed it to the office and fired off a scathing piece.

Dupont promptly refused to print it because, first, he yelled, how dare I leave my post at the criminal courts without his permission, and second, no one gave a fig about my goddamn opinion. Who was I to judge the judge? Did I think he cared what I thought about New York society? And what in the world was that nonsense about the child needing her parents and being consigned to live in a world of strangers? "One day, she'll thank her lucky stars that she no longer has to molder in that hellhole and that Zeller made the right decision."

Trembling with rage, I argued that my colleagues never stuck to the facts, and if I wasn't allowed to tell the whole story—

"Then what?" Dupont interrupted harshly. "You'll take your services elsewhere? Be my guest. Now, write this up short and sweet, or I will turn it over to another reporter. Problem with you, Mrs. M., is that you've gotten too big for your britches. You used to be so grateful for every assignment I gave you. And now, you've forgotten what this job entails."

* * *

The city looked spent as I walked home—as spent as I felt, like a squeezed-out tube of toothpaste. Trees drooped, buildings sagged, the honks of cars and the clatter of carts sounded hollow. Lights shone dimly through curtains pulled close, and trash lay scattered all over. The sidewalks were empty of revelers despite it being a Friday evening. A boy kicked a can across the road while a lingering group of Thaw supporters straggled along, their signs resting on their shoulders, heads bent from the weight, if not of complete defeat, then of incomplete satisfaction. Exoneration, plain and simple, was what they wanted for their hero.

Dr. Morley asked how it went as we sat together for dinner. Paintings of one of his seafaring ancestors and the Chinese merchant, Eshing, stared down at us from the walls.

"They took the child."

"Child?" He helped himself to veal cutlets. "I thought the jury was hung. In the end, I suppose, the outcome was better than I feared. I thought they would definitely vote to acquit. At least a few of them showed some courage.... What is this world coming to? Seems like we can't tell right from wrong when we don't convict a man for murdering another in full sight of a crowd...."

He noticed that I hadn't said much. "What's the matter?"

"I'm exhausted." I left my dinner half eaten and went up early. Took a shower, lay in bed, but couldn't sleep. I was supposed to be an impartial observer, but how was that possible after what I had witnessed? I stared at the ceiling, reliving the moments: the flash of a gray cloak, squeak of patent leather shoes, a dolly's limp hand dragging along the floorboards. And henceforth and forever more, she'd be known as Helen Francis and *taught to forget the six years she'd spent with the Chinese.*

And just like that, it was over. The mighty Mock Duck had been vanquished. He had no winning hand, no eleventh-hour trick up his sleeve. He had left the court just like any other defeated parent. When it mattered most, the man who had outsmarted the law a hundred times had come up empty.

That night, I dreamt of a middle-aged, white woman in a floral dress, a chain around her neck with the entwined initials *HF* dangling from it. The pendant was heavy, the letters curlicued. The woman was perspiring and confused as she wiped her face with her handkerchief and wandered through

Pell, Mott, and Doyers Streets. Everything seemed at once both strange and familiar: the shops, the doors, the signs. She stared up at the window at No. 10, and when a passerby asked if she needed help, she replied with a nervous laugh, I've just lost my bearings. I'm sure I'll find my way soon."

And then the scene shifted to Bombay, and suddenly I had become the stranger—I woke up in a panic, unable to breathe. Despite my best efforts at distracting myself, the tightness in my chest wouldn't ease. I tossed and turned until I finally dozed off again.

After my husband left for work the next morning (he worked a half-day on Saturdays), I laced up my shoes and headed east. I picked up copies of the *Sun, Tribune, Times,* and the *Observer* and sat down on a bench to read. The story was hard to find because the bulk of all four papers were filled with—but at this point, I don't need to tell you.

The *Tribune* placed its account in the "Interesting To Women" section beside *COLD IN SOUTH INJURIOUS TO STRAWBERRIES AND VEGETA-BLES.* The tadpole noted that *Ha Oi seems to be quite reconciled to the change and had discarded her Oriental dress even before her Oriental name. Smiling and happy, she was a strange contrast to the poor little waifs and the strays of humanity, who had stood, a few minutes before, trembling and weeping at the bar. Ha Oi understood not a word of all that was going on and was quite undisturbed by it, save once, when she seemed to get a little frightened, and a single tear overflowed and ran down her cheek.*

He also added: *The Mock Ducks wore the inscrutable expressions of their race, and only by their apparent willingness to spend money in fighting for possession of their foster child did they show how deeply concerned they were.*

In the *Sun,* Pike observed that *A few days in the rooms of the Children's Society worked a transformation. Ha Oi's hair, which had been dyed black, came out golden, her blue eyes lost their slant, and constant association with white children brought back the tongue she had once known.... While she didn't forget Mock Duck and Tai Yu entirely, she wasn't desirous of returning to Doyers Street.*

Pike's story fully subscribed to Ha Oi's transformation—not just that she had always been white, but that she also turned white—that becoming white was a process. He also acknowledged that she would be missed. *No more will she wish the Chinamen "gor si gi" (good luck) as they shuffle into the gambling houses on Doyers Street, and no more will the gloomy, deserted building that used to be her home hear her laughter.*

It was like a fairy tale that had been turned inside out: a beloved daughter leaves home, and as a result of a strange and unaccountable spell, transforms into someone else—someone supposedly better. So much better, in fact, that she can no longer return to her humble village. Her family fights to bring her back, but they fail and lose their golden child forever.

Hornby's account was terse, yet he observed that *Mock seemed very fond of the child, and he and his wife wept when the decision was rendered yesterday.*

The three articles agreed only on a few particulars: that Ha Oi was definitely Caucasian, that Mock and his wife weren't fit guardians for the child, and that John Find, the importer, had committed a gaff when he said he didn't eat off the floor, he ate from a plate.

My watered-down piece in the *Observer* was better than nothing, but it wouldn't set the record straight. It couldn't counter the dust that had been sprinkled into the public's eyes. As far as the other reporters were concerned, Ha Oi had transformed into a white child, and so her fate was entirely reasonable. Not one of the accounts—mine included—asked why Mock Duck's offer to leave the city had been turned down.

* * *

I made my way to the district, which looked deserted. Stores and restaurants were shuttered or only half open. The usual bustle was missing. Hardly anyone was out as I turned up Mott, onto Pell, and over to Doyers and Chatham Square.

The Corsair sat on a crate, whittling a figure from a stick of wood, a black armband tied around his sleeve. "I'd say good morning but it's hardly good," he remarked as I approached. "In case you hadn't noticed, we're all in mourning."

"How are Mock and Tai Yow?" A silly question, but the only one to ask in the circumstances.

They had taken a cab back after the verdict, the Corsair replied, then they went inside their home, and hadn't been seen or heard from since. Even Bedelia hadn't come out to do her usual marketing.

"What do you think will happen now?"

"Damned if I know. But I'll tell you this: They've crushed this district's spirit. It's been sucked right out of us. If they can turn Mock into just another helpless creature, what chance do we have?"

We sat in silence for several moments. The only sound came from his blade as it scraped the wood, and the clatter of the elevated.

"What's next for you," he asked, "now that this is over."

"I don't know," I said. And I really meant it.

"There's nothing left for him to do, is there?"

"I don't think so.… As far as I'm aware, the judge's decision is final."

"Who would think it would end like this?" the Corsair said. "With Ha Oi gone and Mock cut down to size."

I decided to take my leave of Mrs. Woo and thank her for her help.

When I knocked on her door, she peered out, frowned, and whispered, "Why are you here?"

A male voice called from inside. Mrs. Woo replied and then said to me in a loud voice, "You want to have your photograph taken? Please come in."

I stepped inside her home. Her two daughters played together on a string cot—what we'd call a *charpai*. They looked up, smiled shyly, and returned to their game. A black curtain separated the front of the room from the back. A stove stood in one corner beside a mirrored cupboard and beneath a shelf with cooking utensils.

"This way, please." Mrs. Woo ushered me to the back as Mr. Woo appeared from behind the fabric partition. His rumpled shirt was untucked, his thinning hair was pressed against his forehead, and he inspected me up and down before he spoke a few words to his wife.

"He wonders," she said, slightly shamefaced, "why you want to be photographed in those clothes."

"You can take it from the shoulders up. No one will ever know the difference."

"He's a bit gruff," Grace Woo said in a low voice, "but don't mind him."

She brought me to a rotating metal stool covered in green velvet, an adjustable neck-and-shoulder brace stood behind it. Off to one side, a table was stocked with pans of liquid and bottles of chemicals.

"That's where the pictures come to life," Mrs. Woo said. She cranked a painted backdrop from a roll attached to the ceiling. A glorious scene descended: the Great Wall snaking through mountains.

The vista was replaced by New York's harbor—tiny figures dotted the shore, steamers chugged along the Hudson, and Lady Liberty commanded the skies from her island. The final choice was more subdued: an elegant interior of marble steps, Grecian pillars, and a tasteful potted plant.

"Which do you prefer?" Grace Woo asked.

I chose the harbor.

She winched the other backdrops out of view, positioned the stool, spinning it up to the correct height, and set up the brace while her husband tinkered with his camera.

"I don't know if you heard," she said. "We're moving."

"Where to?"

She handed me a comb and mirror.

"New Jersey. My husband has always wanted to live there. And now, after what's happened, he says it's time. In any case, he's been making inquiries there for the past few months."

I removed my hat and checked my reflection. Smoothed the strays in front.

"He's never liked our upstairs neighbor," Mrs. Woo went on as she positioned me correctly. Her husband bent and peered through the viewfinder. Waved his hand to indicate I should shift slightly to the left. "And now that they've taken the neighbor's child, he's sure they're going to come after the rest of us."

Mr. Woo held up his hand.

"Take a breath," his wife said, "then exhale. Keep your eyes open and stay steady. Three—two—one." A flashbulb exploded. "All right, one more time."

Her husband adjusted the equipment.

CHAPTER TWENTY-ONE

"He says it will be good for us. More space, fresh air…safer."

"When will you leave?"

"By the end of the week."

"So soon?"

"He says no point in wasting another minute. So come back on Tuesday to pick this up. We'll keep it ready."

Mr. Woo held up his hand again. Grace Woo counted backward from three, and I tried not to blink when the light went off.

Mr. Woo scribbled a receipt. Apparently, he could write a few words in English.

His wife pulled back the curtain and escorted me out. "Sorry about that," she whispered. "I hope you don't mind. Otherwise, I would have had to tell you to leave."

I assured her that it was all right and waved to the girls. "Good luck," I told her and stepped onto the sidewalk.

"Who knows?" she said. "This may be for the best."

Maybe it was. And maybe, after what had happened to Ha Oi, the Woos wouldn't be the only ones to depart. One by one, the entire neighborhood would clear out.

Chapter Twenty-Two

The rest of the weekend passed quietly. Dr. Morley spent Saturday afternoon trimming and weeding. He had developed a green thumb during his childhood days in Salem and now liked to tend to the pocket-sized garden at the back of our home. The tiny patch overflowed with bushes, vines, and flowers and provided an escape from the noise and acres of steel and stone everywhere else, but maintaining it wasn't for me. I didn't have the patience or the long-term planning that gardening demanded; so instead, I sat on a bench and kept him company.

Apart from that, my husband liked to read, learn about the world, and travel. Before he started working for the government, he'd run a clinic for the poor, which kept him busy. It was what he saw in his practice that made him realize the city needed to undertake sweeping sanitary measures to protect the public's health, and that he wanted to spearhead the effort.

On one of his rare weekends off, we took a trip to Poughkeepsie. We visited the grave of one of my countrywomen, Mrs. Anandibai Joshee, who came to America to study medicine at the age of seventeen or eighteen. She'd worn a sari for the entire duration of her stay and maintained a strict vegetarian diet. I had done neither. Anandibai passed her medical exams, but the combination of the work, her diet, and an early miscarriage (she lost a child at thirteen or fourteen) took its toll, and she passed away at the age of twenty-two, shortly after returning to India.

Her husband sent her ashes back to her American hostess, Mrs. Carpenter, a woman Anandibai loved like a mother, and it was she who had them buried in her family plot. We walked around the gravestone marker that read:

Anandibai Joshee, MD. 1865-1887. First Brahmin Woman to Leave India to Obtain an Education.

It was so simple and yet, said so much. And as I looked at it, I wondered where I wanted my ashes buried. In this country, or back home?

And then there was the question of what I had accomplished during my time here. Anandibai had become a doctor. Her kinswoman Pandita Ramabai ("bai" is an honorific) traveled around the country delivering hundreds of lectures.

I hadn't even been able to help one little girl.

"Archie," Dr. Morley called. "Give me a hand, won't you?"

I held back some branches while he cut the dead growth around them. Then I tried to make myself useful by collecting the debris in a basket.

On Sundays, Clément took the morning off, so I assembled leftovers for lunch. My father had never wanted me to cook, saying that it was woman's work and that I should stay out of the kitchen. Now, I was paying the price since we had to rely on our maid's dubious culinary skills, and yet I didn't mind too much. Dr. Morley was satisfied with meat and potatoes, and I managed with fried eggs on rice, boiled vegetables, and whatever else was put in front of me. As long as I could do what I considered to be my real work, I was content—for the most part.

Afterwards, I tried to write some letters, but could only think about Mock, his wife, and their child. I wondered what they were doing now. Would Tai Yow ever recover from the blow? Had the loss of Ha Oi changed Mock Duck for good, and if not, how would he respond once the grief subsided?

Some days later, I came across a piece in one of the papers which reported that Helen Francis had been spotted at the circus with ribbons in her hair, a rag doll clutched in her arms, "talking gaily" with other orphans from the Society.

I know they say children forget, but not this fast.

And a day or two after that, Shrimpy told me that Mock Duck had been spotted at Foley Square speaking to George Washington Plunkitt, the Tammany philosopher. That didn't ring true either. I stopped by the square on a regular basis, once or twice a week, at least, and I'd never seen Mock there. And besides, what could he possibly have to say to Plunkitt, especially just a few days after he lost his child?

In any case, I planned to allow some time to pass, then return to Chinatown to see what I could uncover.

* * *

Dupont dispatched me to the Catskills as soon as I came in on Monday morning. He didn't say so directly, but I guessed it must be to punish me for my previous defiance.

He displayed none of his usual humor when he told me to go home at once, change into something appropriate, and catch the steamer from the westside docks. And I should hurry if I wanted to return before nightfall.

Cursing under my breath, I took a cab home, dressed in a skirt and shirtwaist, and left a note with Clément telling my husband where I'd gone just in case I was delayed. I didn't like traveling outside the city on my own, and Dr. Morley wouldn't be thrilled by the prospect either. He tolerated my roaming about Manhattan because he believed there was safety in crowds and colors, and even when I had to travel to the Bronx or to Queens to write a story, he worried. In more rural settings, I stuck out like a sore thumb. Still, I didn't have much choice.

I bought my round-trip ticket and waited on the pier for the boat to arrive. Now that the Thaw trial was over, at least for the moment, the *Observer* had been forced to shift gears. The world had continued spinning throughout the weeks and months of hysteria, and it was time to catch up with the rest of the news. Dupont had taken it upon himself to write a piece about the so-called "McClellan Act," which gave New York City the right to take over any lands required for the construction of the reservoir and aqueduct and conferred powers on our youthful mayor that a judge said "the Almighty would have hesitated to bestow on his favorite archangel."

The purpose of the day's trip was to pay a visit to one of the towns that was to be submerged so that Dupont could give his story a bit of local flair.

"Hizzoner's on a roll," the editor remarked before I left that morning. "He's unveiling a statue in his father's honor and, despite the protests, it looks like the groundbreaking in the Catskills is still on schedule." Dr. Morley was pleased to have been invited to both—for being an old friend who'd passed muster, he said. "If Georgie B.'s headed to the top, he needs people around him he can trust." I'd been invited as well—presumably so I could write a word or two for the *Observer*.

The liner arrived, and the passengers climbed aboard. I lowered my veil, presented my ticket, and took a seat under the awning. A few minutes later, we started to move, and my spirits sank as the island pulled away.

I didn't realize how comfortable I felt there until I wasn't there anymore.

The day liner chugged along the Hudson until the familiar skyline was a speck. I'd keep things efficient, I told myself. One quick trip to the town, a few quotes, and then back to New York.

We steamed north, past the emerald-green Palisades of New Jersey, past homes nestled in the woods, past railway lines and lighthouses, Bear Mountain and West Point. A well-turned-out pair whom I'd noticed on the pier eyed me warily, and the woman whispered loudly to her companion, "Who are they letting on board these days, Nathan darling? Can you tell where she's from?"

"I'm not sure," darling Nathan replied. "Maybe a mulatto…from Georgia?"

In my pocket, I carried a letter that had been printed in the *Tribune*. It read:

So the courts have deprived Mock of his little white child, Ha Oi. Well and good. That he loved her and lavished upon her all that money can buy counts for nothing, for has he not been accused or suspected of all the crimes in the code, although none has been proved? "Does not a Jew have hands, organs, dimensions, senses, affections, passions?" wrote Shakespeare. So might he have written of a Chinese, and the answer would have been equally in the affirmative. But what of that? Mock Duck has committed the crime of being of an alien race. Happy little Ha Oi, that she has been dragged from the lap of pagan love and luxury that she may become the drudge of some Christian household and the target of its taunts.

The phrase "crime of being of an alien race" echoed Posner's words at the hearing. The letter was unsigned, and I wondered whether the lawyer or an associate had penned it at Mock's request…and whether the mayor or his wife had arranged for his child to be removed. The loss of Hai Oi and Mock's defeat certainly had a chilling effect on the district. Mock's very existence was an affront to the city's power, and now he and all the rest of the locals had been shown, in no uncertain terms, who really was in charge.

I closed my eyes and listened to the water rushing past.

In her observations on the United States, Pandita Ramabai wrote that the reason that the West showed contempt for the Chinese was simple: fear. China had the most ancient and continuous system of self-rule of any country in the five continents, and it hadn't been subjugated like India. It was still independent and possessed the strength to compete with any Western nation. Mock had shown his strength and independence too, and maybe that was why he had to be crushed.

My destination arrived, and I stepped onto the docks and looked for transport. The water lapped lazily against the shore. There was nothing available apart from a few cars, which other passengers had already booked. And why should there have been? I shouldn't have expected a line of cabs— this was hardly Manhattan. I fumed at my lack of foresight and Dupont's vindictiveness. He'd sent me off without time to make adequate preparations. There was no way on god's green earth that I could walk uphill to the village and back.

A weather-beaten farmer with a horse and open cart clopped over and, for an extortionate sum, allowed me to ride at the back of the wagon. I managed to hoist myself up—he didn't offer to lend a hand—and my feet were barely off the ground when we started moving. He held on to the reins, sucked the wad of tobacco that he nursed in his lower lip, spat fulsomely from time to time, and didn't say much as we headed up into the dense mountains except to inquire whether I'd heard about the upcoming groundbreaking. Hizzoner and a bunch of "good-for-nothin'" city folks would be here.

To which I replied that I had, and he asked, "You ain't one 'em Goner tourists, are ya?"

I'd never heard the phrase before.

"It's what we call 'em in these parts 'cause they're always askin'—will this be gone? Will that be gone? Yes, sir; yes, ma'am, I tell 'em. It'll all be gone. Won't be a stick nor stone left when they're done with us. They're gonna pull up every last tree and bush, and whatever they can't rip out, they'll burn right to the ground."

"It sounds like hell."

"Worse than hell. It's all gonna be buried under water." He spat, gave the reins a snap, and didn't say another word for the next half-hour.

Tent towns for the laborers who would be working on the aqueduct had sprung up along the way. They stretched as far as I could see. Hard-eyed men squatted around makeshift shelters, sharpening knives and axes, chopping wood, and boiling water in kettles on outdoor fire pits. Laundry hung from lines tied between trees. Someone strummed a banjo. A couple of men took turns tossing a knife at a target carved into a tree. The aqueduct would take ten years to complete, and no doubt, even more workers would be required as the monumental undertaking progressed.

"How do they keep the peace here?" I asked. With so many men corralled together, fights were bound to break out.

"Yeah," the farmer muttered. "Eye-talians, first time in this country. Negras from the south. They're swarmin' everywhere. And we don't have police like they do over in the city. They'll come after our women, come after everything." He gave the reins an angry shake. "And all for what? So city folk can drink a glass of water?"

Twenty minutes later, he brought the wagon to a halt at Main Street just long enough for me to slide off, then urged his horse onward.

I surveyed my surroundings. Even a desert would have been more inviting. In the midst of majestic natural scenery, the homes, shops, and places of business stood empty. A screen door blew open and slammed shut on a vacated porch. Grass grew wild on abandoned front lawns. The village was already a ghost town.

I made my way toward the sound of voices. A group of scruffy children sang a chipper tune as they skipped in time to a whirling jump rope.

"Underneath the Hudson, Thro' tubes of massive stone,

They will take the Catskills Water, From its mountain home.

Then 't'will reach the mighty city, On the River and Bay,

Soon there'll be water a-plenty, For the throngs on Old Broadway."

"Hey, miss. Wanna tour?" An enterprising tow-haired lad trotted up to me. "It'll cost ya a quarter." He held out his hand. "I'm Alexander."

I offered him a nickel. He countered with twenty; we finally settled on fifteen.

"You sure drive a hard bargain." He nodded, impressed, as I dropped the coins on his palm. "You from New York?"

"That's right."

"Ah, the big city." The pint-sized Catskills lobbygow nodded sagely. "Most of my customers come from over there. Come to gloat at us, Pa says. But I say, a dollar's a dollar."

"And how many dollars have you earned so far?"

He assessed me for a moment before replying cagily, "A couple." He pointed to a ramshackle building. "That's the schoolhouse. At least, it used to be the schoolhouse. Teacher's left town, and we ain't had school for more'n five months."

I followed him down the road, passing by shells of businesses—a grocer, a general store—until we came to a church. The inside was empty, no pews, no statuary or ornamentation. The pastor had taken them all away. "For safe-keepin'," the boy said, "until we can build a new one."

We wandered over to the cemetery at the back. Broken headstones lay helter-skelter amongst piles of dirt, and deep craters scarred the ground.

"Can't leave the departed behind," my guide explained. "Bad for the water. They pay us fifteen dollars for every coffin. Pa dug up Grandpa, Grandma, Uncle Pete, and Cousin Liz."

I stared at the deep holes. "Where are they now?"

"We moved 'em to higher ground," he replied cheerfully.

I asked why he and his friends were still here.

"We like to play in the streets. No one bothers us. And sometimes, I get to show a tourist around."

"They paid for your house?" Dupont's article said the city paid two hundred and fifty dollars for every dwelling.

"Pa says it's highway robbery. You can't force a man to leave the land he's worked on all his life. But we ain't got no choice. If you don't like it, ya gotta lump it. Eminem domingus."

"Say that again?"

He repeated the phrase.

"Eminent Domain?"

"That's right!" He seemed pleased that I knew the term.

From the graveyard, he escorted me to "the Pride of the Catskills," the highlight of his tour. Bishops Falls was the centerpiece of a picture-postcard-perfect scene that included a covered wooden bridge, the oldest in the mountains, a grist mill, and an old stone house.

"Wondrous, ain't it?" He pointed proudly.

It was difficult to conceive of water being drowned by even more water, gallons upon gallons of the stuff, but that was what would happen right here. In a few years, the dam across the Esopus Creek would be complete, and the spot where we were standing would be submerged nearly five-hundred feet beneath the surface. The reservoir would cover an area nearly the size of Manhattan. It was dizzying. Incomprehensible.

I stared up into the bowl of the sky and imagined myself drowning. Ghostly hands plucked me from the depths.

I told my guide that I had seen enough.

He insisted that my final stop should be the Mountain's End. "You must be hungry. Get a bite to eat before you head back. Don't worry," he assured me, "there'll be plenty of time to catch the ferry."

Famous last words. He pointed me in the direction of the tavern and ran off.

Unused to steep inclines, I felt like a sherpa as I trekked the winding path that took me to the edge of a cliff, where the tavern perched. It must once have been a magnificent place judging from its size, carved roof, and side porch, which offered customers a scenic view.

But the porch was empty, and a few broken tables and chairs had been pushed to a corner. A sign hung off the front doorknob: STRICTLY NO SURVEYORS OR APPRAISERS ALLOWED. BY ORDER OF MGMT.

The door opened with a forbidding creak, and the proprietress, a faded blonde of indeterminate age, grinned broadly when she saw me. "A customer." Two of her front teeth were missing. "We don't get many of those these days. Where you from?"

"The city."

The smile disappeared.

"What brings you here?"

"I'm writing a story about what's going on."

"Wait a minute. Wait a minute." She beckoned me over. "Come sit right here." She patted a spot in front of the counter.

Four gnarled men in their cups huddled around a table. A single drunk might be harmless, but a group of them—

I didn't move.

"Now don't be shy. Alexander sent ya? Come on in."

I didn't like her tone.

"I said, 'c'mon over.'" It grew sharper.

The men were all attention now, ready to see what would happen. A shotgun hung from a post near the bar.

"No, thank you." I turned. The door slammed shut behind me, the roar of her laughter mixed with that of the men as I ran, boots pounding the dust and pebbles.

I reached Main Street, which was empty, no sign of the children, no sign of anyone, and although it was still light, that would soon change.

Trying to control the tide of panic that threatened to overwhelm me, I waited at the crossroads, and angrily wiped the tears that smarted in my eyes. Dupont had sent me over to teach me a lesson, and I'd come up here like an idiot. And now I'd be done for like an idiot too. Either at the hands of that lunatic and her friends, or at those of the workmen in their tents less than a mile away.

Maybe I'd hide overnight in one of the abandoned cottages, or I should just call it quits and lie down in one of the empty graves. I berated myself for my stupid decision to leave Manhattan, and then for my decision to come to America in the first place. I should have stayed in India, where I was always surrounded by people I knew. I never should have left.

I felt completely unmoored, the way I had during my first few days on the endless ocean. As though I was in the middle of nowhere—which I was—and wishing I could turn the ship around.

I had never possessed Ramabai's sense of calling nor Dr. Anandibai's sense of clarity and purpose. The letter that the prospective medical student had written to Mrs. Carpenter in America came back to me:

> *You have every reason to think that a very distant voyage will be hazardous to a girl of eighteen because the world is full of frauds and dangers, but wherever I cast my glance, I see nothing but a straight and smooth way.*
>
> *I fear no miseries...I have nothing to despise. The whole universe is a lesson to me... Rest assured that I am happy wherever I am on the face of this earth.*

If only I shared her unshakable serenity and confidence.

Maybe it was thirty minutes, maybe three-quarters of an hour, maybe a full hour, but I repeated her words like a mantra dozens of times before a cart finally appeared. It was the same farmer from that morning.

He didn't seem to recognize me, or if he did, he didn't care.

Neither did I.

He barely slowed his wagon. "Hop on."

Chapter Twenty-Three

I rarely fell ill but now I took to my bed. My husband chalked it up to the rigors of the journey. "You should have told Dupont no. There's no reason for you to have gone. A woman on her own up there.…" He shuddered with indignation. "It's not worth whatever story he wants."

That, plus the strain of the Thaw trial, he said, had done me in. Probably I was also upset by what had happened to the child in Chinatown. He agreed that she shouldn't have been taken from the Mocks, but wondered whether a better life might now be possible for her.

I slept on and off for the better part of forty-eight hours, waking only to take the medicines he prescribed and the broth that Clément prepared. At some point, Dupont sent someone over to collect my notes, but I was so tired that I didn't even bother to look them over to make sure they were coherent.

When I returned to work on Thursday, I felt a bit calmer, if not exactly refreshed.

"Glad you're back," Dupont said with a wolfish grin. "The exertion of that trip proved too much? Never mind. We'll keep you close for the foreseeable future. I just thought… since you care so much about the plight of displaced persons and whatnot that the situation might be of interest."

The editor couldn't leave well enough alone. When he found a sore spot, he had to keep poking at it.

He planned to run the Catskills story over the weekend to warm up our readers for the groundbreaking that would soon follow. He'd print it on two facing pages with diagrams and illustrations to show the ingenuity of the construction and its massive scale. The pyramids of Egypt and the Roman aqueducts, he said, were the only worthy physical comparisons.

"Only thing is—most of the marvel will be buried deep underground." He chuckled. "Poor Georgie B. It's hard to get credit for a masterpiece that's hidden."

He instructed me to describe what I'd seen to our sketch artist. The extent of the reservoir and its depth. He already had drawings prepared to show the size of the tunnels that would be dug beneath the earth (they were wide enough for a horse and cart to drive through, with plenty of room to spare), the means by which they'd be channeled under the Hudson, and how construction would take place deep within the city's bowels with minimum disruption to traffic and surface movement. The final paragraphs were reserved for a description of the town that I'd visited, the way it looked at present, and the effect its demolition would have on the residents.

"They're going to tear out every last tree and bush?" Dupont asked.

"And burn whatever they can't pull up."

"Superb."

* * *

Shrimpy came over to my desk later that afternoon, pink-faced as usual and breathless. He'd been out and about and heard rumblings. Hizzoner was on his way to Chinatown along with a group of bigwigs. Something important was about to happen. Did I want to go?

What a question. I hurriedly finished the advice column I was working on, reached for my hat, paused for a moment when I realized that Georgie B. would see me in my trousers, and decided that it was worth the risk. Hizzoner in Chinatown was an event I couldn't miss. I would just have to stay off to the side and try to remain inconspicuous.

We arrived to find a gaggle of dignitaries milling around Chatham Square. Representatives from the American Architectural League, the City Beautiful movement, the Playground Association of America, and so on. The gentlemen had come armed with binoculars and walking sticks; the ladies wore sturdy boots and no-nonsense hats and had brought along canteens of drinking water. They looked as though they were headed on safari, and Mock Duck, no doubt, was their prey.

Cool and fresh on a hot day, Georgie B. strode in on foot, accompanied by a flustered Engineer Webster, whose shirt was damp with sweat.

The mayor had also brought along an aide and two policemen as escorts. He shook the pooh-bahs' hands, thanked them for coming, and headed up Doyers. He didn't seem to notice Shrimpy or me trailing behind.

Georgie B. stopped when he approached the bend and stationed himself in front of the Opera House. The padlock was gone; it seemed ready again for business.

I looked up and saw Mock's window, right on the curve. A curtain moved slightly and remained cracked open. It couldn't have been the breeze; it had to have been him, watching.

Beaming from ear to ear, the mayor apologized for assembling everyone on such short notice, but he had good news to share. A "vital stumbling block" to the creation of the park in the district had been removed, and he wanted to deliver the tidings himself.

Engineer Webster had completed his preliminary studies, Georgie B. said, and had come to the conclusion that it wasn't a subterranean stream, rather some other minor issues that were causing problems. These could easily be resolved with proper planning, and would only slightly increase the project's overall cost.

"Hear, hear." The invitees applauded.

"I never doubted that the plan to create a park in this area was feasible in a timely manner," Hizzoner declared. "And I would not have hesitated to hire an outside firm to provide a second opinion had it proved necessary. Fortunately, Engineer Webster discovered the error himself"—he thumped the perspiring engineer on his back—"so we can move ahead at the pace we originally envisioned.

"Webster assures me that the drawings will be ready in exactly seven days"—he emphasized the last three words—"in time for this month's Board of Estimate meeting next Friday.

"Ladies and gentlemen,"—the mayor stood proud—"I am not a betting man, but I believe that it is safe to say that by the end of this summer, everything you see around you will be gone, only to be replaced by a new green lung that will provide much-needed relief to our city's poor."

The curtain at No. 10 fell closed as the aristocrats hurrahed.

The mayor asked for suggestions for names for the future park.

Franklin Square, Jefferson Square, and Celestial Fields were proposed. Someone suggested Mandarin Grove, but Hizzoner didn't care much for that one.

Tom Lee's grandnephew, William, appeared out of nowhere and ran in the direction of Pell Street, presumably to break the news to his great-uncle. Faces looked down from the windows above, but the locals must have known to stay away, because there was no one on the street apart from the mayor and his entourage.

I couldn't help but be impressed by the pressure that Georgie B. had applied on Webster. The threat of bringing in an outside opinion must have forced the engineer to reconsider. That, or something similar. Things were falling into place for the general's son.

Shrimpy returned to the *Observer* to write the piece, but I stayed on to collect my photograph from Mrs. Woo. The family would be leaving the following day.

When I knocked on their door no one answered. And then I noticed that it was locked from the outside.

A chill of apprehension crept over me. As I stood on the street, deciding what to do next, Daniel O'Reilly came out the front door, nimble and light on his feet as ever.

I let him pass and went in search of the Corsair and found him at his corner on Chatham.

"Well," he said ruefully, "that was quick. I thought we'd been spared, but"—he sighed—"not for long."

"What's O'Reilly doing here?"

"Beats me. He's been by a couple of times. Probably paying his condolences, and angling to see if there's anything else he can do to earn an extra buck."

"And the Woos? Have they left for New Jersey already? I'm supposed to pick up a photograph."

He paused his whittling and gazed at me with his one good orb. "They've gone, all right. But not to Jersey. Mr. Woo was taken to Bellevue."

"What happened?"

"I'm not sure. Something to do with those chemicals he uses.... They splashed in his eyes. I heard he might lose his vision."

Chapter Twenty-Four

The hospital on the East River by Kips Bay was a maze. It consisted of hundreds of corridors, dozens of waiting rooms, pavilions, and special wards for everything from maternity to mental hygiene, surgery and a special zone set aside for tubercular patients. Bells clanging, horse-drawn and gas-powered ambulances pulled in and out of its emergency wing, bringing the poorest of the poor, victims of injuries, street accidents and illnesses who had been refused by private hospitals, and yet were unfailingly met by Bellevue's dedicated team of emergency physicians and trained nurses.

I'd been there several times as a reporter and hated everything about it: the stench of rubbing alcohol, the enamel pans filled with blood and slop, the patients' gut-wrenching howls. Not to mention the faces in the waiting room, some teary, others more stoic, but all desperately seeking answers as they pelted the staff with questions in every language under the sun. Everywhere you went, you came across armies of doctors in white coats, nurses in their starched caps, orderlies pushing patients on gurneys, or carrying out refuse in buckets.

It took me a while to find Mr. Woo. Several questions, some greased palms, and many wrong turns were involved. I steeled myself before I arrived at the burn ward. I smelled it before I saw it and certainly heard it before I came to it. The wretched cries of patients whose bandages were being peeled from raw skin were enough to turn my stomach.

I'd been to the morgue, seen corpses on metal tables, water pouring from the showers above and flowing into the drains on tiled floors. But they had all been dead. These poor souls were still conscious.

I began to feel faint, still I continued, past medics and worried relatives, and into a long room lined with rows of beds, each one separated from its neighbor by a curtain.

"Who are you here to see?" A doughty nurse stood in my way. "Only family members allowed during visiting hours."

"My husband." I pointed wildly to a bed in the distance. I must have looked so distressed that she believed me.

I tried not to hear the screams as bandages were changed, tried not to breathe in the smell of charred flesh mixed with ointment and pus, when I found Grace Woo sitting beside a metal bed at the far end of the hall. She had her head down, chin resting on her hands.

Mr. Woo lay unmoving on the mattress, his body covered by a thin, white sheet, eyes covered by white gauze.

"Mrs. Woo?" I approached her.

She looked up slowly. "What are you doing here?" Her face was ragged. She was barely recognizable as the striking woman I'd first seen at Mulberry Bend Park.

"I heard about the accident."

"Accident?" She laughed bitterly. "Fifteen years he does this work, and suddenly he has an accident? I don't think so."

"What happened then?"

"It's none of your concern."

"I'm sorry." I backed off.

She apologized. She wasn't herself, she said. Then added that the doctors told her Mr. Woo might never see again. She sounded as though she still didn't believe it.

For a few moments, neither of us spoke. She looked away, adjusted the rolls of gauze on the table beside her, then continued: "Mock's friends believe Mr. Woo wrote the letter to the Gerry Society. And now that Ha Oi is gone they've taken their revenge."

"Mock's friends did this to him?"

She nodded.

"But how could Mr. Woo have written the letter—and why? He barely speaks English."

"That's what I told them."

"You were there?"

"With the girls."

I was stunned. She must have thought I was an idiot.

"You're in over your head," she said in a flash of anger and disdain. "You don't know the district. You don't know who you're dealing with. And you don't know the first thing about us. It's time for you to go back home."

I stumbled through the corridors, past wards and orderlies, families, and other lost souls. I climbed stairs, turned corners, reached dead ends, and turned around before somehow making it out.

Chapter Twenty-Five

The train hurtled toward Washington, D.C. Dr. Morley and I had taken a ferry to New Jersey and caught it from the depot there. Once the Pennsylvania Station was complete, with its tunnels running beneath the river, that extra step would no longer be required.

Now, we shared a compartment with the mayor of New York City, his wife, and an aide. Dr. Morley had been invited to attend the unveiling of General McClellan's statue, and thanks to an apparent run on tickets, we had been granted the unexpected honor of traveling with the McClellans. I wondered whether we'd be asked for any favors in return.

Although, when he heard I where was going, Dupont wanted an article out of it—so maybe it was I who was being calculating and using them.

During the first fifteen minutes or so of pleasantries, I congratulated Hizzoner on the progress he'd made in Chinatown.

"I promised the people it would happen, and it did," he replied.

"It certainly took some doing," his wife said. She wore a smart, amethyst-colored traveling suit with military-style piping on the cuffs, collar, and hem. "More than I would have expected from that kind of place…but the mayor prevailed in the end."

Lady Mac had brought along a stack of newspapers and magazines, and once her husband turned to his work, she turned to hers. She carefully perused each publication, circling articles of interest, and then cut them out with a pair of sharp, pointy scissors that she carried in her purse. The blades snipped neat rectangles of text, which she attached with a pin to a blank slip of paper, on which she wrote a note in her rounded, sloping hand.

A note like the one she sent to the Gerry Society? I could picture the words: *Dear Sirs, It is with great dismay that I inform you...*

Even if she hadn't, I couldn't believe that Mr. Woo wrote the letter. I didn't think his linguistic skills were up to the task, and even if he hated his upstairs neighbor, he couldn't have been such a fool as to risk Mock's wrath.

I wished I had seen the original—it might have contained a clue to its author. But with Ha Oi firmly in the Society's care, neither Pisarra nor anyone else would allow me to see anything.

Telegraph poles, fields, and farmhouses flashed past Dr. Morley's window. He was absorbed in a medical article. Something to do with the effect of improved ventilation on disease. He scratched his beard while he read, turned to me, and smiled.

His kind and intelligent face was my anchor, and I felt guilty about misleading him. I hadn't told him that I'd interviewed Mock—and since my conversation with Mrs. Woo, I was glad of that.

I had been forced to acknowledge the truth of what she'd said: I didn't know the district, and I had no idea who Mock really was. I had heard the stories, sure. But up to this point, they had just been stories. I'd never met one of his victims. Now, the cruelty that had long been his trademark was hitting home.

* * *

A friend of the mayor's sent a car to meet us in Washington. After a quick break to freshen up, we drove directly to the location on Columbia Road where the ceremony would be held. The broad avenues of the capital never failed to impress, although at this time of year (we were already in June), it was sweltering, and the mosquitos of the bog on which it was built were out in full force.

The traffic crept along at a snail's pace because certain streets and avenues had been blocked off to accommodate the parade, and from our windows we could see veterans of the War of the Rebellion hobbling along. Men missing legs, arms, eyes, waved flags and cheered for Little Mac, their beloved general.

Together, this ragtag band had scrimped and saved to collect the funds for the monument that paid tribute to their commander.

Georgie B. reached for his wife's hand. Lady Mac crossed herself. We parted ways at Columbia Road. The McClellans joined the other dignitaries on the dais while Dr. Morley and I took our seats in the stands reserved for guests.

In short order, a band began to play, and the veterans took their seats or marched along in line.

A blessing was said before the president approached the podium. Theodore Roosevelt put on his pince-nez, held on to his lapels, and surveyed the gathered soldiers. Roosevelt was young, just shy of fifty. His rise to the highest position in the land had been meteoric. He served as police commissioner of New York City, assistant secretary of the navy, briefly as governor of New York State, and after less than a year as vice president of the United States, an assassin's bullet launched him to the presidency, where he'd served since September 1901.

His patrician background wasn't dissimilar to Hizzoner's. If the Republican from New York could do it, then why not the Democrat? Even if our mayor had been born abroad while his father recovered in Europe from the loss of his bid for the presidency.

That question grew more insistent as we watched the parade. Perhaps that explained why Roosevelt seemed to go out of his way to sideline the younger man.

Rumor had it that the president ignored the speeches that his aides drafted, and this occasion didn't prove otherwise. His eyes drifted over his notes, and then he abandoned them. He saluted the general's wife, barely acknowledged the son, and discussed the exploits of other great military leaders.

He spoke about the importance of bearing children and his distaste for birth control, calling it "worse, more debasing and destructive than ordinary vice," and recommended to the befuddled, elderly troops that they should aim for four offspring each—the ideal number for most couples. Afterward, his secretaries came around and handed members of the press "true copies" of his words for publication. Naturally, the rambling about families and birth control had never been part of the speech, and we were left with words that were cogent and to the point.

Georgie B. wasn't given an opportunity to speak, but he stepped forward and pulled back flags to unveil a bronze sculpture of the general on his steed, one hand holding the reins, the other on his hip, staring resolutely into the distance. The sculpture stood on a massive granite base, almost double the height of the statue itself. It was decorated with emblems on all four sides, and proud eagles held the ends of laurel garlands in their mouths.

The Army of the Potomac threw their hats in the air and roared.

Rifle shots went off, a canon blasted. "The Star-Spangled Banner" played. The general's son and namesake stood on the dais, his hand on his heart, basking in his father's glory.

We returned to New York that same evening. No one spoke much on the journey home. We had a quick meal in the dining car and then returned to our compartment, where both the McClellans leaned back and closed their eyes. She fell asleep with her head resting on her husband's shoulder. My husband dozed off reading his papers, and I looked out at the lights punctuating the darkness.

* * *

Dupont inquired about my trip to D.C. the minute I stepped in on Saturday. (I worked on weekends depending on the need.) He wasn't the least bit surprised that the president had veered away from his prepared speech and said whatever popped into his mind. "They say whatever they want to say, but we print what we're given." He directed me to summarize the event in a few paragraphs. "And throw in a description of the horse. To make it meaty."

"Aye, aye, captain." He certainly had a bizarre sense of humor.

The weekend brought a letter from my friend Cyrus Chenoy and his sister, Meher. They had taken a break from business in Bombay and were traveling in London. They planned to visit Rome and Venice afterward, but Meher also hoped that her brother would bring her to Paris; she longed to see the Eiffel Tower. "And then," she wrote, "perhaps we can come see you in

America."

Cyrus's grandfather had visited the United States during the war. He'd been impressed by New York City's grid-like streets and how they allowed you to find your way around so easily; he'd traveled to Lake George with his manservant and met the son of President Van Buren at a hotel. Later, he met President Lincoln and was amazed at how, in one part of the world—India—it was difficult to meet the lowliest official, while in America, he was able to meet the highest official in the land, even during times of war. He said that throughout his visit he was treated with courtesy, some curiosity, and kindness.

The stories of his travels had always thrilled me and fueled my desire to travel to America. Cyrus had made the journey and met Dr. Morley and me in New York, but Meher hadn't.

I wrote back and told her she should visit soon. That nothing would make me happier. I would take time off from the *Observer* to show her around. And—I thought but didn't write—I would wear skirts or saris the entire time. It would do me good to take a break from my current ways.

The doorbell rang and, grumbling to herself as to who it could be on a Sunday afternoon, Clément went to answer it. She returned to the sitting room looking flustered.

"It's for you, Mrs. Morley. A China-woman, and an Irish. The Irish says they know you." Clément sounded doubtful.

I looked out the window: Tai Yow and Bedelia stood on my doorstep.

Dr. Morley had gone to meet an ailing friend, but he could return at any minute.

I had no wish to have anything more to do with Mock Duck, but Tai Yow looked so wan that I decided to take the chance, and told Clément to show them in.

They entered, Tai Yow moving unsteadily, like an invalid.

"Will you be wanting tea, madam?" Clément asked, her nose out of joint. She was clearly put out by my visitors.

"That'd be nice," Bedelia replied as they perched on the edge of the couch. Bedelia's eyes darted from the books to the carpets and paintings. Tai Yow didn't appear to be looking at anything in particular. She wore her formal black gown and had lost even more weight than before. For the first time, I noticed strands of white glimmering through her jet-black hair.

"I am so very sorry about what happened," I said. And added, "Tai Yow doesn't look well at all."

"She's been layin' in bed constantly," the maid replied, "not sleepin', but starin' at the wall. She finally roused herself yesterday and ate more than a morsel. But she hasn't said more than two words since last Friday."

"I wish I could have done more." I could see the dolly's limp arm dragging across the floorboards.

"Don't we all. They'll take care of her. That's what I've been prayin' for each day. And I think they will." She spoke as if to reassure herself. "They'll take care of her." She breathed deeply and crossed herself. "Nice place you've got here." Her eyes fell on a photograph of my husband and me on our wedding day. "And that's Mr. Morley?"

Dr. Morley came off well in his best suit, his beard trimmed, hair swept back, a carnation in his lapel. I'd worn my mother's red sari and gold necklace. We'd had the photograph taken right after we were married by the officiant in a small church in Brooklyn. A friend from medical college had been Dr. Morley's witness, and Miss Osiroff had been mine. I would have liked to have taken the seven circles around the sacred fire, but you make do with what you have. Since it wasn't the fashion to smile, we hadn't, but the day had been momentous—filled with incredulity at our daring and anticipation for the future.

"Yeh makes a handsome couple," the maid observed.

I asked how I could help them. "My husband will be home soon."

Clément brought in the tea, nose in the air. I'd hear the complaints as soon as they were gone. Tai Yow didn't want anything, but Bedelia helped herself to a cup, plopped in three lumps of sugar, stirred vigorously, and took a sip.

"Mr. Mock wants to see yeh," the maid said.

"Me? What for?"

"Somethin' he needs help with—on the rascal's behalf."

My response was firm. I was sorry that he sent them both all the way, but

I couldn't. In fact, I could no longer have anything to do with Mock Duck or the family.

"So when it suited yeh—"

I interrupted forcefully. "That's before I fully understood what he's capable of."

"And what does yeh mean by that? What is he capable of now?"

Tai Yow had cottoned on to the rising tension because her gaze went back and forth between me and her maid.

"I heard what happened to Mr. Woo."

"What about it? It was an accident. A terrible accident. Are yeh sayin' Mr. Mock's to blame?"

"Mock or his friends."

Bedelia sat up straight. "Did Grace Woo tell yeh that? The brazen hussy. And to think I ever thought well of her."

"Are you saying she's a liar?" My back was up. "She saw them herself. They hurt her husband in front of her and her daughters."

"And why would Mr. Mock's friends hurt Mr. Woo?"

"Because they think he wrote the letter to the Children's Society."

"Oh." Bedelia put down her cup. "What she ain't tellin' yeh is that Mr. Woo borrowed money. Plenty of money—for his gamin', for his house in New Jersey. For everythin'. He even borrowed from me. I'm not the type to do anythin' about it, but some fellas are. And if he borrowed from them, and never paid back… who knows what could happen."

"I didn't realize you had visitors." My husband appeared in the doorway. "And who's this Mr. Woo?"

"They're just leaving," I said.

Tai Yow seemed to grasp the gist, because she was already struggling to her feet.

"Are you all right?" Dr. Morley asked, taking a step toward her. "You don't look it."

"She'll be fine, sir," Bedelia said. "We'll take care of her." She shot me an aggrieved glance. "Now that we know who our friends are."

I wanted to do something for them. Something, anything. Just not help

Mock Duck. I searched around in desperation, and my gaze fell on a figurine of Ganesha, the elephant-headed god and remover of obstacles. My mother had given it to me as child, it was one of the few mementoes I'd brought along when I left the country. I pressed it into Tai Yow's hand. She didn't even look at it.

She didn't say anything, she didn't do anything, but she was angry. Her chest moved up and down beneath the ruffled silk, the corners of her mouth curled downward, and her eyes blazed. "Well, thank yeh for your time, Mrs. Morley, Mr. Morley," Bedelia said. "We're sorry if we troubled yeh in any way."

She went to hold on to her mistress's elbow, but Tai Yow shook her off.

"Now, now dearie, don't you worry," the maid murmured as Tai Yow headed out ahead of her.

"What was all that?" Dr. Morley asked as the door closed firmly shut.

I started to explain—and for the first time in what felt like ages, we fought.

Chapter Twenty-Six

Graziano's bootblack stand operated at full throttle. The chairs were full, the shoe-shine boys buffed and polished as though their lives depended on it, and the peanut gallery bubbled with the latest. The gossip that day had to do with Silent Charlie, the tight-lipped Tammany boss. Apparently, he was ticked off that the huge construction project in the Catskills hadn't landed his men any jobs.

"Not a single one," someone remarked.

"Never thought Georgie B. would do such a thing. That turncoat."

I stopped by on my way to work, bought a cup of chicory-laced coffee from one of the nearby carts, and waited for Plunkitt to begin his sermon. The previous evening had been difficult, and I wanted to put it behind me. Dr. Morley couldn't believe that I'd gone to Mock's home and, worse still, that I'd kept it from him. "You went behind my back, Archie. Anything could have happened. And now that monster knows where we live."

"That was his wife and maid. Tai Yow and Bedelia are hardly about to—"

"This is no time to be flippant!"

I'd never seen him so distressed. Yes, I could be difficult, I was stubborn, headstrong, all those things, but in the past, he'd managed to make light of our differences.

I apologized as best I could. Said that I saw the error of my ways—which I did—and offered to extricate myself from reporting entirely. Maybe it was time for me to find another line of work. The words came out in a rush.

He cut me off saying I should stop being dramatic. It didn't suit me. And he didn't want me to give up being a reporter. All he wanted was honesty, and a promise that I wouldn't consort with criminals. Could I manage that? Could I manage not to have anything to do with Mock Duck, or anyone else in his orbit?

I said I could, and I would. And I meant it.

Since my conversation with Mrs. Woo, Mock Duck's hold on me had been loosening, and then, while I was speaking to Dr. Morley, it let go completely. I felt light, free. I hadn't realized how much Mock had been lurking at the back of my mind and preying on my thoughts since the shooting at the theater. I finally felt ready to move on.

I sipped my coffee and watched as Plunkitt stretched his arms and shook out his legs like an athlete, limbering up before a sprint. Then he climbed onto his rostrum.

"I want to talk to you today about the difference between politicians who make a fortune out of politics by keepin' their eyes wide open and political looters. Now, listen carefully because this is important: The looter goes in it for himself alone—he doesn't consider his organization or his city. As for the politician, he looks after his own interests, the organization's interests, *and* the city's interests all at the same time. See the distinction?"

Hoots and hollers. He seemed to be referring to the difference between Tom Lee and Mock Duck...or maybe Charlie Murphy and George B. McClellan—with Murphy as the politician, and traitorous Georgie B. the looter who only looked out for himself.

The key to getting the most out of Plunkitt's talks, I'd discovered, was not only to take in what he said explicitly, but also to read between the lines. You had to combine the news of the day with his sermons to discover a hidden level of meaning, which perhaps he didn't care to reveal out loud.

"Now, do you know why Philadelphia, which is ruled almost entirely by Americans, is more corrupt than New York, where the Irish do almost all the governin'?"

The crowd roared, "No."

"The Irish was born to rule, and they're the honestest people in the world. Show me the Irishman who would steal a roof off an almshouse! He don't exist. Of course, if an Irishman had the political pull and the roof was much worn, he might get the city authorities to put on a new one and get the contract for it himself and buy the old roof at a bargain—but that's honest graft. It's goin' about the thing like a gentleman, and there's more money in it and no penal code."

One of the philosopher's chief lessons was the inextricable link between jobs and votes. Like the tongs, Tammany looked after new arrivals, whom no one else seemed to care much about. They found Irish and other newcomers work, and a place to live, and such. However, unlike Chinatown's residents, Tammany's new arrivals would one day be able to vote—and out of loyalty and gratitude, they voted the way the boss wanted. That gave the organization enormous sway at the polls, which (along with a bit of ballot stuffing) was the source of its power.

Murphy kept his part of the bargain by bringing in votes for Democratic candidates. But by refusing to appoint the boss's cronies to plum posts, and then deepening the blow by failing to offer jobs on the aqueduct, Georgie B. had shown that he was willing to tear up the age-old compact.

What would happen next? I'd need to keep my ear to the ground and return to the bootblack stand to find out. That was what aggravated me when the papers only talked about Thaw, Thaw, Thaw. There was always so much else going on in New York City. So much burbling right beneath the surface. And if you looked away for even an instant, you could miss it.

* * *

A day elapsed, during which I congratulated myself on maintaining my resolve and not thinking about Mock, his request, or his family for an instant. On Tuesday, Dupont greeted me with a Cheshire-cat grin and said he had a surprise. One that I was sure to love.

"What is it this time?" I hung my hat from the row of hooks on the wall.

"Really? No 'Thank you, Monsieur Dupont, I am forever in your debt'?"

"Tell me what it is, please."

He sighed theatrically and then said he was dispatching me to Chinatown. "No," I burst out.

"What do you mean, no?"

"I'm sorry. I can't go."

"Can't or won't, Mrs. Morley? A couple of days ago, you would have jumped at the offer. What happened? I thought Tom Lee and Mock Duck were your closest associates."

I didn't bother to reply.

"Well, I'm disappointed. I thought you'd see this as a peace offering, a thank you for your excellent report from Washington. Loved the description of the steed, by the way. Some of your finest writing…. Anyhow"—he turned businesslike—"I'm not asking, I'm ordering. Our readers appreciated the descriptions of the desolation in the Catskills, and since you've become an expert in such matters, I'd like you to provide a final glimpse of the district before it's reduced to rubble. So hop to it."

"What exactly do you want from the piece?"

"Just do what you always do: observe."

"No need to talk to anyone?"

"Not necessary. Just make sure you capture the essence. The sensation of being there. The exodus that is only now beginning, but which, in the long run, will empty the neighborhood, and be the best outcome for everyone."

"Fine." I unhooked my hat. "And after this, please think of Shrimpy when it comes to reporting on Chinatown. I'm sure he'd be good at it."

"After this, there won't be any Chinatown left to report on. And Mrs. Morley—focus on your own work and allow me to do mine."

I jammed on my hat and left. I already had a plan of action sketched out. A few minutes on Mott, a few on Pell. No time at all on Doyers. Write everything up, and that was that.

Chinatown's demise would't be good for its residents, but it would suit me personally. Of course, I would miss it. But there would be no need for me to return anymore. What was over was over. I had put the district and its struggles behind me.

I arrived on Mott in a prickly mood. Five days had passed since Georgie B.'s announcement, and the city hadn't wasted a moment. Like a body being prepared for surgery, walls and sidewalks had already been marked with the inscrutable notations and arrows of surveyors. Official signs told residents that they should prepare to leave soon. "Going Out of Business" placards hung in shop windows.

Two men passed by pushing barrows filled with personal belongings. A stoic child followed, holding his grandfather's hand. A woman brought up the rear. She carried an infant on her hip, a striped sack in her free hand.

Dupont was right; the exodus had begun.

The door to Tom Lee's tobacco shop was open. "Is that you, Observer?" his voice called from the darkness. For an old man, he sure had sharp eyes. "Come on in."

One final time, I thought to myself.

The On Leong chief stood proud in his jacket and waistcoat, chatting with a cadaverous white gent at the counter.

They were surrounded by boxes. One of Lee's assistants stood on a ladder, untying the dangling bunches of tobacco leaves.

"So this is it? Everything's moving fast."

"Nothing to gain by waiting," Lee said. "Board of Estimate meets on Friday. Webster will submit his drawings, and then"—he dusted off his hands—"it's really over."

"End of an era," his companion said. "My grandfather remembers this place when it was just an orchard. Then came the homes, then the first Chinese moved in. Wo Kee had a store right on Mott, if I remember correctly."

"That guy." Lee exhaled a cloud of smoke. "Had a room upstairs for fellas to sleep, everythin' they want to buy on the street level, and a gaming setup in the basement." He gestured to the gent. "This is Mr. Charles Bacigalupo, Chinatown's undertaker. Mr. Bacigalupo says he'll take care of us wherever we go. Ain't that right, Carlo? You'll come out to Red Hook or Williamsburg or wherever?"

The undertaker doffed his hat. "For you, Mr. Lee, anything." He turned to me. "Tom Lee's been one of my longest and most faithful customers. We go way back. Even got Mr. Lee's own funeral planned, down to the last song."

"Yeah," Lee said. "Six black horses, wreaths of white roses, brass band playing 'Closer My Lord to Thee.' It's gonna be something. Thought they'd parade me down Pell and Mott before they lay my bones to rest, but I guess it's gonna hafta be someplace else now. Won't be the same."

"Not the same, but still magnificent," the undertaker murmured.

William sat in the corner, sketching in his notebook.

"Sad to leave, William?" I asked.

He bit his lip as he shook his head no. Trying to appear strong.

"William gonna miss his school and his friends," Tom Lee said. "But we'll find another place. We'll build another Chinatown, just you watch."

The boy didn't appear convinced.

"Problem is," Lee went on, "because Tom thought we were gettin' a break with that underground water, he didn't look for new land. Bad decision. Turns out, it wasn't a break, just a hiccup."

He rolled his cigar anxiously between his fingers. "Yeah. Tom's gotta do somethin'. Gotta move fast or else some of these fellas, they'll be out on the street."

"You're a good man, Tom Lee," the undertaker said.

The On Leong chief shrugged off the compliment. "Ain't got no choice." He beckoned to his assistant and handed me a box of cigars.

I tried to refuse the gift, but he insisted—for Mr. Morley—so I tucked it under my arm and wished him good luck.

"Write something good about us," he said as I headed out the door.

A group of surveyors took care of business on Pell. They peered through their instruments, jotted notes on clipboards, and barked orders at underlings, who slopped white paint symbols on the sidewalks and walls.

Little children watched the curious activity.

"Ayy!" An elderly grocer, stubble dotting his chin, yelled at one of the men whose paint had splattered on an open basket of fruit.

"Shut your trap," the underling retorted, thrust his brush in the can, and was about to make another mark when the grocer yanked him away, the underling shoved back, paint spilled, and the old man lost his balance and fell to the ground with a thud. The basket tipped over and gooseberries scattered everywhere.

The grocer's assistant ran out of the store and helped his employer to his feet. The old man's slippers were covered in white. His forehead was grazed. He shook off his tunic and the affront to his dignity, spat out angry words.

The assistant ran back inside, brought a broom from the store, and started to clean. Locals looked on silently, and the surveyors, unbothered by the incident, resumed surveying.

I knew what would come next. It had happened over and over again. Eviction notices. No more water, electricity, or other city services. The juggernaut was in motion.

It was getting close to ten, but already hot, so I popped into the Pelham Café for a quick something to drink. A striking young waiter sat behind the piano at the café, banging out a tune.

"My sweet Marie from Sunny Italy

Oh, how I do love you.

Say that you'll love me, love me too.

Forevermore, I will be true.

Just say the word, and I will marry you."

"Not bad," I remarked to the bartender.

"That's our Irving," he replied, handing me a glass of Coca-Cola.

"Packing up soon?"

"Any minute now. The city's barreling along like there's no tomorrow. I tell you though, it'll be a shame when this neighborhood's gone. There really ain't any other place like it." His attention shifted, and he gazed over my shoulder. His mouth opened a fraction in surprise.

I swung around. Mock Duck was walking toward the bar.

"You're late." He didn't look pleased.

"Are you talking to me?"

"I told Bedelia you should come at nine-thirty, and now look at the time."

"She didn't tell you my reply?" I explained that I wasn't in the neighborhood for him. I was there strictly on *Observer* business.

He noticed the cigars. "Good chat with Tom?"

Instinctively, I pulled the box closer. "That's none of your concern."

"So are you coming? You're going to want to see this."

But I didn't want to see anything. And I didn't want anything to do with him. I told him so in no uncertain terms.

Meanwhile the singing had stopped, and everyone was watching us.

"Well, I'm not going to keep standing here like some animal in a zoo," he said. "You do what you want. It's your loss." And he walked out.

* * *

To hook a fish, you dangle bait. To hook a reporter, you dangle something they don't know, throw in an ultimatum, and just reel them in.

It sounds weak, I know. But that's all it took. My resolution not to speak to Mock lasted all of twenty-four hours. In my defense: I hadn't sought him out, he'd come looking for me, and I was just as susceptible to his powers of persuasion as the next person. Like John Find said at Ha Oi's hearing, he knew exactly what to say to get people to do what he wanted.

Now, I found myself following as he strode confidently toward Doyers. Nothing about the way he conducted himself gave the impression that he'd lost his beloved child just eleven days before. He walked briskly and with purpose, veering neither left nor right and completely ignoring the surveyors.

Five minutes, I told myself. Five minutes. I would look at whatever it was he wanted to show me and leave. No loitering. No getting dragged into anything else.

Doyers Street hadn't yet been touched by the city. They were saving the best for last. We slowed down at No. 10, and oblivious to the watchful eyes of Mr. Woo's photography shingle, Mock pushed open the door and took the stairs up.

No sign of Bedelia in the kitchen. No sign of Tai Yow in the front room. The highbinder must have realized I was anxious because he said, "Bedelia's gone to the market, and my wife is sleeping. Her journey uptown yesterday took it out of her."

Mrs. Wardell's sketch of Ha Oi hung over the child's bed. I was struck again by the spark in her eyes and her impish smile. They would henceforward belong to a girl named Helen Francis.

The very thought still felt unreal—as though someone had waved a wand and abracadabra, she became Helen, and we were all supposed to agree that it somehow made sense. That somehow a child could be transformed just like that.

A vase of flowers and a burning stick of incense stood on a shelf beneath the picture. That weekend's edition of the *Observer* lay on the mattress, open to Dupont's double-page, illustrated story on the Catskills Aqueduct; *The By-Laws of Municipal Government, Unabridged Version* was tucked off to one side.

"Look," I said, "I can't stay long."

"All I need is a minute. Bedelia told me what Mrs. Woo said. And it's bullshit. Her good-for-nothing husband couldn't write a letter to the Society if his life depended on it. Now, Grace Woo—she could. She certainly could. Not that I'm saying she did. Everyone tells me she loved my daughter."

I took a deep breath. His crisp, matter-of-fact delivery, coupled with his willingness to believe the worst about his neighbor, the mother of Ha Oi's closest friends, was even more chilling than if he'd been furious. "I thought you had something to show me."

He opened the drawer to the bureau. I took a step back.

"Please," he said, mildly annoyed. "I'm not going to hurt you. Haven't you realized that by now?" He carefully pulled out a rag doll.

The same doll with the button eyes and checkered dress that Tai Yow had given to Ha Oi the first time she stood by the pen and that Ha Oi carried everywhere she went.

"How did you get it?" I feared the worst.

"Someone who sweeps the sidewalk outside the Society's headquarters found it in the ash can. He knows me and brought it over. They must have taken the doll away from her. The one remembrance she had of her family, and they took it away.

"That's what you do when you really want to wipe out the past—when you really don't want someone to remember. And they say I'm vicious." He stared at the doll for a few moments and carefully propped her on the bureau, so she sat there, watching us.

"Now," he went on. "I have work to do. And that's where you come in. I need someone to keep a record of what happens next. And sometime in the future, I need them to write about it. Are you willing?"

"No."

My response threw him off. "Are you sure?"

"One hundred percent."

But he quickly regained his footing. "I could have gone to any other reporter in the city, but I chose you. Do you know why?"

"Because I'm the only chump who was willing to believe you?"

"No. Because you're the only chump who looks beyond the obvious."

Not a bad job of flattery, but I wasn't falling for it.

He looked up at the cuckoo clock. "It's getting late. I should have left already—"

"What are you going to do?" I pictured bullets flying across Fourth Avenue; Pisarra, Butts, the judges, and everyone who'd wronged Mock falling in a hail of gunfire. The Opera House Massacre all over again, this time on the streets of Manhattan.

"Not what you imagine."

"Why all the secrecy, then?"

"Some things just don't work when they're out in the open." He turned to leave and glanced over his shoulder. "So what's your decision?"

Chapter Twenty-Seven

I could tell you that I stood my ground and decided not to go. That I showed him he no longer had any power over me, that I could see through his maneuvers. That would have been the sensible course of action; I would have maintained my sense of dignity and pride—and been much the poorer for it.

Refusing him felt like I was cutting off my nose to spite my face. Instead, I would see what Mock had planned, pride and my husband's trust be damned. I'd figure out how to regain them later. And if I couldn't? I didn't have time to consider that possibility.

Mock was already out the door, and I had to make up my mind in a split second. Like a puppy in search of its master, I scampered to catch up with him.

An associate appeared from a side alley and joined us as we made our way down Doyers to Chatham Square, where he hailed a cab.

"Where are we going?" I asked.

Mock didn't reply but told the driver who pulled up. "Fourteenth Street."

We hopped in the back with the friend in the middle.

"What's on Fourteenth?" I said after a few minutes.

Silence. The associate stared ahead, and Mock looked out the window, hands loosely clasped in his lap, thumbs circling each other, round and round.

The cab pulled up in front of the Big Wigwam. That's what they called the actual Tammany Hall, or The Society of St. Tammany, or the Columbian Order, to give it its formal name. A chair-manufacturing concern stood to its left, and to the right, a player piano showroom played Strauss's Blue Danube.

Mock stepped out of the cab, waited while his friend paid the fare, and together, they walked toward the entrance.

"What business do you have here?" I asked urgently. "You've got to tell me. If you want me to write about it, I've got to know what it is."

"Patience, Mrs. Morley. Patience."

We entered beneath an ornamental cornice bearing the words "Tammany Society," the dates 1789 and 1867, and tucked beneath it, a massive statue of the Lenape chieftain, Tamanend, after whom the entire enterprise had been named.

Chief Tamanend, feathers sprouting from his head, cape swinging from his shoulders, bow in hand, also presided over the foyer. Carved beneath this second statue was the organization's motto: "Freedom Our Rock." Arrows pointed visitors to offices, a concert hall, club rooms, library, and other amenities.

I wondered what the chief would have made of his likeness being used to welcome hordes of newcomers to the island. It was probably just one of the many indignities and injustices heaped on him and his people.

A sentry, perplexed at the sight of the motley assortment of visitors, inquired who Mock had come to see.

"Charles F. Murphy."

I couldn't quite believe it. Did Mock hope to bribe or cajole Murphy to help his cause—did he still think there was some way to get Ha Oi back? As far as I was aware, even the mighty Tammany boss didn't possess that power.

The guard scratched his head. "He's expectin' you?"

"Yes," Mock replied coolly, he had an appointment.

The sentry waved us in. It seemed likely that he didn't recognize the highbinder; if he had, he probably wouldn't have allowed him through without an escort.

We walked past a row of glass-fronted display cases like those in newer school buildings. A series of maps charted the city's growth from a tiny outpost on the tip of Manhattan to a bustling port town to a mighty metropolis spanning five boroughs.

Leaflets advertised Tammany's activities: Reading and Writing Lessons—All Ages Welcome!, job training, citizenship classes, health and hygiene sessions, weekend picnics, and a Punch and Judy performance.

Portraits of Tammany-backed mayors followed the notices. The last one showed Georgie B. looking stern and serious; he had started out as a Tammany mayor, even though he eventually strayed from the fold.

Then came portraits of the chiefs, which stretched back to Aaron Burr and Martin Van Buren, but quickly gave way to a cast of more rough-and-tumble characters. There was the legendary Boss Tweed, who bought a quarry in Massachusetts in order to supply the city with marble for the construction of a new courthouse—at a hefty markup, of course. "Honest" John Kelly, who was anything but. Boss Croker, who had initiated Georgie B. into politics, and then—to avoid charges of wrongdoing—fled to his castle in Ireland. They say he was a scoundrel through and through, but a charming one. And finally, Silent Charlie, his face behind rimless glasses as smooth, cold, and unyielding as polished marble.

Murphy was a comparative unknown; he'd only become boss four or five years ago, in the aftermath of Croker's hasty departure. Silent Charlie kept his opinions to himself, played his cards close to his chest, and all the press really knew about him was that he put loyalty above all other considerations. His supporters joked that Murphy valued his privacy so highly that he wouldn't sing the national anthem out loud for fear of committing himself in public.

We climbed a flight of stairs. Made our way down a corridor. Diligent men in suits banged away at typewriters in one of the rooms; in another, fellows in rolled-up shirtsleeves printed pamphlets. In a third, a group of women studied home cookery while children played on the floor.

At the end of the hall, a discrete wooden panel no larger than any of the others bore Murphy's name chiseled in neat block letters. Mock's comrade knocked.

The clack of typewriter keys ceased. "Come in."

A motorized fan on the windowsill ruffled a secretary's mousey brown strands, which he tamped down as we entered. A glass paperweight in the shape of a clover held a sheaf of loose-leaf papers in place. The edges rustled in the breeze.

Mock introduced himself and told the secretary who he'd come to see.

The employee took in the black tunic and trousers. "May I inquire on what business?"

"I'll tell that to Mr. Murphy directly."

"I'm afraid the chief is busy at the moment. Did you make an appointment?"

"I was told he would see me this morning."

"By whom?"

"What?"

"Who told you he would see you?"

Mock paused. "A friend we have in common."

The secretary's eyes roved back and forth. "And with you are?" Unlike the mayor's shiny, attractive staff, he appeared to have been selected precisely for his drab, unexceptional appearance.

"Billy Wong," Mock said. "And a reporter from the *Observer.*"

"The chief don't care for reporters."

"Don't worry"—Mock took a seat on the bench opposite the functionary's desk—"neither do I."

Murphy's man wasn't amused. "Just a moment." The legs of his chair scraped against the floor. He pulled at the ends of his jacket, eyed us suspiciously as if we might pinch something in his absence, put his ear to the door of the adjacent chamber, and, apparently satisfied with what he had or hadn't heard, knocked.

If there was a reply, it was inaudible, but he waited before he entered and closed the door behind him with a firm click.

Mock didn't say a word. The seconds ticked by.

The secretary reemerged a minute or two later, closing the door after him. "I'm afraid you've been misinformed. The chief is busy all day and cannot see anyone."

"That's all right," Mock replied, unperturbed. "He'll have to come out sometime, won't he? We'll wait. Go ahead with your work. We won't disturb you." He crossed one foot over the other at the knee, leaned his head against the wall, and closed his eyes as though he was about to take a nap at a railway station.

Murphy's aide went red in the face and began to tremble. "There are no guarantees. When Mr. Murphy says he's busy—"

"Understood." Mock's tone shut him up.

The functionary reluctantly returned to his desk and, with a loud sniff of disapproval, scrolled a fresh page into his machine, lifted the paperweight, turned over a sheet of notes, and resumed typing. The cuffs of his shirt refused to cover his wrists. He kept tugging at them, and seconds later, they would slide back up beneath his jacket. Every now and then, he tossed a surreptitious glance at us. Arms crossed, Billy Wong kept watch by the door.

I sat at the far end of the bench. Mock's breathing slowed, and amazingly, he appeared to be asleep. He was able to switch himself off, seemingly at will.

The typewriter clacked, the fan whirred, perspiration prickled on my forehead and on the back of my neck, but despite the heat, not a bead of sweat moistened the highbinder's brow. I recalled a story my mother told me about a god who pretended to be mortal, but his inability to sweat and the fact that his feet were free of dust gave him away. Sometimes, being better than everyone else has its drawbacks.

I knew I was testing my luck by coming here. Possibly jeopardizing my marriage and everything else I'd built for myself in New York.

The secretary snapped. "Are you sure you wouldn't like to make an appointment? You could be here for hours. And even if Mr. Murphy does come out, he might decide—"

Mock slowly opened his eyes. "I'll be fine." He took a deep breath, linked his hands together, rested them on his stomach, and drifted off again.

A couple of men carrying folders entered and then exited the boss's chambers. They turned to Mock curiously but didn't say a word. I still couldn't figure out why Mock wanted to speak to Murphy, what that had to do with Ha Oi, or the book and newspaper lying on the bed, and whatever it was that he wanted me to write. Meanwhile, back at the office, Dupont must be wondering where I'd disappeared to. It didn't take over two hours to conduct a quick survey of the neighborhood.

A fellow from the Sanitation Department came through. He was followed by a contractor well known for failing to fix streets on the city's dime. Then a representative from the Bell Telephone Company. They all introduced themselves to Murphy's secretary in hushed voices.

The hands on the clock moved to half-past noon. Mock kept dozing.

I coughed. The highbinder opened an eye. "Still here?"

"Yes," I hissed, considering whether to leave. There was still time to salvage my dignity, my marriage, and my employment. And yet, after all this, I'd never forgive myself if I didn't uncover what Mock was here for.

At one o'clock sharp, a chipper delivery boy brought in packages and lunch for Murphy. The secretary paid, conveyed the necessary to his employer, and informed us that it was time for his own lunch and that visitors would have to wait outside until he returned.

Mock rubbed his eyes and yawned, rose leisurely, and scratched his stomach. We stepped into the corridor. His friend hurried off and reappeared a few minutes later carrying a chair.

"Want to sit?" The highbinder offered, but I declined. He lowered himself into the seat.

"You better give me something," I said, "or I'll be fired."

A stream of women, their children in tow, poured out of one of the meeting rooms. "Look Ma!" a little girl cried, pointing. "It's a Chinaman!"

"He looks familiar," someone else said.

"It ain't Mock Duck, is it?"

"No. That can't be him."

"It is, it is. I seen him in the papers."

"Pipe down." Embarrassed whispers. "He can hear us."

"Can he understand?"

"What's he doin'? Is he a friend o' Mr. Murphy?"

"Let's move it along. No need to dawdle," the man in charge instructed, even while he ogled the visitor.

Mock looked over at me. "You like your job?"

"Enough to mind if I lose it," I muttered. "Can I ask you a question? How did you know that I would join you?"

"I didn't… But I took a chance that you would, and you did." He changed the topic. "You know, I wanted to travel the world once."

"Like Hieun Tsang?"

A smile escaped him. "You heard about him?"

"He came to India."

"I wanted to be a monk myself, take a vow of silence, and leave the messiness behind."

"And why didn't you?" I couldn't tell whether he was pulling my leg.

"Oh, I was ready. And I would have, right after I came out of Bellevue. Being close to death puts life into perspective. I was planning to announce my decision at the banquet."

"But then you met Ha Oi."

"Exactly. She and her mother needed someone to look after them."

"Surely you don't look after everyone who needs your help."

"I don't."

"Why them, then?"

He exhaled deeply. "You want the truth?"

"I'd prefer it." With Mock you never knew what you were getting. I'd begun to suspect it was never outright lies; rather, something hazier.

"I have no idea. I simply don't. I just saw her running around, little braids flying, and changed my mind. And I've never regretted it. Not for a minute… What brought you to New York anyhow? Were you born here?"

I explained that I traveled to America when I was nineteen, accompanied by a missionary friend of my father's.

"They let you go so far away?" He looked shocked. "I don't allow Ha Oi to cross the street by herself."

"I was much older."

"Still." He shook his head in amazement. "Where are your parents now?"

I explained that they had passed away and that I had married an American.

He nodded. I thought our conversation was done and was surprised by how easy it had been to talk to him, but it turned out he was just getting started.

He asked about the duration of the journey from Bombay to New York, what the steamer was like, and about all the ports of call. I described my first-class cabin, my homesickness and sea sickness, and said that it had taken a month to sail from the Arabian Sea to the Red Sea, and then via the Suez Canal into the Mediterranean, and finally to England.

"First class? Your parents must have been rich."

"Not really. They thought that was the best way for me to travel since I was on my own."

We discussed the Suez Canal, how the boats inched through the passage, how the air was so still and the sun beat down so heavily that I doubted that I was even breathing.

"Look, Mock," I said eventually, "all this chitchat is well and good. But we've been here for hours, and I'm going to have to tell my editor something." I asked again why he needed to meet Murphy.

And again, he said that I would have to wait.

Billy Wong returned with two glasses of water. I hadn't eaten lunch and was starving, and I drank the glass he offered me greedily.

Mock wanted to know if it was usual for women from India to travel to the United States on their own. I told him about Anandibai and Ramabai. He was particularly fascinated by the young doctor. Despite being married at nine and only learning English in her teens, she possessed an almost preternatural sense of self-worth. When asked in an American questionnaire, *If not yourself, who would you like to be?* She had answered simply, *No one.*

"How do you know that?" Mock demanded.

I replied that I read it in a biography written by an American lady who also mentioned that one of Anandibai's classmates at the medical college was a young woman from Foochow.

"Foochow? Probably it's easier to go to that college from China than from Chinatown, don't you think?" He stared at the children's drawings pinned to one of the boards in the corridor. "I would have liked Ha Oi to become a doctor.... Maybe it's better this way... maybe she'll be able to do more in her new life."

A uniformed copper clutching two lads like puppies by their scruffs strode up to Murphy's door and knocked. There was no reply.

"Let's go, boys," he told his charges without loosening his grip. "You should be glad you missed the chief. Next time, you won't be so lucky." He noticed Mock and shot him a dirty look. "Don't want to end up like this one."

Mock watched the policeman retreat with his prisoners. "You know why boys like that make trouble? To prove to themselves that they still matter. They make noise not so much to bother others—although there is that—but to remind themselves that they're still alive."

His associate reappeared with a packet of nuts and passed them around. Mock tossed a couple of cashews into his mouth and chewed slowly. There was still no sign of Murphy's secretary.

"You miss your home?" Mock asked.

"Sometimes."

"You plan to go back?"

"Eventually."

"Will your husband go with you?"

"He says he will." That is, if he would even speak to me after what I had done.

"I know Ha Oi misses us. And she'll miss us today and tomorrow. For a month, six months, a year… But then we'll start to fade. And in four years or twenty-four years, with Chinatown gone and nothing left to remember us by, she won't even believe we existed."

"You can't know that." I wanted to reassure him but somewhere deep inside, I knew he was correct. There were things in my own past that I couldn't be sure had actually happened—and I hadn't been torn from my family at the age of six and taught to forget those years.

If and when Helen returned to Jefferson Park or Celestial Fields or whatever they decided to call it, there would be nothing left to remind her of her former home, her parents, and the life they had lived. Her past would be irretrievably gone.

Murphy's secretary returned, keys jangling from a bunch at his waist.

"Still here? You really don't give up, do you?" He fingered the right one and unlocked the door.

Mock rose to his feet and stretched his shoulders. He looked at me intently. "So, you're with me?"

This time, it was I who didn't answer.

We took up our former places—him on one end of the bench, me at the other, Billy Wong by the door.

The secretary scowled, turned the fan back on, and resumed his never-ending typing. What was he composing over there, the next installment of *War and Peace*? I wanted to inquire but held my tongue.

The typewriter barrel flew back and forth. The clock on the wall kept ticking. Mock's eyes closed again. He didn't appear to be sleeping now, just lost in his own thoughts.

I thought how easy it was to talk to him. How effortless and comfortable, as though he understood me and my experiences. And he didn't ask questions that got my back up.

It's one thing not to know about the world; it's quite another to ask strangers about themselves and their homelands in a way that betrays the questioner's prejudices and small-mindedness. Even soft-spoken Dr. Anandi, when asked whether it was the custom for desperate Hindu mothers to drown their babies in the Ganges, replied with asperity that it was about as true as if she inferred that it was the custom of American mothers to commit infanticide based on the number of abandoned and murdered babies that came across her dissecting table.

The only other person in New York to whom I could speak so freely, without censoring myself, or worrying how I would sound or where my thoughts would lead (apart from Dupont, with whom I mainly discussed work) was my husband.

And as for Mock's observation that it would be easier to study medicine as a foreigner from China than as a resident of Chinatown, he probably was correct about that too. The student from Foochow had come to America of her own free will; she must have had financial means and status, while a girl from Chinatown would be assumed to possess none of that. She would be assumed to be one of a despised class.

Or, as I had learned from my own experience, a few of anything could be tolerated and sometimes, might even seem desirable. Too much could cause panic. I was able to get by and mix in polite society because I was well off, well educated, and fluent in English. The only other Indians I knew of in New York were travelers, businessmen, and students, as well as some Bengali lascars who'd married Black and Mexican women and settled in Harlem. But if thousands of my countrymen arrived in the city without a penny in their pockets and settled together in a tight-knit group with their clan loyalties, their squabbles and desires—that would be different. The enclave would become its own territory with its own rules and customs. It would become threatening.

It would become Chinatown.

The bell on the secretary's desk rang. Mock's eyes flew open.

Murphy's aide sprang to his feet, and seconds later, a broad, hefty figure filled the doorway. Sun streamed through the window at the rear, casting a shadow across the chief's face, but his silhouette was brightened by an otherworldly glow.

"Mr. Duck, Mr. Murphy will see you now—" the secretary began.

Mock was already there. I made a move to follow, but the functionary blocked my path. "No reporters allowed."

And without so much as an apologetic look or a backward glance, Mock Duck entered the boss's chambers.

Chapter Twenty-Eight

It took all my willpower not to scream in frustration. Mock had done it again; he knew exactly how to manipulate people, and he'd played me like a sitar.

I stood by the door, trying to listen. The secretary ordered me to step away.

Everything began to grate: the hum of the fan, the gurgle as Murphy's peon cleared his throat, the incessant clack of the typewriter.

I was a fool, more than a fool to come here—because I knew better. And as for Dupont, he'd give me the boot. Gone all day with nothing to show for my time? I might as well hand in my resignation.

Five, ten, then twenty minutes passed. I could barely contain myself. Every now and then, I thought I heard a few words. *Make him choose... One or the other...* And something about an agenda.

Finally, the door opened, and Mock walked out, slightly flustered but satisfied. "Let's go," he ordered. And when I opened my mouth— "No questions now."

He strode swiftly down the hallway, down the stairs. Past the photographs of the bosses and the city, past the statue of Chief Tamanend, and onto the sidewalk.

"Here's the thing," he said before I had a chance to speak again. "Charlie Murphy wants me to keep my lips sealed. He doesn't want me telling anyone."

I stared at him in disbelief.

"You made me wait...all day...for nothing?"

"Look—"

"You knew he wouldn't allow a reporter in. Yet, you wanted me there."

"I wanted you to *see*," he said.

"See *what*?" I was yelling. "Will you stop talking in riddles?"

Traffic flowed by, honking and rattling. The player piano showroom belted out some hideous jingle.

"I know you can do it. I know you can piece it together… just like you did with Webster." He hopped into a cab that Billy hailed, and the two of them drove off.

* * *

"What in god's name is the matter with you?" Dupont took the trouble to stand up behind his desk. He leaned forward, palms resting on the paper-strewn surface, and bellowed, "You're skating on thin ice, Mrs. Morley. This is a business, not some charitable organization. We have stories to write and bills to pay, or haven't you noticed? I don't know what took you the entire goddamn day, and I don't want to know. All I will say is that I expect a treatise from you tomorrow, and it better be good. More than good, it better be the best damn thing I've read. Do you hear me?"

Looking neither left nor right, I put on my hat and slunk out, certain that the lads were exulting over my comeuppance. When I passed Shrimpy, he whispered, "Hey, Mrs. M., did you hear? They arrested two fellows for the Opera House Massacre. A fellow called Yee Toy and another guy they call the Scientific Killer. Nothing to do with Mock. Both men said they planned it on their own."

I whispered back a thanks and continued on out. All right, so Mock had been telling the truth for once, but it hardly seemed to matter. I was a victim of my own curiosity and over-confidence. I thought I would be able to manage the highbinder, but he had managed me from start to finish.

I began the long walk home. It took about forty-five minutes. Usually, I enjoyed watching the city as it transitioned from day to evening, but that day, I was just avoiding getting back home. Everyone, from the shabbiest street urchin to self-important businessmen, seemed happier, more content, and more sensible than me. They knew where their responsibilities lay and they fulfilled them. They didn't go off on whims, following any old tangents and strangers' commands. My father would say, *Don't get carried away. Follow the right path, Archana.* What right path? No one gave me a map.

I spent the first twenty minutes or so feeling sorry for myself, then I tried to concentrate and focus on the issue at hand.

Piece it together, Mock said. *Just like you did with Webster.* That meant, first of all, that I had been correct. Mock knew the engineer's son and had been working on him from at least the day of the Board of Improvement hearing, if not sooner. And it was he, perhaps via Webster Jr., who convinced the engineer to declare that the streams constituted a challenge.

Mock planned his moves several steps in advance, like an expert chess player. And now he was playing another game, this time with Charlie Murphy as a partner. I was supposed to figure out what his moves meant, where he was headed, but how could I do that if I didn't know what his final goal was?

I assumed it must have something to do with his daughter, but since I didn't see any way he could get her back, it had to be something else, a quest for revenge, most likely, and in that case, the questions were: against whom, and how?

* * *

For once, Clément served something close to a masterpiece for dinner. She'd bought fresh spices from the market and managed to prepare a flavorful curry laden with an assortment of vegetables.

I came into the dining room in my slippers. Even after all these years, I hated tight-fitting footwear, and one of the first things I did when I came home was take my shoes off. Clément had been shocked when she first started to work for us, but she soon got used to it.

Dr. Morley was in a good mood. Milk pasteurization was looking like it would happen, and other initiatives that he'd proposed for the benefit of the public's health were being given serious consideration. But the best news of all was that the groundbreaking in the Catskills was set to proceed in a few days. He had feared that, for some reason or other, it would be postponed. That's what seemed to happen to most worthwhile initiatives.

"Think about it, Archie," he said, his eyes sparkling. "Once the entire population of this city, and especially the poor—the ones who suffer most from diseases like cholera, polio, dysentery, and typhus—can drink clean water from their taps for the cost of pennies, then in a single stroke we will have done away with so many of our problems, so much unnecessary suffering. Babies, mothers, the elderly…they need clean water desperately. Clean water and clean air, in the long run, that's what will enable our city to thrive."

He took a bite of his dinner. "This isn't bad at all."

I served myself some curry and rice. It was time to be honest about what had happened that day. He listened in silence. Then all he said was, "I'm disappointed in you, Archie. You're playing with fire. And I fear…that we'll both go up in flames."

* * *

Sounds of the city kept me awake: the roar of motors, clop of hooves, a couple arguing, and then a drunk singing and a crash as he fell over an ashcan. Dr. Morley was immune to those kinds of disturbances; his solid form rose and fell with every breath as I lay there, unmoving in the darkness, thoughts churning. Finally, I slid from beneath the covers, slipped on a robe, crept down the stairs, unlocked the front door, and sat on the front step. A breeze rustled the trees and provided some respite from the heat while the electric streetlamps bathed the leaves in a ghostly glow. None of my neighbors' lights were on. On my own and in the open, I could think more clearly.

Why had Mock made me accompany him to Tammany Hall? He'd known that Murphy wouldn't allow a reporter inside, so why go through the rigamarole of having his wife and maid fetch me? He wanted me to be present despite Murphy's restrictions. Why? So that I was aware that something was going on regardless of whether or not I could be privy to the details?

What had I heard from the room? *Make him choose...* make who chose? And something about an agenda.

The only agenda I could think of, apart from Mock or Murphy's personal agenda, was the agenda of the Board of Estimate. It was always published in advance, and the Board, which consisted of the five borough presidents, the city's comptroller, the president of the Board of Aldermen, and the mayor, followed it to the letter. They would meet in three days to approve Webster's drawings, among a host of other proposals, and they would vote, as they always did, in unison. None of them had any reason to oppose the Chinatown plan. Moreover, Chinatown's fate had nothing to do with what would happen to Ha Oi....

I stared into the darkness. Nothing made sense.

* * *

Dr. Morley didn't say much over breakfast. Just drank his coffee, ate his eggs and toast, read the *Journal* from front to back in silence, and left for work. I finished my tea, dressed in my uniform, and set off for Foley Square. When all hope is lost, only one alternative remains: consult an oracle.

I felt sure that the peanut gallery would be buzzing about Mock and Murphy's meeting. And that Plunkitt would have something to say about it as well—if not directly, then in his oblique, read-between-the-lines way. Mock had spent all day at the wigwam, had been seen by a copper, the fellow from Sanitation, not to mention Murphy's secretary and the guard out front. But from the moment I arrived, the piazza was strangely quiet. In fact, there wasn't so much as a peep or a whisper or a whimper about the Tammany and tong leader's meeting. And in and of itself, that felt suspicious.

Looking sharp in a green waistcoat and black top hat, the bard hefted himself onto his crate.

He glanced at his scribe, the faithful Will Riordan, who had his traveling desk open and pen poised, then he checked the time and cleared his throat. "With a heavy heart," Plunkitt said, "I must discuss a serious matter today."

This was it. The skin on the back of my neck prickled.

"I must discuss a matter of great import to this city," he went on, "and to the republic at large: Ingratitude. 'Ingratitude?' you say. 'Plunkitt, that's hardly a topic worthy of your attention.' I reply, 'hold your judgment.'

"There is no crime so mean as ingratitude in politics. But every great man from the beginnin' of the world has been up against it. Caesar had his Brutus, that king of Shakespeare's—Leary, I think you call him"—scattered chuckles—"had his daughters go back on him. Let me tell you: It's real proof that a man is great when he meets with political ingratitude. But the ingrate in politics never flourishes for long."

He must be referring to someone.

"The politicians who make a lastin' success are the ones who are always loyal to their friends—even up to the gates of the state prison!" Plunkitt went on. "Boss Croker"—Georgie B.'s mentor—"used to say that tellin' the truth and stickin' to his friends was the political leader's stock in trade. Nobody ever said anything truer, and nobody lived up to it better than Croker. That's why he remained the leader of Tammany Hall as long as he wanted. It's the same with Charles F. Murphy."

It was the first time that day I'd heard the boss's name mentioned.

"Murphy has always stood by his friends even when it looked like he would be downed for doin' so. Remember how he stuck to McClellan in 1903 when all the Brooklyn leaders were against him, and it seemed as if Tammany was in for a grand smash-up?! It's men like Croker and Murphy that stay leaders as long as they live, not backstabbers like Brutus."

Of course, he was talking about McClellan! And I began to wonder… could Mock and Murphy be banding together to take down the mayor? From Tammany's perspective, he was nothing if not a backstabber, who was leaving his friends in the lurch.

"Now I want to tell you why political traitors, in New York City especially, are punished quick. It's because the Irish are in the majority. The Irish, above all people in the world, hate a traitor. You can't hold 'em back when a traitor of any kind is in sight, and, rememberin' old Ireland, they take particular delight in doin' him up."

Hollering and foot stamping. Murphy would enjoy nothing more than to see Georgie B. fall. And Mock too, I thought, recalling how the mayor stood opposite No. 10 and announced that he'd forced Webster to recant. It wouldn't bring Ha Oi back, but it would show the world that Mock wasn't a man to be crossed lightly, and maybe it would serve as a balm to distract from his loss.

I approached the bard as soon as he finished. Will Riordan was blotting his notes, and Plunkitt stood with his back to me, combing his mustaches while he checked his reflection in a hand-held mirror. I told him that I was a great admirer of his talks.

"Most kind." He continued his grooming, curling the tips of his whiskers just so. "We'll be publishing my sermons in a single volume for the edification of the public. I hope you will purchase a copy. That's why I employ young Will to take dictation."

"I certainly will, Mr. Plunkitt." I asked whether I might speak to him about a different matter. Still with his back to me, he indicated that I should continue.

Had he heard anything about Mock Duck's meeting with Charlie Murphy yesterday, I asked.

His shoulders stiffened. "Mock Duck and Mr. Murphy?" he said after a second. "The Hip Sing Tong and Tammany? You must be mistaken. What could they possibly have to say to each other?" The bard slid his comb into his jacket pocket and turned to his scribe. "Have you heard anything along those lines, Will?"

The scribe shook his head. "No, sir."

"You see? Will hasn't heard anything either."

I cast about, trying to figure out how to breach the wall of silence, and remembered Shrimpy telling me that Mock had been spotted at Foley Square talking to Plunkitt himself in the week after his daughter was taken.

I suggested as much to the Tammany man. "Does that ring a bell?"

He didn't reply immediately and then, with more force than was strictly necessary, belted out a single word: "Preposterous!"

* * *

"What do you have for me, Mrs. Morley? What do you have?" Dupont looked up from his papers.

The truth was that apart from the description of the district that I'd handed in the previous day, I had nothing.

"Let me make something clear," the editor continued. "I took you on when no one else would have you. I've kept you here over the lads' objections. At one point, our esteemed publisher even intimated that I may have lost my judgment—lost my fucking mind, as he so eloquently put it—but I defended myself—and you, no thanks needed—by insisting that you were reliable, that you didn't refuse assignments, and that you worked harder than the rest of these lumps." He raised his voice so that the lumps could hear.

"But you disappear, you give me nothing—"

"Mock Duck went to Tammany Hall to speak to Charlie Murphy."

That got his attention. "What?"

"That's what Mock did yesterday. And that's what I was doing yesterday. I was with him."

"You're joking. I heard something of the sort—that he was at the wigwam with a reporter, but I didn't believe it. And I certainly didn't think the reporter was you."

I assured him he'd heard correctly.

"Well, don't keep me in suspense. This could be the story of a lifetime! 'Tong Boss Meets Tammany Boss.' What are they plotting?"

"That's what I'd like to know." I told him I wasn't allowed in the room, but that I saw Mock go in, and the two men must have spoken for at least twenty minutes.

"And you kept this from me for twenty-four hours? Are you a fool, Mrs. M.? Tell me everything."

I did. It wasn't much.

"So we don't know what they talked about, and we don't know why." Dupont exhaled loudly.

"That's right." I told him I suspected it might have something to do with the mayor and explained my reasons.

"All right. All right." He drummed his fingers on the desk. "Well, what are you waiting for? Go find out what they're up to, and make it quick, before someone else scoops us."

* * *

The prospect of eviction hadn't yet turned Pell, Mott, and Doyers into the Main Street in the Mountains, but they were headed in the same direction. In just one day, the streets looked emptier, the shops looked vacant, there were paint markings everywhere, and the district felt drained of hope.

"William," I called to Tom Lee's grandnephew, who skulked along, dragging his satchel behind him.

He came over, presenting a brave face but with red, puffy eyes.

"What's the matter?"

The boy shrugged his bony shoulders.

"You're upset about what's going to happen and that your friends are leaving?"

The childish face crumpled. "It's all my fault."

"That's not true."

He didn't reply.

"Are you thinking about the day the mayor's wife came to visit your school? Were you one of the children who tried to convince her not to tear down the neighborhood? There's nothing any of you could have done to change the course of events. The mayor had already made up his mind."

"That's not it," William said. He wanted Ha Oi to get taken so that it would teach Mock Duck a lesson, after what he had done to William's pa and great-uncle Tom. "And then she did get taken." The words tumbled out. "And then all this happened. It's my fault."

I patted him awkwardly on the shoulder, crouched down, and tried to explain that wishing for something to be true and actually taking steps to make it come true were completely different. It was normal for Willian to want to punish Mock after what he had done to his family.

Then a doubt stole over me. "You only wished it, William—am I correct?" He nodded.

"You didn't do anything… like write a letter to the Gerry Society, for example?"

He shook his head no.

But I couldn't stop. "Maybe you thought you were helping your uncle?"

"I said no!" He flashed me a wild stare and ran off.

Even though I wanted to believe him, part of me couldn't. He was a young boy who'd seen more than his fair share of horrors.… Then again, what was the matter with me? Had things gotten so desperate that I needed to accuse a child?

I traveled down Doyers toward Chatham. That crooked, narrow street was like a funnel, sucking me in. I came to No. 10. Someone had taken down Mr. Woo's photography shingle.

Had Mock's friends really blinded the photographer—or had he been punished by thugs to whom he was in debt, and Mrs. Woo cooked up the story about the letter to save face?

Was it even true that she and her daughters had been witnesses? I hoped not.

The trouble was, I suspected I would never really know. There was so much going on here that I could only guess at.

Across the street, the doors to the Opera House were locked and bolted once more. I pictured that unforgettable scene: benches tumbled helter-skelter, backdrop punctured with holes, bodies littering the floor. The place had barely reopened, only to be shut down again. Shrimpy had a piece about it this morning—how the two perpetrators had confessed.

"Come to pay your final respects, then?" The Corsair looked up from his whittling.

"Mind if I join you?"

"Sure." He pulled up another crate. "No need to look so distressed. Nothing lasts forever. We can only be certain of two things: change…and kicking the bucket."

"Now, you've become a philosopher." I managed a laugh.

"Well, I plan to remain here, park or no park, and dispense my pearls to whoever will listen."

"You'll tell Chinatown stories?"

"Whichever stories pay the bills."

I asked if he'd heard anything about the Woos.

"Just that Mr. Woo will never see again. Whatever got into his eyes burned right through them. The girls have been sent to New Jersey to live with their aunt, and Mrs. Woo came by last night to pack their things."

That explained the shingle.

"Did you hear rumors that Mock's friends might be behind it?"

"Behind what happened to Henry Woo? No, no. That was an accident.… Shit." The Corsair nicked himself with the whittling knife and sucked his finger. "So what's next for you?"

"I'm trying to figure out what Mock Duck and Murphy are up to."

"Weren't you there?" He must have seen me get into the cab with Mock and then heard about the rest.

"You think they let me join them?"

"You have a point."

"My guess is that they're gunning for McClellan," I said. "They probably want to bring him down a peg or two."

"I wouldn't complain about that. Mr. Hoity-Toity No-More-Goddamn-Chinatown deserves it. What's the latest on Hizzoner, anyhow?"

I replied that the mayor was headed to the mountains for the groundbreaking. I pictured the journey up the Hudson, the broad river with its strong currents, the winding road, blazing sun, armies of workers at the ready with shovels and pickaxes…no police.…

A growing sense of dread filled me. I stared at the lobbygow.

That was it.

Far from his usual stomping grounds, there was no better place to teach Georgie B. a lesson than on his trip outside the city.

Chapter Twenty-Nine

<u>BOARD OF WATER SUPPLY OF THE CITY OF NEW YORK</u>
Order of the Day.
Thursday, June Twentieth. Nineteen Hundred and Seven.
9:00 Steamer "Albany" leaves Pier A, Battery, North River
12:00 Luncheon on the Steamer
1:00 Conveyances leave Cold Spring for Place of Ceremonies
1:30 Exercises
* * *

PROGRAM
Star Spangled Banner....B.W.S. Glee Club
Welcome and Address....Hon. J. Edward Simmons, Commissioner of the Board of Water Supply.
Presentation of Spade....Hon. Charles N. Chadwick, Commissioner of the Board of Water Supply
Address and Turning of First Sod....Hon. George B. McClellan, Mayor of the City of New York
Benediction Praye....Rev. M.J. Lavelle, Vicar General of the Diocese of New York
* * *

3:00 Steamer leaves for Storm King Crossing
6:30 Due at Pier A, Battery, North River

D r. Morley and I climbed into the cab that would take us to the pier. I studied the card that detailed the order of events, trying to predict the best moment to try something underhanded. An incident on the steamer, an accident on the drive, or perhaps something more subtle during the mayor's address and turning of first sod?

The previous day, I had returned to the *Observer* after my conversation with the Corsair and shared my suspicions with Dupont. I told him I thought Mock or Murphy's men might get up to something in the Catskills.

The editor liked the sound of it. He seemed to relish the possibility of danger and wanted to send one of the lads in my stead, but I insisted that I'd be able to get to the bottom of things, and that as a guest of the mayor, I could move about freely, while other reporters who wanted to attend would have to make their own way there and be herded into a separate enclosure.

"I should send two of you," he said.

But I persuaded him that wouldn't be necessary. Having another reporter from the *Observer* there would only slow me down. He didn't appear entirely convinced but eventually relented.

After some internal back-and-forth, I also shared my fears with my husband. He'd been aloof when we started dinner but softened as the meal progressed. I said my piece while he sipped his port.

"What do you envision, Archie?" He put down his glass. "Someone pushing Hizzoner overboard? His car malfunctioning in the mountains? I don't mean to seem dismissive, but it sounds a bit absurd."

"When you put it like that, it does."

But after a few minutes, my worries resurfaced. I asked him to call the mayor's office and urge Georgie B.'s aides to be cautious. He grumbled that I shouldn't have been in a position to suspect any of this in the first place.

"And if something happens, you'll be glad I was."

We arrived at the pier at a quarter to nine. Although Dr. Morley did eventually make the call, I saw no sign of extra security. However, smartly attired staff checked invitation cards as they greeted guests at the head of the gangplank. Key figures in municipal government milled about the deck, as well as others involved in the heroic project since its inception—lawmakers, engineers, architects, advocates and experts. Three hundred and sixty in all.

Dr. Darlington, the Health Commissioner with matinee-idol looks, waved to my husband. Dr. Morley introduced us, and the commissioner held out his hand. "Mrs. Morley. A pleasure."

I'd worn a skirt and jacket with a hat, its light veil pulled back for the occasion, and I briefly shook his outstretched hand with my gloved one.

"Dr. Morley tells me you're from Bombay?"

I said I was.

"I'd love to visit someday. Do a tour of India and the East Indies. Trek in the Himalayas for a few weeks. Have you been, Morley? You must go."

More pleasantries followed, then he inquired whether he could borrow my husband for a few minutes. I slipped away, skirting round the edge of the crowds and bent over the rails. The water was calm, unlike my thoughts. I scrutinized the waiters serving cups of tea and coffee to the assembled dignitaries. I scanned the shore, half expecting a horde of Tammany hooligans to storm the vessel or some suspicious types to sneak onboard via a rope ladder. But neither occurred. I felt both foolish and yet unable to give up my vigilance.

Trumpets sounded a fanfare to announce the McClellans' arrival. Smiling and waving, they greeted their guests, who applauded as the perfect couple ascended the gangplank. He radiated energy, courage, and confidence; she glided along silently beside him, a pillar of strength and discretion. One day, their likenesses would be emblazoned on postcards—The Hon. George B. McClellan and Mrs. Georgiana McClellan, President and First Lady of these United States.

A mere six years ago, President McKinley hadn't survived an assassin's bullet. Maybe someone would gun down the mayor, and they would claim it was another anarchist.

I scrutinized the waiters again for any sign of suspicious behavior. There was one who seemed shifty; he approached the McClellans, reached his hand into his pocket, as they were quite unaware— "No," I cried, and dropped my glass.

The waiter rushed over, pulled a small towel from his pocket, and wiped up the mess. I apologized. Something had startled me, I said. I didn't know what.

Georgiana McClellan looked over and mouthed the words, "Are you all right?"

My husband came to check on me. "You're skittish. Don't worry so much. Everything will be fine."

I smiled, breathed. I couldn't allow myself to embarrass him in front of his colleagues.

A crew of tugboats sprayed a celebratory shower from their nozzles, and the droplets sparkled like diamonds suspended in the air for an instant. With a deep toot, the steamer pulled away from the dock.

The vast expanse of the Hudson glittered under the sun, and a mass of green hugged the palisades of New Jersey. The deck buzzed with a sense of unfettered optimism, anticipation, and excitement. We were about to witness the birth of a once-in-a-lifetime enterprise, one that would benefit New York City in perpetuity, one that had been achieved with no shortage of blood, sweat, and effort. And I was still anxious.

A warm wind blew across the back of my neck, and I held on to my hat. Dr. Darlington led my husband around, and Dr. Morley shook hands with practiced ease, speaking with conviction when required and bending forward to listen attentively. He was in his element.

A waiter passed around cookies, but I couldn't eat. Georgie B. chatted with well-wishers, pressing palms, recalling the many misadventures that had finally brought him to this momentous day. "But," he added with a smile, "it's not over until it's done."

Indeed, I thought, as I wiped the perspiration from my face with a handkerchief.

"Do you anticipate any complications?" someone asked.

The mayor's upbeat demeanor didn't vary for an instant. If anything, he exuded even more confidence as he replied, "If I constantly worried about everything that might go wrong, I would never be able to put a foot forward. So I prefer to look toward the future, to the great things we can accomplish when we work toward our goals without fear or favor. As my father taught me, generals lead from the front!"

"Hear, hear!" His listeners applauded.

Georgiana McClellan came over, all graciousness and smiles. I congratulated her on her husband's success.

She accepted the compliment modestly. "I hear you've been sounding alarm bells. The mayor and I do appreciate your concern." Her smile hardened even as her hand rested like a butterfly on my arm. "But let me assure you that no harm will ever come to my husband. Not while I stand beside him."

I didn't appreciate her tone. "Well then," I replied sweetly, "we have nothing to worry about."

"I did hear some rather surprising news, however—that Mock Duck was at Tammany Hall the other day. And that he spoke to Mr. Murphy at some length, and he brought along a reporter.… That wouldn't happen to have been you, would it?"

All of a sudden, the sun's glare became overpowering. I couldn't think how to answer.

"Are you all right, Mrs. Morley? You look a bit unwell."

"It's being on the river. I should sit down."

"Oh yes, do find yourself a seat in the shade." She offered to help me, but I insisted she join her other guests.

I found a seat and caught my breath. It was one thing to risk my own reputation, but I didn't want to jeopardize things for my husband. This was his world, he was part of it, and he deserved every success he could get.

He joined me a few minutes later. "Enjoying yourself?"

I assured him I was.

"And don't worry about Georgie B. He knows how to take care of himself."

We passed towns and houses dotting the river and pointed out the school that he and Georgie B. had attended, as well as Washington Irving's home, nestled amongst trees right behind the railway tracks. Dr. Fischer, an American missionary and my father's friend, had loaned me copies of *Rip Van Winkle* and *The Legend of Sleepy Hollow* and I had read both in a single gulp. They contributed to my vision of America as an untamed land, full of unusual characters.

A lunch of sandwiches and fruit was served at noon. I began to relax. By the time we arrived at Cold Spring, I wondered whether my fears were unfounded and whether I'd misjudged the tong and Tammany leaders' plans. But the trip wasn't even halfway over.

We climbed into waiting automobiles and carriages, which jolted us to our destination—the valley of Indian Brook, three miles inland. Dr. Morley and I were seated with a Board of Water Supply commissioner and a businessman. The McClellans led the convoy in a motorcar up front.

We passed the army of laborers, their tents assembled in orderly rows. Some of the men raised their hats and cheered in foreign tongues as the mayor's entourage waved from their car windows. Someone could hurl a rock… someone could fire a pistol.

"Most of the fellows are new to the country and don't speak a lick of English," the commissioner said as we rattled along. "I've been telling Hizzoner that we must find a way to maintain peace in the mountains—not that we've had any troubles yet. He says first things first. If we try to iron out every wrinkle beforehand, we'd still be doing the laundry."

The businessman chuckled. "Wise man, our mayor."

A cart of Irish workmen pulled up alongside aside our vehicle. They wore liberty cap badges pinned to their chests and passed a bottle amongst themselves.

"Rowdy bunch," the commissioner said. "Wonder where they're off to."

"Are they Tammany men?" Dr. Morley looked out the window. "Have you hired them?"

The commissioner craned his neck to get a better view. "I thought we hadn't, but we must have. There are three more cartloads right behind us."

"I don't like the look of them," Dr. Morley said.

"Our foreman will sort it out," the commissioner replied. "Frasier can handle anyone."

Dr. Morley glanced at me. I looked ahead but squeezed his hand. There were plenty of officials here; if something were to go off course, they would take care of it. Or so I hoped. I didn't see what else I could have done.

Troops of engineers, foremen, and laborers had gathered at the "Place of Ceremonies"—the first parcel of land to be acquired for the project. Dark-eyed men, some white, others black, some with caps on their heads, others with caps in hand, silently observed us as we took our seats. And to one side, stretching as far as the eye could see—horses, heavy machinery, a mountain of shovels, and crate upon crate of dynamite carelessly covered with sheets of tarpaulin. Enough to blow us all to kingdom come.

The mountains closed in.

"I don't think it's safe," I whispered to my husband.

"You've said your piece. There's nothing we can do now."

The program began. We stood at attention for the Board of Water Supply Glee Club's rousing rendition of "The Star-Spangled Banner." Georgiana McClellan reached into her purse and pressed a handkerchief to her lips. George B. McClellan pressed his right hand to his heart.

Whatever was going to happen, I wanted it to be over fast.

A shot went off. My heart leaped from my chest. Dr. Morley and I exchanged glances. An aide whispered in one of the dignitary's ears. The dignitary nodded. Apparently no cause for alarm. The program continued.

The Honorable J. Edwards Simmons delivered his welcome address, comparing the heroic undertaking to timeless construction works carried out by the civilizations of Rome, Babylon, and Egypt. Then the Honorable Charles N. Chadwick presented the mayor with a silver shovel especially forged for the occasion by Tiffany & Co.

A low rumble began as Hizzoner stepped forward to accept the gift—I braced myself—and a thunderous blast ripped through the mountains. The force was so great that the benches and dais shook, and a couple of precariously seated attendees stumbled. Everyone looked about anxiously.

Another blast followed the first. It was just as strong, but this time, we were prepared. Then, a third. The roar pummeled my ears.

Georgie B. raised his hand and asked for calm while an aide rushed off to make inquiries.

"I'll be back," I told Dr. Morley.

"Where are you going? Don't be silly, Archie."

"Wait for me. I won't be long." Suddenly, I was hit by the full force of what he meant to me—but now was not the time.

I moved as quickly and unobtrusively as I could to the staging area some distance behind the dais where the construction equipment and dynamite had been stored. Attendees couldn't see it because a backdrop with the words *Catskills Reservoir and Aqueduct* obscured their view.

The Irish contingent had gathered there, and one, who appeared to be the ringleader, was in the midst of a heated argument with another fellow I took to be the project foreman. The Irish worker had his mug right up against the foreman's, and his mates crowded around holding shovels, crowbars, and pickaxes. Angry words were exchanged. I remained off to the side and in the shadows.

From the dais, the commissioner addressed the guests. "Our mayor leaves no detail to chance. He will be right back in a few minutes."

Moments later, Georgie B. strode toward the group.

I wanted to yell at him to be careful but could only watch as the Tammany ringleader went up to Hizzoner and spoke with some heat. A few words floated in my direction.

Choose...one or the other... Words I'd heard spoken before—in the Tammany boss's chambers.

Georgie B. went pale. His hand scrunched into a fist, and he looked ready to wallop the guy.

The Irishman kept talking while the mayor, fists clenched, stared at the mountains as though they held some deep, dark secret. Maybe he understood the full implications of what he was facing, or maybe he was in shock and desperately thinking how best to respond.

The foreman tried to intervene, but Hizzoner had made up his mind. He spoke a few strong, sharp words to the Irish laborer and strode back to the dais.

In retrospect, his forced smile when he announced that the blasts were just some locals mishandling fireworks and that the situation had been resolved, seemed understandable. His wife's brow creased with worry, but ever the statesman, the general's son gathered himself and addressed the crowd.

"Why do four million Americans who comprise the greatest municipality of the New World contribute without protest all the treasure required for this gigantic enterprise? The answer comes spontaneously to our lips. It has been demanded and ordered by the people for the people.

"When I first came to office on January first, 1904, I found myself confronted with a possible water famine in our city and nothing practical done for its avoidance.

"The imminence of the peril was appreciated by the few who had studied the matter, but the public at large did not understand its seriousness, nor was there any public sentiment in favor of its speedy solution."

The mayor no longer betrayed any distress. He continued as though whatever had gone on back there, whatever conversation he had entered into, hadn't affected him in the slightest.

He enumerated the steps taken by his administration to facilitate the construction of the reservoir and aqueduct. The laws passed, the patient and painstaking process of bringing together government officials, politicians, engineers, and businessmen and reaching a consensus. The health benefits that clean water would bring to every citizen of New York.

My husband and several others rose to their feet and cheered wildly.

"As the years merge into decades," Hizzoner continued, "and the decades into centuries, when time has thrown its kindly veil over the bickerings and the differences and the quarrels which seem so much to us and after all are so futile and so petty"—he glanced around meaningfully—"when friend and enemy, when traducer and traduced have passed away, when our very names have been forgotten, when this great work, conceived in honesty and completed, God willing, in honesty, shall be administering to the health and happiness of millions yet to come, then God grant that those who shall see it may say, 'It does not matter how they were called to do this thing, or who they were, or what they were, it is enough that they did their duty.'"

Hats flew into the air. The crowd rose to its feet and huzzahed. The laborers' band burst into a song to the tune of "Auld Lang Syne":

"Our young mayor shall ne'er be forgot

Who put our project through

Who knew the unwashed city's need

And gives us work to do.

There'll be much drink, there'll be much wash

For New York's family;
So take a cup and drink it up
To the health of Georgie B."
The mayor stepped inside the cordoned-off enclosure. Photographers trained their lenses as he bent, and a flurry of flashbulbs went off as he pierced his shovel into the soft, dark earth and cut out a neat square of sod. Then he straightened and declared: "Now, I, the mayor, in the name of the people of New York, declare this work begun!" And he surveyed the scene with as much pride as a general with his troops before they charged off into battle.

Chapter Thirty

The journey back to Manhattan was more subdued. And if the mayor had lost a little of his vim, if his smile had lost some of its luster, one could chalk it up to fatigue and the natural letdown after the culmination of a hard-won accomplishment.

Dr. Morley and I sat side by side on the steamer, our chairs pushed close together. I apologized for keeping things from him and putting my work first. I had a feeling, I said, that I would be wrapping up soon at the paper. Or at least, stepping back. He wouldn't get far in his career if mine drew too much attention.

"That occurred to me, too," he replied. "But let's not make any rash decisions."

We hailed a cab at the pier. I dropped him off on Eighteenth Street and continued to the *Observer.*

"Anything happen?" Dupont was still at his desk and all agog.

"Don't you ever go home?" Apart from Shrimpy, who was always first in and last out, there were just the two us.

"You know what they say—you have to sleep on newsprint and eat ink to succeed in this business."

I filled him in on what I'd witnessed and the "mishandled fireworks."

"Ha! Likely story. What do you think the Tammany thug was threatening?"

I said I couldn't be sure, but it seemed that the mayor had been given a choice, maybe an ultimatum.

Dupont thought for a second. "Probably something to do with jobs.… But we can't print that without evidence. For now, just write 'Mayor McClellan informed those who had gathered that…' So it's clear the explanation about fireworks isn't coming from us."

I was about to return to my desk and start typing.

"The Board of Estimate meets tomorrow," he said.

"And?" No reply. "You want me to cover it?" If he wanted me to go he would never say so directly. He usually sent the lads. Not that anything out of the ordinary ever happened at the meetings. If a project made it as far as the Board, its approval was all but guaranteed. And since no one except for the members and a single recording secretary were allowed inside, it turned into an opportunity for reporters to sit on the City Hall steps and chew the fat while they waited for news from within.

"Listen to the schedule." Dupont raked his fingers through his thick head of hair and began to read. There was the IRT's proposal for changes in the routes of the subway lines; the Atlantic Telephone Company's application to maintain and operate the poles, wires, and appliances necessary for the installation of a telephone system throughout the city; the issuance of several million dollars of corporate stock for the erection of a new penitentiary on Rikers Island; over a million dollars toward improvements to the Metropolitan Hospital on Blackwell's Island; and of course, the demolition of Chinatown and the creation of a park.

The dustup in the Catskills couldn't be all that Mock had in mind; there had to be more. "I'll go."

"I didn't ask you to."

He didn't need to ask. We were thinking along the same lines.

"Fine," he said after a second. "If you insist. But just this once."

* * *

The usual scrum of tea-and-coffee sellers, oyster carts, peanut stalls, and a vendor grilling meats—as if preparing burnt offerings—filled Foley Square, which was bustling the next morning, a few minutes before eight o'clock.

Clerks traded gossip with lawyers, lawyers joked with judges, politicians swapped favors with Wall Street financiers and businessmen. The wheels of

New York City were being greased so we could keep moving onward and upward.

I had a feeling it was going to be a momentous day—though I couldn't be sure how. If anyone apart from Mock and Murphy had any inkling, it would be the Tammany bard.

"When I retired from the State Senate," Plunkitt began, "I thought I would take a good, long rest, such a rest as a man needs who has held office for about forty years and has held four different offices in one year and drawn salaries from three of them at the same time."

Will Riordan scribbled furiously as the crowd chuckled. *Come on, come on, get to the point,* I thought.

"Drawin' so many salaries is rather fatiguin', you know, and as I said, I started out for a rest, but when I seen how things were goin' in New York State, I said to myself: 'No rest for you, George. Your work ain't done. Your country still needs you, and you mustn't lay down yet.'"

All right. This was going to be good.

"What was the great, big black shadow hanging over us? It was the primary election law, amended so as to knock out what are called the party bosses by lettin' in everybody at the primaries. But have you ever thought what would become of the country if the bosses were put out of business, and their places were taken by a lot of cart-tail orators and college graduates?"

He had to be referring to McClellan—who else was a college graduate among that lot?

"But look at the bosses of Tammany Hall in the last twenty years," Plunkitt continued. "What magnificent men! They built up the grand Tammany organization, and the organization built up New York. Suppose the city had to depend for the last twenty years on irresponsible concerns like the Citizens' Union"—a reform group, I assumed—"where would it be now?"

The oracle stared at me, his eyes blazing into mine. He wanted to tell me something.

"Then see how beautiful a Tammany city government runs with a so-called boss directin' the whole shootin' match. *The machinery moves so noiseless that you wouldn't think there was any.*"

I nearly fainted. It was brilliant. It was poetic. Whatever Mock and Murphy planned, it would be almost imperceptible. Or like the 'fireworks' in the mountains, it could be explained away as something else.

The oracle pointed his finger at me. "Of course, newspapers like reform administrations. Why? Because these administrations, with their daily rows, furnish as racy news as prizefights or divorce cases. But *Tammany don't care to get in the papers.* It goes right along *attendin' to business quietly* and only wants to be let alone. That's one reason why the papers are against us."

I needed to sit down in order to make sense of my swirling thoughts. Silent, mysterious, private—that was Murphy. Mock was also someone you couldn't pin down. What they were doing would happen so quietly—or maybe it had already happened—that I wouldn't be able to hear, see, or smell it. But then again, it must leave some ripple, some trace, or else Mock couldn't expect me to write about it.

The prophet ended on a thunderous note. "The men who put through the primary law are the same crowd that stand for the civil service reform, and they have the same objects in view—the destruction of party rule, the downfall of the constitution, and hell generally."

He tipped his hat and bowed for several minutes while the square reverberated with applause.

"That was quite a talk," I said to the man standing next to me.

"Yeah," he agreed. "He wants to call it 'Bosses Preserve the Nation.'"

I hurried back to City Hall. The Board of Estimate and Apportionment would meet behind closed doors in Room 16 at ten on the dot. Even though he'd pretty much suggested I cover the meeting, Dupont had made me promise to keep a low profile and do nothing that might embarrass him or the paper. "You're just there to pick up whatever crumbs they drop."

Reporters from other publications had gathered on the front steps, smoking and shooting the breeze. The stairs were littered with cigarette butts, and a new luxury liner docked at the harbor seemed to be the chief topic of discussion—apparently its first-class cabins and dining rooms were quite the sight.

No one seemed to care much about the groundbreaking in the Catskills.

It was quite literally yesterday's news. And as for the day's meeting, I only heard a few complaints about the proposed alterations to the subway line.

Board members' vehicles—"bored members," Shrimpy liked to joke— began to arrive at a quarter to. First, Bird S. Coler, Borough President of Brooklyn. Short hair combed back, center part, eyebrows joined in the middle like some mythical demon. Next, Bermel of Queens, corrupt to the gills, but looking rather respectable with his clean cheeks and handlebar mustache. He would flee the country the following year in the hopes of evading arrest for widespread corruption. Then, Haffen from the Bronx, and Cromwell from Richmond County, a real blue blood, son of a shipping magnate and educated at Yale, and probably honest—or so they said.

Finally, Ahearn of Manhattan, a Tammany man through and through. Probably not at all pleased with Georgie B. since the mayor's office had started an inquiry into his conduct, the results of which would be made public the following month and revealed inefficiency, neglect, waste, and— again, every politician's bugbear—corruption.

The five *avatars* of New York City were followed in quick succession by Comptroller Metz and Patrick McGown, president of the Board of Aldermen. The mayor was already inside. The group was complete and would soon begin its deliberations.

At that moment, it felt as though the gods were convening at Mount Kailash in the Himalayas to determine the fate of millions.

To compensate for the complete lack of transparency, a week or so after each meeting, the particulars of every application and its results would be published in a lengthy official report, down to the type of glass used, thickness of pipes, choice of tiles, and the height of doors on subway kiosks, for instance. But the report never told you what discussions had been had, or which levers had been pulled to bring a particular project to fruition.

The reporters never waited for the official minutes, in any case. The lads would corner the attendees as they left, and usually, someone would slip them a nugget or two, or the recording secretary could be relied upon to share a few morsels. Although there were never any surprises, the approvals for each project still needed to be confirmed. That was the game that had to be played, the dance that had to be danced, so that the public could believe something of significance happened in the room, and that the outcomes hadn't been decided long in advance.

I was toying with a twig, breaking it into pieces and aiming them at pebbles, when I caught sight of Dan O'Reilly and ran to speak to him before he reached the newsmen.

I asked what brought him to City Hall that morning.

"Oh, just keepin' an eye on things," he replied, his gaze darting here and there.

"Any things in particular?"

He chuckled. "You might say I'm just an observer myself."

I wasn't deterred and asked whether he had come on behalf of Mock Duck, or maybe Charlie Murphy.

"Whatever gave you that idea?"

"Can we expect something to happen regarding Chinatown?"

His eyes narrowed. Maybe he was a bit perturbed. "I'm under no obligation to disclose my whys and wherefores to you, son." He appeared to spot someone he knew and slipped away.

The minutes crawled by with excruciating slowness. If something didn't happen soon, I would tell Mock he had me beat. That I couldn't figure out what in the world he was up to, and if he wanted me to record it, he better come into the open and spit it out.

That probably wouldn't go over too well, but it was all I had left. I'd pursued the matter as far as I could. I had done enough.

Finally, someone called from inside—the proceedings had come to an end. A general scramble as everyone surged through the portico and waited for the doors to Room 16 to open.

Manhattan Borough President Ahearn stepped out first, followed by Queens, the Bronx, Brooklyn, and Richmond County. The *avatars* were no doubt starving after an arduous morning's work and ready for lunch.

"Done," Ahearn replied to the reporters who crowded around asking about telephone lines and subways. "Approved," Haffen said when cornered about the penitentiary on Rikers Island.

"What about Chinatown?" I yelled from the back. But they had already made it to the front steps and would be whisked away by their aides and automobiles. The other reporters would return to Newspaper Row and type up their stories, or, in the case of the reporters from the *Herald* and *Times,* to Herald and Times Square, respectively.

Just as I was about to admit defeat, the doors to Room 16 opened again, and a harried lackey carrying a sheaf of papers under his arm emerged.

"You must be the recording secretary," I said.

"What if I am?" He kept walking.

"Was Chinatown approved?"

He stopped in his tracks. His cheeks turned bright red, and he looked ready to explode. "I can't say anything."

"Can we step outside for a minute?"

"I really shouldn't."

"You seem disturbed." It was an understatement.

"You can say that again."

"Let's just go out for a minute. If you decide not to talk, that's your business."

He glanced over his shoulder to make sure no one was watching and followed me down the front steps to the park. I chose an inconspicuous spot under a London plane tree.

"Something go wrong?" I prompted.

He tried to control himself, then spat it out. "I've been working here for eight years. Eight years, I've been preparing the minutes for these meetings. And every month it's the same. We print an agenda and follow it. To. The. Letter."

"But not this time?"

"That's right. They took it off."

"Who took what off?"

"They took Chinatown off."

"Could you please explain?"

"It wasn't there.... Someone typed up a different agenda, and that's all there is to it. It never came up in the discussions...." He appeared on the verge of tears. "No one ever types up a new agenda. That's *my* job."

"I'm sorry to hear that."

He didn't reply; just sniffed.

"So what does this mean for the district?"

"It means they didn't vote on it."

"Chinatown stands?"

"Yes, for this month. But you know how it is. Once something is postponed, other items take priority. The old project gets swept under the rug, and soon enough, they're on to the next big thing."

There will be questions," I said. "No one will forget this."

"No." He sounded shrill. "It won't be in the minutes. It won't be in the records. And if it's not in the records…it's as though it never existed." He caught himself. "We never had this conversation. And if you report otherwise, I will deny it." He stalked off, a bundle of wounded pride and nerves stretched to breaking.

I raced back to the *Observer.*

"No," Dupont said after I filled him in.

"No, as in you don't believe it?"

"No, as in I will not print it. I cannot print a story in which nothing happens."

"What do you mean nothing happens?" Our voices were raised, and the lads were listening, but for once, I didn't care. "They took it off the agenda."

"And that is not a story, Mrs. Morley," the editor roared. "Removing an item from an agenda isn't a story. Don't try to teach me my business. And don't tell me you think this two-bit, murdering hoodlum has managed to give everyone the runaround and save Chinatown in the process."

"But he has. Don't you see? That's the choice the mayor was given. If he wants the construction of the aqueduct to go forward without a hitch, he has to abandon Chinatown. The only person who could have swapped out the agenda without questions being raised is Georgie B." I was guessing, but it made sense.

"That's ridiculous." We stood there, glaring at each other. "What's in it for Murphy?" he said finally.

"He takes Hizzoner down a peg or two and forces him to give up his most popular, vote-getting project. If it was approved, Chinatown could have been done by the end of the summer. As it is, it may never happen. And the aqueduct will take years."

The editor paused. "So you're saying none of the members of the board inquired about the changed agenda."

"If they did, I'm sure the mayor was perfectly capable of coming up with some reasonable explanation."

"No, no, no. I don't like it."

"Why not?"

"Too convoluted." Dupont sounded like a man who had made up his mind. "And Mock Duck couldn't have suggested a plan like that.... He doesn't have it in him."

Chapter Thirty-One

And that's how it goes sometimes. People see what they want to see; they believe what they want to believe. When the minutes of the meeting were finally published, and Chinatown wasn't mentioned, Dupont didn't say a word. And when Chinatown remained standing two, three, ten years later, did anyone remember that its demolition was supposed to come up for a vote, but didn't? I have no idea.

I'll tell you this. Save for a tiny piece buried at the bottom of page five in the *Tribune*, none of the papers reported on it.

Titled *HAIL THE SAVIOR OF CHINATOWN*, it read:

"Dan" O'Reilly, the Idol of the Chop Suey Belt, and Rice Wine Flows.

"Dan" O'Reilly, fresh from his career as counsel for Harry K. Thaw, is now the Idol of the Celestials of Mott Street. "Old Tom" Lee joined with the friends of the "good" Mock Duck yesterday to do honor to the savior of Chinatown—that's what they are calling "Dan" now.

Borough President Ahearn has wanted to wipe out the Doyers Street pestholes for some time and make a park out of the noisome dens of Chinatown, but "Dan" O'Reilly came to the rescue. He fought for the preservation of the chop suey belt until his efforts were crowned with success, and the Board of Estimate decided that there would be no park. All day yesterday big vermilion banners hung from the windows of the Hip Sing Tong, at No. 12 Pell Street, bearing the congratulatory message....

This was followed by a mangled series of words, which apparently meant, "Oh, what a beautiful time we're having. Come in and celebrate." The story concluded:

> *Everybody did, until the evidence of overconsumption of rice wine overflowed into Chatham Square.*

The piece was sandwiched between "Hot Needle Revives Contortionist" and "S.I. Ferry House Open At Last."

***

I turned my steps to Chinatown after my dispiriting conversation with Dupont. The scene wasn't quite as the *Tribune* described it, but it certainly was festive. Fireworks crackled, banged, and squealed through the air, although it was still daytime. Locals banged spoons against pots and pans, hooting and dancing. Restaurateurs brought out vats of food and drink; waiters from The Pelham Café began to sing. Actors from the theater arrived in colorful robes; men, women and children sobbed and embraced each other with relief.

Dapper in a crisp linen suit and straw boater, Tom Lee stood on one side of Chatham Square, graciously inclining his head and accepting residents' thanks and blessings.

"It was nothing," he said modestly to someone in English, "All in god's hands."

"Hey, Observer!" The old man reached into his pocket and pulled out a Havana. His nephew, Lee Toy, stooped down to light it. "Didn't wanna say so before, but I knew this would happen. Minnie Rose has been livin' in the pews these past two weeks. Tom's got friends down here"—he gestured to the ground—"but she's got friends up there." His cigar poked the heavens.

I asked what he thought accounted for the board's sudden shift.

He replied that Hizzoner and the Manhattan Borough President and all the rest, must have seen reason in the end. All the donations that he made over the years must have counted for something. "What goes around, comes around. Ain't that what they say?"

William was dancing frenziedly with a friend, sticking his arms into the air and making silly faces when I tapped him on the shoulder. He swiveled and froze.

"Hey," I said. "I'm happy for you. You don't have to leave now. You get to stay on with your friends."

He didn't reply, just stared at me, horrified, said something to his mate, and the two darted away, giggling.

William probably said I was some crazy lady—and I didn't blame him.

Mock came out with O'Reilly at his side. A few paces behind, Tai Yow, wearing a silk robe, the dragon pendant around her neck, leaned on Bedelia's arm for support.

Mock wrapped his arms around his chest and stood in the corner opposite Tom, observing the festivities warily.

Bedelia beckoned me over with a wave. "Tai Yow wants to thank yeh for your efforts. She knows you've been busy on Mr. Mock's behalf lately. None of this"—she gestured around her—"will bring our rascal back." She sighed. "But still, it's somethin'."

I was shocked by the change that had come over Ha Oi's mother. Usually alert and aware, her cheeks sagged, and her face was vacant. She looked frail.

I told Bedelia to let her know that I wished her good luck. Though Tai Yow didn't answer, the maid did. "She wishes yeh the same."

I wondered whether this was how it would be from here on out—Tai Yow would go through the motions with Bedelia as her mouthpiece and support, or would she eventually recover and start a new life?

The maid adjusted the thin shawl over her mistress's shoulders, and the two continued to watch the festivities. Or at least, Bedelia did. I couldn't tell what Ha Oi's mother was seeing. What I remember most clearly is the shallow up-and-down movement of her robe as she breathed; the rest of her remained motionless.

"You pulled it off." I moved over to Mock. O'Reilly had drifted away. And before the highbinder could deny it, I added, "McClellan was given a choice up in the mountains. In return for trouble-free construction in the Catskills, he'd have to give up his plans to demolish this district."

Mock blinked. I like to think he was impressed that I had met the challenge he had set. "I did no such thing," he said finally. Then he relented just a bit. "If I did anything. *If,*" he repeated, "it was to give our friend on Fourteenth Street a few ideas."

"They certainly seem to have worked."

No response.

"You must be pleased. Chinatown's been saved."

"Perhaps." He blinked. "But I couldn't save the one person who matters most." He looked away, and then added simply, "But if she comes back and sees these streets—maybe she won't think we were just some people she dreamed up."

I looked toward Doyers, that one-of-a-kind alley. Tried to picture a middle-aged Ha Oi in a dress and leather shoes, clutching the "HF" pendant around her neck, desperate to understand why the bend in Doyers felt so familiar— almost as if she could walk up it with her eyes closed... almost as if she had lived here once.

"Come with me," Mock Duck said.

We left Tai Yow and Bedelia. Turned up the curve, past the wooden double doors of the Opera House, and stopped in front of No. 10.

"You won't forget our arrangement? Not today or tomorrow, but someday you will write about this?"

I nodded.

He pushed open the door and entered. It closed with a creak. I never saw him again.

* * *

Many years later, Georgie B. wrote to my husband saying he died that day in the mountains. That he had made decisions that marked the start of a glorious new era for the city, but the beginning of the end for his political career. He should have known you can't have everything. You have to pick and choose your battles, and he had tried to do too much, on too many different fronts.

The letter was postmarked from Hizzoner's alma mater, Princeton, where he was by then a professor. He would serve out the rest of his term as mayor, but was never again elected to public office, even though he angled for governor—while Murphy went on to become one of Tammany's longest-serving bosses.

Although I didn't realize it at the time, if that day in the mountains was the beginning of the end for Hizzoner, it was also the beginning of the end for me. I wish I could tell you something dramatic occurred: that the lads rioted, or Dupont erupted, or even that Lady Mac complained about me. Nothing of the sort. Over the course of six months, during which I completed my assignments but without my customary zeal, I sensed that the time had come to move on. I was tired and felt that the avenues around me were closing. As the city grew, and the new century progressed, and everything became more formalized and rule-driven, there would be less and less room for someone like me to maneuver.

I handed in my resignation. Dupont wasn't surprised. In fact, he seemed to expect it. "We had a good run, Mrs. M.," he said. "To be honest, I'm surprised you lasted for as long as you did."

I told Dr. Morley that I needed to get back home and see if there was anything left for me there. He asked me to wait, then he wrapped up his work at the health department, we packed our things, sold the house, and set sail four months later.

Dr. Morley had no regrets about leaving. He said Georgie B. had become a changed man after the groundbreaking in the Catskills. He was obsessed with getting the better of Murphy, almost to the exclusion of his other responsibilities.

My husband and I settled in Bombay near what was once the mansion of the great Baghdadi Jewish trader, David Sassoon, and soon became the Masina Hospital. While I stayed home and wrote and read, Dr. Morley treated patients. Apart from Cyrus, his sister, and a few medical colleagues who didn't ask too many questions, we kept to ourselves. I resumed wearing saris every day but sometimes missed the freedom of trousers. From time to time, I would put them on and wander through the streets of Bombay, reliving my former life.

On occasion, I borrowed copies of American newspapers from the library, scanning them for news about people I knew, but Tai Yow and Bedelia were never mentioned. And Mock, who left New York at the end of '07, had fallen out of the news as well. In 1912, Dupont told me in one of his infrequent letters that the highbinder was finally convicted—for running a lottery. His punishment: a couple of years in Sing Sing. Either he was extraordinarily lucky or he was, as he always maintained, innocent. I would never know, but it seemed appropriate, that after everything, he would only be sentenced to a few years in prison.

Around the same time, Dupont quit the *Observer*. I thought he was the kind of man who would keel over at his desk and have to be carried out feet first covered in newsprint. He said that the business was no longer what it used to be. Gone were the freewheeling days when he could do what he wanted, hire whom he wanted, publish the stories he wanted. Now he was being nagged about every little detail, and it was time to retire.

I stopped thinking about New York, became involved in the freedom struggle, and in teaching girls to read.

Not too long ago, I came across a piece in the *Times* about Tom Lee's passing. The mayor of Chinatown was seventy-six years old, and he died of natural causes. His wife had preceded him a few months earlier. I was pleased to see that he was given a grand funeral just as he and Bacigalupo had planned, with black horses pulling the hearse and a marching band. The story mentioned the war between the On Leongs and the Hips in which, it said, more than fifty-three men had been killed, but didn't include a word about Mock. He'd been completely forgotten.

Still, it reminded me of my promise.

I unearthed my boxes of files, notes, and clippings and began to write. As my pen scratched back and forth across the page, I was transported once again to the bend on that crooked alley, to the homes that leaned in toward each other. I wonder whether the girl who once lived there will ever read this and realize that he preserved the neighborhood for her. Whether she does or not—and I hope she does—it is a story that has remained with me, a story I promised I would write, and I have done my utmost to do it justice.

—*A.M., Bombay, 1918*

Author's Note

This novel is inspired by events that took place in New York City in 1907. Mock Duck's court case was covered by the New York *Times, Sun,* and later, the *Tribune,* but was overshadowed by Harry Thaw's murder trial. The "Chinese Opera House Massacre" occurred in 1905, but it and other instances of violence between the Hips and the On Leongs fed into perceptions of Chinatown as a hotbed of criminality and lawlessness.

All references to articles in the *Times, Sun,* and *Tribune* are either direct quotes or close paraphrases from those publications. George Washington Plunkitt's speeches are available online, titled *Plunkitt of Tammany Hall: A Series of Very Plain Talks on Very Practical Politics.* Much of the information on the conflict between the On Leongs and the Hips comes from Scott Seligman's *Tong Wars: The Untold Story of Vice, Money, and Murder in New York's Chinatown.*

Pandita Ramabai's account of what she saw in America was originally published in Marathi in Bombay in 1889. It is available in translation as *Pandita Ramabai's America: Conditions of Life in the United States.*

This novel took over six years to write. Along the way, I received feedback and advice from several talented writers and friends. My thanks to them; to Mitch Hoffman, my agent, for his steadfast support through all the twists and turns; to my indefatigable publisher and editor, Shawn Reilly Simmons, for her insights and for bringing this novel out into the world, and to Deb Well at Level Best.

And, as always, to my most honest critics: Daniel, David, Sita, and Tulsi. I couldn't have done it without you.

About the Author

Radha Vatsal is the author of the acclaimed Kitty Weeks mystery novels set in World War I-era New York. Her writing has appeared in *The New York Times*, *The Atlantic*, the *Los Angeles Review of Books,* and elsewhere. Born and raised in Mumbai, India, she earned her Ph.D. in Film History from Duke University and has worked as a film curator, political speechwriter, and freelance journalist. She lives in New York City.

AUTHOR WEBSITE:
  www.radhavatsal.com

SOCIAL MEDIA HANDLES:
  Instagram: @radha_vatsal
  FB: radha.vatsal
  Substack: radhavatsal.substack.com

Also by Radha Vatsal

A Front Page Affair

Murder Between the Lines